Gobble 'til you Wobble

···

S.N. Moor

Contents

Hey Dad

Well, looky looky what we have here. I don't think you're surprised anymore. I will go ahead and say there are a couple more of these in your future. Good news is, you're crushing your TBR this year, since you only get a page per book. #winning

To quickly summarize for you... Everlee and her companions are back from the beach and things changed. Woah. Nothing too crazy, so no need to read... the woah was really for dramatic flair. Any whoozle, Everlee is back and has quit her job to help run a... family-ish business that focuses on love and acceptance. Supes sweet. Everlee's parents finally meet her companions and hilarity ensues after probably one of the most mortifying moments of her life. But our girl rebounds. You can say this book took you on an emotional rollercoaster. You laughed and you cried. As always, thanks for your support, even on the NSFD books!

A haiku dedication for you.
Step out of the dark
Love is love and kink is fine.
Let your kink flag fly

Introduction

Gobble 'til you Wobble is the 6th book of the series. A lot of things changed in Stars and Stripes and now we get to see our favorite fivesome back in the real world. How is Everlee doing with running Allure? Do Jax's walls go back up? You will cry, blush, and laugh with this one.

It's recommended you read Cupid's Contract, Bunnies and Bowties, Rainbows and Unicorns, and Stars and Stripes first. If you haven't read those yet, stop here, because there are spoilers below (the title links will take you to the books).

In **Cupid's Contract**, Everlee meets her four delicious men who give her the time of her life and the confidence she lost after dickface, Rich, destroys her. The only problem is the men make her agree to only sleep with them two times before they part ways. By the end of the arrangement, Everlee gets attached but doesn't know how the men feel, so she honors the agreement against her own desires and leaves. She's scared of getting hurt again.

Bunnies and Bowties, picks up two months later. She's been absolutely miserable, and unbeknownst to her, so have the men. Lizzy, being the amazing BFF she is, gets her back out on the scene, but she runs into her men and things are as hot as ever. She wants to talk with them about a future, but she's already committed to visiting her family for Easter. We get to meet her eccentric brother, Beckett, and her mother and father. Her mother is hellbent on a marriage and grandkids for Everlee and uses every opportunity to remind her, going as far as setting her up on a date with a lawyer. Everlee does her part but is missing her men desperately. The church her family attends is hosting a birthday party for one of their members and during the celebration Everlee comes face to face with her men (while on her date). They were all in foster care together a few towns over from Everlee growing up. Small world. As you can imagine, fireworks ensue, and Beckett picks up on all the sexual tension between them all and calls out she's in a poly relationship. Our favorite fivesome is formed and it is HOT! HOT! HOT!

<u>Rainbows and Unicorns</u> picks up soon after Bunnies ends. This one centers around Memorial Day and Pride Month. Sammie, a woman from the men's past enters the picture with a proposition for them that is hard to refuse. Because of personal reasons, Sammie has to go back to Texas, but offers to sell Allure back to the guys. Allure was their first successful business, a sex club, that gave them the funds to open Vixen and Bo's. Scared of how Everlee will react, they are hesitant to tell her, but when they do, she shocks them when she's excited about it. Sammie sets up a night where our fave five can visit Allure and experience Eden and Infernus (hello fave wood scene), two other areas of the club she added. While at Allure, Knox and Everlee participate in a Shibari demonstration that is... ahem... hot AF and we learn that Knox's nickname in the SEALs was Knots. In the end, they all decide to buy the business, Everlee included, so she's now an official owner of a sex club with the boys. Things continue to progress with the relationship and by the end of the book everyone says they love one another with hints of something more developing between Emmett and Jax. Lizzy is still in wedding planning mode so who knows what she'll decide about her wedding, and we also finally get to meet Betty's husband.

<u>Stars and Stripes</u> gives us our summertime vacation feels! Our fave five head away for a week of fun in the sun, with Beckett, Will, Lizzy and Tony, but when Beckett stupidly invites his and Everlee's mom, things get tense. She never travels alone, so why would she now? Several days later, the knock on the door shocks them all. Dearest Donna took a page out of Ev's book and travelled on her own... to the beach house... the forbidden love nest with Ev and her men. Things are awkward and their bedroom activities are put on hold, but when Everlee's life is in danger and all the men jump in to save her, the cat is out of the bag. Everlee and her mom talk, and Ev admits she's in a poly relationship. With the weight of the world off Everlee's shoulders, she can finish out the week relaxing and Donna can really meet the men. Also, in Stars and Stripes, we see Emmett and Jax's relationship start to heat up as Jax begins to explore the feelings he's been pushing down. Everlee's love and unconditional support give him the courage to explore. What does this mean for the future?

<u>Deal with a Djinn</u> is the fifth book in the series, however, it can be read as a standalone. Like some of our favorite shows do, Deal with a Djinn breaks from the series and our favorite characters are transported to another realm- a paranormal world, where they meet again for the first time. It's a paranormal retake on Cupid's Contract. If you've read the series, then you will likely see Easter eggs that have been planted throughout in this book. Hope you enjoy!

EVERLEE - WHAT DREAMS BECOME

THE MORNING SUN FEELS like needles pricking my eyes. My body is exhausted, and I can't shake the feeling of sleep deprivation.

"Good morning, love." Jax rolls over to look at me.

Looking around the room, my head feels foggy, making it hard to focus.

"Everything ok?"

"Where am I?"

"Ev?"

"Can you growl at me?"

"What the fuck?" Pushing me away, his gaze locks onto me, his expression filled with scrutiny. "How much did you and Knox drink last night?"

"Knox? Drink?" I reach up and massage my scalp, hoping to shake off the haze of confusion that lingers in my mind.

"Yes. You stumbled into my room at like three in the morning. Emmett was plying you both with samples of drinks that he wants to run tonight at Vixen and Allure."

I stare at him, still trying to process what he's talking about.

"For the Halloween parties..."

"It's not Halloween yet?"

He brushes the hair from my face. "Babe? Are you ok?"

"Yes," I say, running my hand down his chest. "I just had the weirdest dream. It felt so real... You all... had powers." I shake my head.

Jax rolls out of bed, not wearing a goddamn thing, and my brain fully wakes up like someone has zapped it with electricity. Damn, he's a dream to watch walk away. The way his muscles tighten and flex. And his ass.

"You're moaning," he calls over his shoulder, in a playful tone.

"Shut up. Let a girl moan."

He chuckles as he walks into the bathroom. When he walks out a second later, he hands me a glass of water and some medicine. "We have to get you ready for tonight. It's your first holiday party since becoming manager at Allure."

Trying not to let my nerves spill out, I swallow down the medicine and stare at him, causing him to laugh.

"You're going to do great. Do you know what costume you're going to wear?" he asks, folding his foot under his thigh and sitting on the side of the bed.

"Well, I was thinking of going with a sexy fairy."

His chin tilts down at me. "I don't want you going as sexy anything."

I wrap my arms around his neck and bring him over to me, the smell of mint wafting through the air when he leans over me.

"Did you brush your teeth while you were in there?"

He side-eyes me cautiously. "Yes. Is that a problem?"

"Yes. I was going to have dirty morning sex with you, but now I can't kiss you because I'm wearing sweaters over my teeth and it feels like I sucked on a chalk stick. I cannot, and more importantly, *will* not kiss minty mcfresh breath."

He grabs my hips and flips me around so my chest is pressed to the bed. "Fine, no kisses for you." He lifts my hips but keeps another hand pressed on my back, holding it to the bed.

"It's really more for you than for me." It sounds like I'm gurgling a mouth full of marbles with my cheek pressed into the bed.

"No. This is for you." He swipes his finger up my center and a little whimper escapes. "And this is for me," he says just before his tongue licks up.

God mother fucking damn it. Before I can let myself sink into the warm feeling of his tongue, I feel something else. The morning bubble love killer floating through my lower abdomen. "You need to move," I say, trying to jerk from his grip.

He licks faster.

"No. Not that kind of move." Oh, my God. This is so mortifying. Why does this always happen to me? As if on cue, the love killer announces itself in my stomach, a little guitar sounding chord that says watch out mother fucker, this trains a' comin'. It was all those damn drinks last night. "Jax, seriously." My voice is tight and panicking.

"No."

Fucking help me. My heart is beating out of my chest while trying not to orgasm on his face. "Jax. Jax. This is not my orgasm call. This is a move your face from my asshole cry."

The fucker is smiling as he continues to spear me with his tongue. I swear to God if I fart in this man's face; I am done for. Pussy farting on Emmett's cock is one thing. Unloading a gas bomb right in the face of a non-combatant, although some could argue that his unwillingness to move is very combatant-like at this very moment, is a no-go.

Tears are streaming out of my eyes as I feel the bubble of destruction inch closer and closer towards its exit.

Towards its freedom.

I'm so busy following that bubble fucker through my system that I've effectively mapped out my entire intestines and completely missed the impending orgasm.

"I'm not fucking you until you come around my tongue."

"Damn you. You know good and goddamn well why I need you to move."

"I do." He dives back in, pulsing his tongue in and out of my pussy while his finger plays on my clit.

"And you what? Woke up this morning and say 'hey! I feel like playing roulette with Ev's asshole. Will she come on my tongue or fart in my face first?'"

"I'm hoping come. But I understand the risks."

Frustration consumes me, and I release a heavy sigh. "Dude. It's like suck and blow. Only you'll be taking a shotgun of flatulence up your fucking nose. So fucking mortifying."

He pauses because he's now laughing. Laughing at my expense. "I can see this really bothers you."

"And I have no idea how it doesn't bother you," I say, pushing up the bed.

"I'm a SEAL. Gas bombs are nothing."

"It's very something when it's coming out of the girl you're eating out. It's like a direct assault. Throw a grenade! Or whatever other military term thing happens."

He crawls up my body, his chest on my back, as his cock hits at my entrance. "Whatever other military term thing?" He chuckles. "Knox and I will take you to a training camp."

"Ha ha. No."

"Ha ha. Yes." He shoves his cock in me at the same time he speaks.

I cry out as his cock presses in, stretching me open. "I..." My words vanish as he drags his cock out and slams it in again.

"No need discussing. Knox has brought it up several times, and I can't wait to see you in gear and a mask."

"Mask? Will both of you be wearing one?"

"You kinky fucker."

"You should have just started with mask." I laugh.

"Shut the fuck up so I can make you come properly," he says with a hint of a smile on his lips. He pushes my face down into the bed. "Stay." He grabs both of my hips and unleashes, plowing into me over and over again.

Moans and wet slaps fill the air while his balls bounce against me. His hand loops around and rubs on my clit, causing my orgasm to slam into me. I clench around his cock as wave after delicious wave pulses through me.

"Fuck Ev," he pants.

I smile, loving how the guys react to me, so I continue trying to strangle his cock until he's moaning out my name and I feel his hot come shoot inside of me.

He leans over and kisses my neck and suddenly I have a flashback to my dream where he marked me, biting me on my shoulder. "Mark me," I whisper out so low, I'm not sure if I even said it.

"What?"

"Bite me," I say a little louder.

His hesitation causes me to doubt whether he will do it, but then he starts to fuck me with a slow and steady rhythm. He pushes my hair to the side and my nipples harden with anticipation. His tongue glides languidly across my skin, leaving a tingling sensation in its wake, before he sinks his teeth into me. Not hard like in my dream, but he bites and sucks while he continues to fuck me slowly. I'm about to come again from this alone. It's so sensual. So erotic.

I don't know how long he does it for, but when he pulls out, he's only slightly hard. He smacks my ass, then crawls backwards off the bed. "I'll be in the shower waiting for you."

"Thank you, daddy," I tease.

"Shut the fuck up," he chuckles, walking away.

By the time I get in the bathroom, I'm one gas bubble shorter and the mirror has fogged, and he is under the rainfall showerhead sweeping his wet hair off his face. A fucking wet dream to look at. All muscles and tattoos. He's growing his usual five o'clock shadow a little longer in prep for the holidays. Apparently, he and the guys are going to shave it all off on November first to kick off no shave

November. They didn't seem super excited when I told them I was going to participate, too. Except for the cooch. That bitch has to stay nice and trim, but legs and armpits... Par-tay time! They also didn't appreciate my joke when I said I was hoping to French braid the hairs by the end of the month.

Jokes on them, though.

The hot water runs down my back when I step in, feeling like lava on my skin. It takes me a moment to get used to, and by used to it, I mean swapping places with Jax. He likes it hot, so he can stand in the stream of lava pouring out right now.

When he finishes rinsing the soap off of his body, he turns the heat down and swaps places with me so he can wash me. When I insist I'll handle it, he ignores me, pressing his finger into my mouth. I bite him, eliciting a deep growl from him that sends a wave of excitement through me.

We're downstairs twenty minutes and two orgasms later.

CALLUM – KNOCKING DOWN WALLS

EMMETT IS AT THE stove working on some omelets for Knox and me when Jax and Ev come down. Ev's eyes sparkled with energy and alertness, in stark contrast to Knox's tired and drowsy appearance. He still isn't drinking much, but Emmett said he was sampling all the drinks last night, and both Ev and Knox were pretty lit when they left. Knox has only got out a series of grunts and groans this morning and is currently laying with his forehead on the island.

"Good morning, you two." I smile, watching Ev walk down.

She rubs her hand up Knox's back, who lifts his head for a second to smile at her, then drops it again. She walks over and climbs on my lap while Jax walks over to Emmett. He places his hand on the small of Emmett's back and whispers something in his ear.

"Morning," she says, laying her head on my shoulder.

"Good morning, love." I give her a small kiss on her still damp forehead. "Did you have a good night?"

"Fucking Emmett," she groans.

"Hey, hey, hey!" Emmett shouts, turning around with a smile spread across his face. "Are you going to defend me?" He cuts his eyes at Jax.

Jax laughs and presses his lips on Emmett's forehead. "Absolutely not. I'd rather watch you two fight it out."

"You kinky asshole."

Jax is still laughing when he walks away and takes a seat at the end of the bar, while Everlee takes the seat between us.

While we were at the beach, I noticed a change in Jax and Emmett. I'd been seeing hints of it for a while. Jax had been grappling with his feelings for Emmett, reluctant to acknowledge them. Part of me believes Jax couldn't shake the belief that he didn't deserve happiness. Or possibly, he was just scared to let anyone in.

We both put them up. Sure, Emmett and Knox were close to us, but not in every way. They are our friends, our brothers. They're safe because we know they'd never break our hearts. If Jax let Emmett in as more than anything but a friend, that would mean Jax was exposing himself and could get hurt. I'm convinced that's why he joined the military. He was trying to put space between Emmett and his growing feelings, literally trying to fight it out.

Obviously, that didn't work.

When Everlee came into our lives, she blew everything apart. When she left, she hurt us, but we did it to ourselves. She was trying to protect herself like we were. We put all the rules in place, and it wasn't until she left, we realized they weren't protecting us. They were hurting us. When we reconnected with her, we all promised that we wouldn't let the trauma of our past dictate the future of our happiness.

It took some time, but Jax finally allowed himself to acknowledge the connection he had with Emmett, beyond mere friendship or brotherhood. Everlee was crucial in proving to him he could rely on others and lower his guard. I don't know if he would call himself bi, because I think for him it's just Emmett. They've always had a bond, a connection on a basic level. Opposite sides of the same coin- the fighter and the lover. The brute and the chef.

Ev and the guys give me a hard time because I'm always so serious. Because of Ev, the guys now call me daddy, which is fucked up, but they don't understand. Being the oldest, I've always taken care of them, and that sense of responsibility is something I can't simply turn off. They are my family and I will protect them with everything I am and everything I have.

When we first got to Mrs. Mary's, Jax was scared and Emmett latched onto us fairly quickly. I'd already been acting like Jax's father for years, so it felt natural to take Emmett under my wing, and then Knox when he came. He was a firecracker, so much anger. When we got to the truth of the matter, he was holding out hope his dad would come back. In some ways, he's still holding out hope, even now. I don't think he would accept him back into his life because it's been so long, but I think he wants to know that he wasn't a mistake. I think that's what we all want, and that's what Everlee gives us. She gives us love, acceptance, respect. She's our shield. And her parents.

Her dad called soon after we got home from the beach and they talked on the roof for close to an hour. We tried to give her space, but Knox... he was a ball of nerves. He told us he was going to shower, but the little shit perched himself at the top of the stairs and listened to their conversation. He was so terrified of her dad not approving of our relationship and talking her out of it, that he couldn't wait to talk to her after. Had he stayed downstairs with us, he would have saved himself a lot of stress because Emmett was texting with Donna the entire time, reassuring us he was ok with it but that he wanted to talk to her- hear it from her. Her mom got to see us all first-hand.

Her mom came up last month and stayed at her place- well, her old place, even though she refuses to claim it as hers anymore since she's moved into our house. Her dad was supposed to come, but something came up at the last minute he couldn't get out of. We were all really bummed because we were looking forward to meeting him in person.

Even though Ev has her own room here, she never sleeps in it. It's really just become her walk-in closet. We all either sleep in the Nest- the room that used to be the voyeur room, or she floats between our rooms.

She's put her touches on the Nest, which I love. Nothing too major, but she's changed out the color scheme, added more pillows, candles and other decorations. The candles are nice... it's like eucalyptus, lavender and sea salt, or something like that. She's told me a dozen times, but I can never remember. It's relaxing and reminds us of the beach, the place that really solidified our family.

Knox yells out, bringing me back to the conversation in the kitchen. When I look at him, he's pumping his fist in the air, hopping around like a lunatic. Jax looks at me. "You good to leave in fifteen?"

I nod. I didn't hear where we were going, but when Knox starts talking about all his gear, I figure it out pretty quickly. Everlee has a look of excitement and worry on her face as she scans the room. Knox and Jax both love playing paintball, while Emmett and I enjoy doing it for them. A few years ago, they bought us our own equipment. It was supposed to be a kind gesture, but when the other players saw we had our own equipment, they mistook us for experienced players and came after us. Hard. I mean, we aren't the worst, but we're not Jax and Knox's level, either.

"Does it hurt?" Ev asks.

"You take four cocks at the same time and you want to know if paintball hurts? I love you," Jax says, pulling her into his arms and brushing a kiss across her forehead.

"Hopefully, you'll still love me when I'm all bloody and bruised."

Knox walks over and wraps his arms around her from behind. "We won't let anyone touch you, love."

She sighs. "No, it's ok. I've thought about doing this for years. I could never find the courage. Now I get to go out with experts."

"You may want to wear two pairs of panties," Emmett says, drying the pan in his hand.

"In case I piss myself? Har har har. I thought you were going to have my back," Ev laughs.

"Not for that love. When you see Jax and Knox in their gear, you're probably going to come."

Everlee bursts out laughing.

"He's not kidding, love." Jax smiles. "We turn straight men gay."

"Look at me!" Emmett throws his hands in the air. "I didn't like dick until I saw them in their gear."

"Lies. You've always liked dick," Knox chimes.

My eyes naturally wonder over to Jax to see how he's handling the jokes and I'm happy to see his walls are still down. Before, they would have shot up so fast, but I think Everlee and Emmett have given him the confidence and acceptance he needed to let himself love and be loved.

"Ten minutes, boys and girl," Knox says, jumping from his chair and running upstairs.

EVERLEE - WHEN THREE PAIRS OF PANTIES ISNT ENOUGH

HOLY FORKING SHIRTBALLS. I'M going to need three, maybe four pairs of panties. Fuck, give me some adult diapers instead. Knox walked down first, followed by Jax, and my knees fucking buckled. You better believe I sure as shit moaned.
Goddamn.
They were both wearing their full tactical gear in all black. Cargo pants, black padded vest and their masks. Shit. Add that to my kink list. Jax's was a dark military green with thin black lens for his eyes and Knox's... his was all black skull face with a place on top of his head to mount a camera. Did I think about what it would be like to fuck him with that mask on while being filmed? Hell. Fucking. Yes. I. Did.
Am I going to make said thought a reality?
Yes. Simply, yes.

Knox slips his mask up to look at Callum and Emmett. "Is that what you're wearing? We bought you both a nice set of gear and you aren't going to use it?"

"When we wear it, people think we know what we're doing. We don't. They don't even use the surrender call."

Knox laughs. "Yea, that makes sense."

"You ready?" Callum asks, putting his hand on my lower back.

"Mmhmm."

His eyes darken, "Words, love."

"Yes, sir." I wink and turn to walk outside. He slaps my ass, causing me to laugh.

"Care for a sixth?" Brady asks, walking outside. The guys must have told him because he is also in his gear, looking as fine as my guys.

"Of course!" I'm dragging him out of his shell, but he's still quiet. He's joined us for dinner several times. I honestly had no idea he lived downstairs until a few months ago, after we got back from the beach. When my parents were here, I'd gone to the cellar to grab some wine and stumbled across another door. When I opened it up, I found an entire apartment. I quickly realized it was Brady's and slammed the door. I tried to talk him and the guys into letting Brady move into the other house, but he wasn't having it.

Despite my best efforts, I haven't been able to figure out his story. But I will eventually. He just seems very private.

Callum drives since he isn't in his gear, while Emmett and I climb into the third row, Jax and Knox take the second row, and Brady slips into the passenger seat.

Yea... I'm won't be able to concentrate. The guys like me in my costumes and I always thought it was... not weird... just... different. But I get it now.

We're at the field forty minutes later. Even though we passed another, they swear by Jimmy's and how it's the best because of the layout. They fit me with a helmet and pads, which they had to change out twice because they didn't like the way they felt, then find me a gun and walk me through how to use it.

Not going to lie, I feel like a badass with my gear and gun and of course Knox, being Knox, takes an usie. He refuses to call it a selfie since there are two of us in the picture. He tried to get one with Jax just before me, but only got a picture of Jax's arm pushing his head away. Knox was excited to show me and thought it was great. Said he was going to frame it and hang it in his room.

Twenty minutes later, the ref goes over the rules for me. The other group we will be against seems to be regulars who are fully decked out. "This should be fun, she says with sarcasm," I mumble through the helmet.

Jax and Callum walk over to the other group and point at me. All I hear is surrender, which seems confrontational and premature. But the leader of the group gives Jax and Callum a handshake before they walk back over.

"What was that about?" I ask.

"We told them the surrender rule applies to you. If they have you dead to rights, they can yell surrender and you must put up your hands and say you surrender. If not, you're going to get pelted. And definitely don't trick them and shoot them to get them out. That is a bullshit tactic that little fuckheads use," Jax chomps.

"Got it. Hands up and surrender and don't be a fuckhead. What about you?"

"We told them surrender rules don't apply to us. Take us out."

"Yay," Callum deadpans.

"Aww boo boo." I rub his cheek.

"I'm tellin' Lizzy you called someone else your boo boo," Knox chimes, walking up looking hot as fuck. With his helmet perched on top of his head and his paintball rifle cradled in his arms, he looks every bit the hot badass.

Knox and I have grown pretty close over the last several months since I've taken over co-managing Allure with him.

When we got back from the beach, I gave my resignation, then fear set in. I've never managed a business and was still very new in the sex world, but the guys were there supporting me every step of the way, and of course Lizzy was cheering me on. She was super excited for me, but I'm sure the little shit was just excited to say her best friend owns a sex club, though she can't really tell anyone that.

I'm making my sex club library room come to life with the guys' help. We ran some numbers and determined we could make the same amount of money with two demo rooms instead of three, so we converted one of those rooms into the library. Sticky page rules apply. No masturbating while holding a book. If you need to get off, they must go into a room and plug the book into the read aloud mode. I did extensive research and got some of the most desirable male voice actors to come and read a catalog of books for us. When I say those rooms have been a revolving door... wow. Knox also had the idea of having the voice actors record other sayings that users could listen to. Things like, good girl, dirty whore, shut the fuck up and take this cock like a good girl, and crawl over on your knees and suck my cock until I come down your throat, just to name a few.

When news of the Book Nook spread, membership increased by ten percent month over month, and this month we're projecting close to twenty percent!

Needless to say, it was the shot in the arm I needed to give me the confidence I could do this. It's made date nights a little hard, so we just take the time whenever we get it. Vixen is open five nights a week now and they're still packing out every night, with a wait to get in. Everything is absolutely perfect right now, which scares me, but I'm trying to focus on the positive.

"Ev!" Callum calls, pulling me back to the present. "You want to play with us or the other team?"

I look at the other team, then him.

"Get your ass over here," he laughs.

"Jimmy is going to take us to the back field, while the other team goes to the front."

Outside is a large ATV looking vehicle, so we all climb in with Jax in the front. Once Jimmy begins driving, the two friends catch up on what each other's missed. When we get far enough away, Jimmy gives pointers about the other team. Apparently, they come every week and are effective. They're composed of four active military, and one retired. The sixth member on their team is a renter. Apparently, renter means someone who is fairly new to the world. Jimmy discusses military and tactical movements, which confuses me, but Jax seems to understand. They seem fairly close and, given Jimmy knows Brady and Knox, I have to assume they served together.

We're at our starting place ten minutes later. Before Jimmy pulls off, he tells us the game starts when the horn blows in about five minutes.

My heart is racing.

This is only paintball, not real guns. How did Knox, Brady, and Jax do this?

Jax and Knox huddle us up and start going through strategy and tactics. It's amazing to see them like this- focused and so in-sync. Literally where one ends, the other picks up like they are reading off the same paragraph. No jokes or jabs.

Watching them is electrifying and erotic. They both pull their masks down at the same time, grab the back of each other's neck and tap helmets. Something they've probably done one hundred times.

"Go paintball!" I say, thrusting my fist in the air. Whenever I find myself in intense situations, I inevitably make them awkward, as if it's second nature to me. I'd say it's a talent, but I'm not sure that's what anyone else would call it.

"Dork," one of the men says. It's hard to tell who said it because their masks muffle their voices. But if I had to guess, I would say Emmett or Jax.

A horn blows in the distance, signifying the start of the game. Heart racing, I jump into the air and pull my mask down.

Emmett grabs my hand and pulls me to the side, while Jax, Knox, and Brady head off towards the other team, knees bent, back hunched, moving with a stealth precision.

Focus Everlee.

Focus.

Callum follows Emmett and me to the side. "There's a bus this way. We can hide in it and potentially snipe them when they come through."

"Sure." I shrug, having no clue what I'm doing. I blame the men for looking so delicious. We move quickly, but not nearly as quietly as the other guys. Twigs break up ahead and we all freeze. There's no way they could have made it over this way that quickly. A moment later, a squirrel jumps from the branches in the tree above us.

I point at the ground a distance in front of me and tap the trigger twice. The thip thip sound bounces back just before the guys turn to look at me.

"What was that for?"

"Just wanted to see what it felt like so I could be ready."

"Precious," Emmett teases in a high-pitched voice.

"Fucker."

"Ooh... still precious, with a potty mouth."

I'm still chuckling when we reach the bus. The bus, once white, is now covered in a mix of spray paint, words, pictures, and paintball splatters.

"Should we all be in the same place? If someone comes, couldn't they make us all surrender or shoot us?" I ask.

"Yea. I'll stay outside," Emmett says, pointing his gun up and stepping around the back of the bus.

"I'm going to wander up," Callum says. "I'll bird call if I run into anyone."

I climb into the bus and give a quick look around to make sure no one else is already in here. After the fact, I realized the other group would have to move with super speed to get here, but it made me feel like I knew what I was doing, if only for a second.

Clear.

I sit in the driver's seat and let my gun hang from my neck strap and pretend like I'm driving the bus.

A flock of birds takes off to the sky in the distance and I freeze. They're getting closer or that's our guys. I'm not sure which. Either way, my heart beats faster, and that's when I see them. A member of the other team is creeping through the woods, looking right at me, and here I am with my hands on the wheel, freaking playing around.

He just stares at me and I stare at him, although he can't see me since I have a mask on.

I try to bird call to warn Emmett without moving, but it comes out as a garbled mess. Maybe if I keep pretending to be a dummy, then he won't shoot. I mean, why else would someone be sitting in the open with their hands on the wheel? The guys are going to give me so much shit about this.

He keeps walking closer, gun pulled up, but I don't move. The closer he gets, the faster my heart races.

Where in the fuck is Emmett?

The guy is too close for me to bird call and if he climbs on the bus, he will realize I'm not a dummy. Well, not a stuffed figure. I'd argue that I'm a dummy for getting myself in this situation to begin with.

Just as he's about to round the front of the bus where the door is, I hear a whistle. The guy stops and turns around and in the distance a body peaks out from behind a tree.

Emmett.

He fires three shots at the guy, hitting him in the side and in the leg.

"Fuck!" the guy yells and drops his head. "Good shot."

A second later, another shot echoes and I see a member of the other team walking out from behind a tree with his gun pointed at Emmett, and my heart sinks. He got

Emmett. "Good shot!" Emmett yells, holding his hand and gun in the air.

"Well, shit." Now it's just me, because Callum has walked on. With limited time, I need to switch my position. As fast as I can, I adjust my gun, pointing it at the door while my hand remains on the trigger. With my elbow propped on the open bus window by the driver's seat, I maintain a firm grip on the wheel with my right hand. I lean into the wall and cock my head at an awkward angle so it looks like I'm a dummy who fell over.

Shit! The man is looking at me. Did he see me move?

His gun goes up as he stares.

Waiting.

I don't think he did.

Look like a dummy.

Look like a dummy.

I slowly relax my fingers so they are hanging over the wheel, not gripping it.

He's stepping closer.

A ruffle of leaves tries to pull my attention, but I keep my head still and my eyes frozen on him. He's curious, that's for sure.

Don't move.

But fuck, Everlee, breathe.

He's not close enough to see your chest plate move.

Another wind blows and the guy pauses and looks over his shoulder. He's right by the doors now, hand on the handle, ready to climb in. I take this moment to make sure my finger is on the trigger because as soon as he sees my gun, he'll know.

But he'll be so close. The angels on my shoulders have it out. I don't want to hurt him, but they aren't playing surrender rules.

Fuck.

The doors open.

Before he can get his gun back up, I fire twice. Hitting him in the chest.

"What the-" He looks up at me and chuckles. "Nice shot, renter."

"Thanks."

He slings his gun around to his back and walks back towards the exit, which is somewhere up ahead and to the left.

A moment later, the horn blows.

"What the fuck does that mean?"

As if answering my question, a voice responds into the air, "One player from each team remains."

"Mother shitballs."

"Constant movement rules apply."

What happened to the other guys? How, out of all the members on my team, am I the only one left?

I climb off my perch and slither out of the school bus, gun up and head on a swivel. My heartbeat is racing, but this calmness sweeps across me. I'm dialed in to everything around me. My ears hear everything, but eyes feel like they see more.

I have no idea how big this course is or where I'm going, but I know I need to stay hidden. Channeling my inner SEAL, I hunch over slightly, like I saw Jax and the guys doing earlier, and move forward.

I'm moving at a snail's pace, cautiously clearing each section, but the progress feels agonizingly slow. I've always pictured these games to be fast. This is almost torturous, just waiting to be shot. Although, they aren't supposed to shoot me, but will they remember? Are they going to expect me to be the only one left?

Some minutes later, I'm coming to a clearing with tall grass and scattered leaves. This is a bad idea. Standing with my back on the tree, I slink down, then turn to look. It's almost like my body or my mind senses danger- like I can feel him out there watching, but where? Constant move rules apply, so he can't perch in a tree to wait for me.

The refs stand is up ahead and further in the distance I see the other team members gathered on a deck. Based on their movements, I can tell they have binoculars and are watching me. Suddenly, this feels very Hunger Games like. *Let's watch the renter get taken out by the professional.* Only the announcer in my head obviously has an accent.

For good measure, I flip the bird at whoever is watching me and when they throw their head back laughing, I know it's Jax. A second later, the other guys are standing beside him and they're passing around the binoculars. If only we weren't in the middle of a paintball field with others watching... I could have a lot of fun with this. Perhaps we could recreate this at Allure.

A breaking twig up ahead startles me. Trying to stay out of view, I sink all the way to the ground and roll to the opposite side. In the distance, just beyond the field, he's walking slowly. I take aim and fire.

One.

Two.

Three.

Miss. Miss. Miss.

Shit!

He sinks to the ground. He knows where I shot from, but doesn't see me.

"Come out, renter!" he yells, firing a shot into the woods, high and to the left of me.

He's trying to scare me. I stay my ground and don't move. There's nothing here to provide cover except the trees and the few bushes.

I stare at the field, but there is no movement. No sound. My heart is nearly pounding a hole out of my chest.

Shit! Shit! Shit! I know he's moving. That's what I should be doing. The competitive side of me wants to win this for the guys, but the other part... she wants to just stand up and yell surrender.

Fuck it. Channel your inner badass Everlee. Carpe diem!

Move with purpose.

I press up just a little so I can get a better view of the field, but still stay tucked behind the tree. There's movement to the left, but I don't know if it's him or the breeze blowing the tops of the grass. Was my shooting that bad that he thought I was nowhere close to where I am?

Or was it that good? The smartass in me chimes, knowing there was no way I meant to shoot that bad. I tuck behind the tree, then turn to press my back against it, taking in a few deep breaths. I peek around the edge again and clearly see him, well, some part of him, crawling low to the ground. Probably a leg. All of the sudden, I'm reminded of the game battleship. Should I fire and aim for some part of him, not knowing if it's the upper, middle, or lower part? Or do I wait and get a clearer shot?

I glance at the guys in the distance with their binoculars trained on me. A smile spreads across my face as I fully flatten on my stomach, legs spread wide. Planting my elbows on the ground, I hold up the gun and narrow in on my sights. The shots fired earlier were quick and unplanned.

My dad's hand rests on my shoulder, and he whispers so low that I barely hear him, "Everlee, take your time and breathe."

My gaze narrows on the buck out in the distance, heart racing. It was the first time my dad let me go hunting with him. I'd been wanting to go for the last several years, but the timing was never right. He would usually bring a deer home and we would eat on it all winter.

He gives my shoulder a slight squeeze. A little nudge to shoot. I know I can make the shot. I've made it on cans a hundred times before. My finger slides over the trigger, my breathing steadies.

A shot echoing somewhere else in the field startles the deer, and he runs off.

My dad sighs beside me and I remove my finger from the trigger and look at him, a tear on the rim of my lid. "I'm sorry, dad. I waited too long."

"It's ok darling. We will find you another one." He rubs the top of my head.

We didn't find any more that trip and I never went back out with him. I was scared I wouldn't be able to pull the trigger again.

Not today, though.

The man moved more into the clearing and I saw his side and legs. He was getting closer to the tree, so he slowed down.

My finger slides over the trigger and my breathing steadies. The memory of the shoulder squeeze pulses through me.

Pull.

Thip! Thip!

The man cries out and grabs his leg and a second later the horn blows, signaling the end. I walk around the tree as the guy is standing.

"Good shot renter."

"Thanks."

"How did you get from over there to where you were? I never saw you move?" He lifts his mask and sets it on his head as we walk back to the rest of the group.

"What do you mean?"

"Your shot pattern."

"Lucky pattern, I guess. I never moved."

He laughs. "Well done. First time?"

"Yes. It was a little more nerve wrecking than I thought it was going to be."

"But fun?"

"Yea. Though if I got shot, I would imagine not so much. I'm sorry for your leg."

He bats his hand in the air. "It's ok. It'll heal."

The guys are running up to me a minute later. Knox gets to me first and lifts me into the air. "Way to go, babe!" He has blue paint spattered across his neck. "That shot. Holy shit. I watched the entire thing, and I literally saw you sink into the zone."

"I may have shot cans in the backyard growing up."

Jax, Callum, and Emmett each give me a hug, while Brady gives me a knuckle bump.

"Who's ready to get some lunch, then head to work?" I ask, and the men grumble.

It's not new to them like it is for me. The desire to work and make it better, bring in more business, come up with more ideas. It is all-consuming and wonderful. Addicting. If I didn't love the men so much, I'd probably sleep at Allure.

"I say we go back home for lunch. There's something I want to snack on," Emmett says.

My eyes cut to him and I blush.

"In front of Brady?"

"What are you thinking about? Perv." He winks, then walks away.

EVERLEE - MAY THE FUCK BE WITH YOU

I'M DRYING UP THE last dish from lunch and putting it back in the cupboard when I feel a pair of hands on my hips. The familiar scent, citrus with a hint of spice, in the air confirms that it's Emmett.

"Nuh- uh buddy," I say, turning in his arms, but he doesn't back away, so we're chest to chest, with his hands gripping the counter beside me. "You called me a perv."

"Did I?" He leans in for a kiss, but I duck under his arm and walk behind him to stand at the island.

When he turns around, his laughter fills the air. "You're going to make me chase you?"

"That's Jax's thing. I didn't think it was yours."

"Someone say my name?" Jax asks, sauntering into the room, fixing the cufflink on his shirt. He drapes his jacket over the back of a barstool, then pauses to look at Emmett and me.

Sin.

Emmett thinks so too.

Jax looks between the two of us and smiles. "What do we have here?" Jax removes the cufflinks he just finished putting on and lays them on the counter and starts rolling up his sleeves.

"Jax," I say breathlessly. "Unfair."

He smiles, a dark smile. "What's unfair?"

"You're both tag teaming me."

"Is that what we're doing?" Jax looks at Emmett. "Are we tag teaming her?"

"Well, I was planning on solo tagging her, but the more the merrier."

"Solo tagging?" I ask, taking a step away from him.

He shrugs. "I was going with the theme."

My eyes catch Jax moving behind me. Fuck, they are boxing me in. Stove on one side, island on the other.

"Ev," Jax whispers, noticing my eyes glancing all around. "Don't do it."

"Don't do what?"

"Whatever it is you're thinking?"

"You're making me. You're trapping me in a corner."

They both pause and ask in near unison, "Do you want us to stop?"

I look at both of them and sigh. They know the answer, but I love that they still ask. "What do you think?"

They smile. "I think I want to lay you on the counter and eat chocolate off your body until you come," Emmett says.

"Well, tell me what you really think," I tease, panting.

He takes a step closer, and when I step back, I bump into something hard. Someone hard.

Emmett's eyes pump as he closes the distance between us. "My favorite kind of sandwich," he says, lifting my chin and pressing his lips to mine. Instantly, I kiss him back and hate myself. I was trying to play hard to get and lasted two seconds.

His hands slide under my shirt and grab my breasts, while Jax's hands slide around my hips and into my pants.

"No panties," he scowls.

When Emmett stops kissing me so he can take my shirt off, I turn my head. "You're surprised?"

"Not at all." His cock presses into my back, at the same time his finger dips inside of me.

Emmett lowers his head and sucks my breast in his mouth while his hand plays with my other nipple.

"A little help, E," Jax calls, sliding his hand around my throat.

I love it when he grabs me by the throat. So domineering. He rarely gets rough when we're with others, but he gives me little tastes- teases.

Emmett slides down my body, planting kisses the entire way as he hooks his fingers in my pants and slides them down. He pats my ankle and I step out of my pants, still unable to look down because of the clamp Jax has on my throat. "Taste her E," he commands.

Emmett also loves when Jax is demanding, though I've never seen Jax be super rough with him. Just words.

Emmett's hand brushes between my legs, and I feel him pull Jax's fingers out. He must suck them, because Jax lets out a moan in my ear, at the same time his cock thrusts up into my back and his grip around my throat weakens. A second later, his finger is back on my clit at the same time Emmett's tongue licks up my wet center.

Jax leans down and whispers in my ear. "Put your leg over his shoulder. I want you to fuck his face and my finger until you come."

I obey, lifting my leg onto Emmett's shoulder. My head presses back into Jax's chest as waves pulse through my body. This feels so fucking good.

Jax's fingers release from my neck and he turns my head to face his. "Kiss me."

Tears threaten the edge of my eyes, because I'm so fucking turned on. It's a new thing that happens to me. Not all the time, but sometimes when I'm over stimulated, my eyes water.

My arm tightly coils around Jax's neck, pulling him closer to me. His tongue presses in without waiting and he kisses me hard. Consumed by desire, my body instinctively reacts, fucking his finger and Emmett's face while my other hand latches into Emmett's hair. The intensity builds as Emmett's hands tighten on my ass, causing my knees to buckle and a low moan to reverberate within me. Our kiss intensifies until it's a frenzy of tongues and fingers as my orgasm smacks into me. I break free from the kiss to let out a loud fucking moan.

"Fuck her with your cock, E. Now," Jax commands.

Emmett stands, pushing his pants down, and notches it into me, pressing in seconds later.

"Oh, goddamn," I whimper.

He holds it there, feeling my pussy pulse around him, still coming off my orgasm.

"Kiss me," Jax says. "I want to taste her on your lips."

I slide my head out of the way and watch them kiss. Slow at first. Jax licks Emmett's lips, then presses his tongue in slowly. Emmett rocks his body faster and faster into me.

"Jax. I need your pants off now. I want you to fuck my face while Emmett fucks my pussy."

He kisses Emmett for another second, then pulls away and looks at me, eyes wild. He loves it. Loves kissing Emmett. Loves fucking Emmett. And loves when Emmett sucks his cock.

He still hasn't sucked Emmett's yet, but we're getting closer. I was actually hoping this weekend would be it. I have some plans to help if he needs it, but I don't think he does. Sometimes when it's just the two of us at night, he asks about it. Not about Emmett's cock specifically, but about sucking cock. I think he's been so hesitant because he doesn't want to be bad. What he doesn't understand is there's no way he could be. Everything he does is perfect. Another moan escapes, like a siren calling out for her cock.

"Fucking now, Jax," I command.

He smiles and I know exactly what he's thinking. He's told me before how cute he thinks I am when I try to top him. His eyes twinkle with humor as he mouths back, 'Fucking now, Jax.'

I glare at him, causing him to chuckle.

"Oh, I can't wait to fuck that pretty little smirk off those lips." He bites at the air in front of me as he pushes down his pants. "Turn around and bend over, princess. My cock is waiting for your mouth." His nose brushes mine.

Emmett pulls his cock out and spins me around. He glides his hand up my back, between my shoulder blades, and pushes me over. His hands wrap around my hips as he glides his cock back into me. Fuck, his piercings feel so good. He presses in deep and the pressure is almost too much to take like this. A whimper escapes from my throat and he backs off a little. I can usually take him deep if I am sitting on him, but bent over... can't happen.

Jax's hands play with my hair for a second before they tighten at the root. "Open wide, princess."

His cock slides in slowly, and I suck him as far as he will go until he's hitting the back of my throat. They pull out at the same time, at the same speed, and something about that just hits me in all the right ways. When they push in again, the arousal on the tip of Jax's cock coats my tongue.

They're being slow. Deliberate. And it's driving me wild.

They both shift, leaning forward, and I know if I were to look up, I'd see them kissing. I can tell because as their kiss deepens, so do their thrusts. They become faster, less in-sync, more erratic. My hand moves up and cups Jax's balls as his hands tighten in my hair. A second later, Emmett's finger is playing with my clit and I hum out in greedy satisfaction around Jax's cock.

"Oh baby," he whimpers.

"In the kitchen? Seriously?" Knox whines, walking in. "And right before work? For shame."

I cut my eyes as far as I can, and see him watching me with a smirk on his face. I'd make some smart-ass comment, but Jax's cock is stuffing my mouth full.

Knox continues, "Well, one of us will ensure that the team is prepared for a successful night."

I release Jax's cock and hold my hand in the air, flipping him off.

"Ohh fuck me? I say fuck you. Which I'll be doing later. Best believe it, shortcake." He walks over and gives me a kiss on my forehead, then grabs Jax's shoulder. "No less than two orgasms, but make it snappy. She's a working woman now and I need her with me tonight. Big night."

Jax thrusts slowly as Knox stands there and watches.

"Can I expect to see you at the club tonight?"

"You want Emmett to come after Bo's and you want Callum and I to come after Vixen?"

"Yes. Ev rented out a room for us. Darling angel that she is. Rather vixen."

"Well, how can we say no, then?"

"Excellent. You can't." He squats down and looks at me. "May the fuck be with you."

"You're an idiot." Jax releases my hand to push him over.

"Not cool dude," Knox stands back up before grabbing my nipple and pinches. "Love these things."

"I'm going to get you molds of them for Christmas."

"Excellent! It will go great with the mold of Emmett's cock I'm getting you." Knox is laughing as he bounces through the kitchen and out of the back door.

"That's a brilliant idea!" Emmett announces, his thrusts slowing as he thinks through whatever it is he's thinking about.

"Care to share? Your idea," Jax inquires.

"Well, I can't tell you in front of Ev. That would ruin the surprise."

"I'm fairly certain she's put it together."

"No."

Jax takes his cock out of my mouth for a second, so I answer, "Molds of all your cocks." Satisfied with my answer, he presses his cock back in.

"Damn."

"Come on, baby. Come for daddy," Jax says and I cut my eyes up at him.

He winks at me and starts thrusting faster, causing tears to stream down my face, while Emmett's finger works my clit.

"She's getting close," Emmett moans out. His hips rotate inside while his piercings nearly vibrate against my walls.

I press back, sucking his cock in and let him grind deep in me, causing tingles to sweep up my spine. One more time.

BAM!

Waves of pleasure crash around me as my orgasm peaks. I latch my hands onto the back of Jax and pull him into my mouth, sucking him so hard as I ride my orgasm. His cock is my fucking drug. A second later, Emmett, then Jax are releasing inside of me and my muscles turn to mush.

"Goddamn Ev," Jax says, pulling his cock out of my mouth.

"Sorry," I mumble, whipping my chin.

Emmett grabs the back of my neck and spins me around, kissing me deep, licking and sucking the remaining come out of my mouth. When we break apart, I catch Jax staring at Emmett's cock, sucking his bottom lip.

He hasn't tasted him, but I know he wants to.

"Tonight." I pump my eyebrows, and he looks at me knowingly, then at Emmett. He gives a slight nod and Emmett looks between the two of us and smiles. "I'm going to clean up so I can get to work. I've got some exciting things planned I want to try, and I think it will be perfect for Jax's first time."

"Ev..." he says cautiously, with a hint of giddy excitement on his face.

"Don't sweat my pet."

JAX - NEVER CLIMB INTO A SHOWER AND EXPECT NOTHING

THE MUSCLES IN MY stomach tighten with nerves and excitement. Even though it's still been months since I've come out to my family, I still get nervous around Emmett. I know he loves and accepts me and he's been so patient while I figure out who I am and what I want.

Less really with what I want, because I know what I want. I want Ev and him. Some say you can't truly love more than one person, but I call bullshit on that. Look at all the parents that have more than one kid. Why is it ok for them to have equal love for their children, but an adult can't? Society has put those constraints on people, made them feel like they can and should only love one.

No. My heart has always had a place for Emmett in it, and I was too blind or too scared to see what that place really looked like. I tried to say it was friendly, that we were brothers, but somewhere I knew, even if I didn't want to admit it.

It's weird.

I've been so guarded with my heart my entire life, allowing myself to only really love Callum. We were a team. Mrs. Mary had a special place, but I don't know if I would have ever admitted it was love. I couldn't. If I loved her, then she would leave.

It wasn't until Everlee that everything changed. I wanted to love her. I wanted her to know that love from me. She's so accepting and... with her, I can be anyone. She taught me that. Once I opened myself up to the idea of loving her and letting her in, it's like the rest of my walls crumbled.

The tucked-away corner of my heart where my feelings for Emmett were hidden started to grow. I still wouldn't call myself bi, even though I guess that's what I am. Right? I love Everlee and I love him, even if I haven't told him yet. But I feel it inside of me. With him, I have a desire to explore and try things I've never wanted to do with a man before. My mouth waters at the thought of him in it, and I want to know what it feels like to have him inside of me.

No one else but him.

God, he's been so good and so patient with me.

Fear has consumed me for years. Fear that this was going to feel wrong, or scared that it wouldn't.

I push open his bathroom door and the steam has fogged the mirrors.

"Hello?" He swipes his hand across the glass and a smile pulls at his lips. "Hello."

I have no intentions of coming in here other than to be near him. Since Everlee has shown me love and acceptance, it's like I have this need to make up for lost time. I've talked to her about it a little and she tells me to take it slow, that it's not a race and we have forever. But... I don't know.

He pushes the door of the shower open and smiles at me. "Come back for more?"

"Not really. I just wanted to spend some time with you." I smile.

"Time?"

I nod and wrap my hand around the back of his head and pull him in for a kiss. He takes two steps backward into the shower, pulling me with him so the rainfall is falling down on us.

When we break for air, he hands me the loofa and soap. "Are you ready for tonight?" he asks.

"Tonight?" My heart gives a jolt in my chest as nerves get the better of me. Images of me on my knees in front of Emmett evoke a fiery blend of passion and apprehension.

"The party. Can you manage Vixen's until closing and then join us at Allure?"

"It will be a long night." But a good night.

"Here. Let me," Emmett offers, taking the loofa from me and turning me around.

It smells like him. The soap. Was that my subconscious reason for coming in here, because I wanted his scent to be on me? Torturing me? Making me want him all night?

His lips gently press against my back, sending shivers down my spine, as one of his hands glides the loofa across my chest, while his other hand softly massages.

"Emmett," I murmur out, leaning my head back as his hand travels further down. "No funny business."

"None," he mumbles against my skin, inching his hand down further.

Fuck. He knows what he's doing to me.

"I'm simply just washing your body. Getting it clean for Everlee."

A low grumble rattles in my chest as my stomach tightens with anticipation.

"You're so kind."

"It's the least I can do for her, really." His hand slides down my shaft, splitting his fingers.

A tingle runs up my spine and down my legs.

This was a bad idea. Why did I think coming into a shower with him would not end up in some sort of release?

You knew it would.

With a gentle touch, he cups my balls in his hands, lathering them up with the soapy suds cascading down my body.

"So dirty here."

I have no words. My throat seizes as feelings of pleasure dance over my skin.

He runs his hand back up my shaft, squeezing at the head, then sliding his fist back down again.

"Damn it, E."

Abandoning the loofa, his hand roams over my hip, sending shivers of pleasure down my spine before wrapping around my erect shaft.

My head falls back onto his shoulder. "You ass," I murmur out and turn around, shoving him back against the wall, letting my cock rub along his. God, his fucking piercings. I take his mouth in a passionate kiss, pulsing my tongue in unison with my hip thrusts. I feel like I'm going to explode right now. He feels so good.

He pushes me off, then starts to drop to his knees, but I stop him. "No."

He looks at me, confused.

"Not right now. I want you to do it when I can do it back to you and... I want Ev there. I want her to share in this moment with us," I say, nibbling on my bottom lip.

"I love that."

"Yea? I don't want you to think I need her there... to... you know. I just... I think she has something planned... I mean, I'm sure she'd understand if we-"

"Jax." Emmett grabs my face to silence me. "I don't think I've ever seen you like this... so unsure. But it's cute. I really don't mind waiting for Ev. I want her there too."

"You do?"

He chuckles. "Yes. I love her so much and to experience this first with her. Watching her, watch us, turns me on almost as much as we turn her on, I'm sure."

"That must be a lot."

"She loves watching us." He chuckles.

"Should we take a video and send it to her?"

"She'd fucking lose her mind."

"Maybe next time... when we aren't in the shower."

Emmett pumps his eyebrows. "In the meantime, though. I need to finish cleaning us."

I watch his hands move down to both our cocks as he clasps his hands around them.

My hands lay over his and squeeze. My hips are rocking just a second behind his, causing my cock to rub along his piercings. They are a fucking dream.

"I can't wait to feel your cock inside of me," I mumble out.

Emmett pauses for a second. "Me either." He leans forward and kisses me.

Our hands and thrusts slow, mimicking our tongues. The hot water rushes over our body as our kiss deepens. He drops his hand and grabs my face, kissing me deeper. With need. My body presses against his, pinning him against the wall while our cocks seek friction and touch. God, I need more. I want to take him in my mouth so badly right now. Make him come so fucking hard.

As more desire edges into me, I press harder. Without warning, Emmett's finger slides down and brushes over my ass. My cock jerks into him, but we don't stop. That was his way of giving me a chance to stop him, but I won't. I need him. I need this release. Like I need water.

He presses his finger against my forbidden entrance, and my balls tighten.

More.

I need more.

I mimic him and slide my hand between the wall and his body and swipe over his ass.

He doesn't stop me, so I press gently. We don't have any lube, only soap and water, which doesn't do a lot, so we're both really slow. Really just applying pressure, because that's all we need right now. I'm so close to the edge, and I have to imagine he is too.

"I don't know if I can wait," I whimper out.

"You can. And will." He presses his finger in just a little, and it's all I need. My hips jerk forward and I grab our cocks with my other hand and pump so fucking hard until I'm shooting all over our chest and crying out.

My mouth is salivating as I watch his cock pulse just before he comes.

"Oh my God." I pant out, stroking our cocks until we're done.

"Fuck."

"Tonight, E. I'm so fucking ready."

He smiles.

EVERLEE - RUNNING A SEX CLUB

FORTY MINUTES LATER, I'M walking into Allure. The lights flicker and dance, casting long shadows on the walls, a foreshadowing of what's coming in a few hours. Meanwhile, people scurry around, diligently putting the finishing touches on the decorations. This is the first time Allure has done a themed event, so it needs to be perfect.

Knox is so excited. Almost over the top. He had to have an eight-foot-tall spider with a diameter of almost twenty feet wide. Its legs are only a few feet off the edges of the room, but it looks good.

The corners of the room have large spider webs placed in them, adding to the spooky ambiance, and they filled the welcome bowl at the front with candy, fruit roll-ups, and a variety of masks.

I can't wait. I just hope the guys are up to it after they close Vixen. We've done this a couple of times over the last several months- rented a room in Eden or Infernus. Tonight, we're in Eden. Infernus booked up months ago, which makes me want to add another room, but we're trying to figure out where to put it. There is some space at the back, but it would be much smaller than the others, so Knox and I are working on a theme that really fits.

After the beach, I was nervous and doubted my decision to manage a sex club, but it has turned out to be a great decision. It was a little awkward at the going away party when everyone was asking what I was doing. Liz said I should have made up something like sailing around the world or opening a bookstore, but I didn't. I honestly didn't think it would come up that much, but damn. It was like the entire topic at the office. Then a few of us went out for drinks where they let the alcohol take over and started coming up with lots of ideas about why I couldn't or wouldn't tell them. A few said a sex club, but that usually got so many laughs that by the time they stopped, the group was on to something else.

"There you are!" Knox yells from the second-story balcony just outside of our office.

He looks good. Black pants, black jacket over a burnt orange shirt. It's his Halloween outfit. Well, not the one he's going to wear later. He won't tell me what that one is.

I bought some fairy wings at the store on the way here. Brady drove me since Knox had already left, and when he saw it was a sex store, he stayed in the car. I don't know why he's so uncomfortable with that, but not the club we work at.

Anyway, they didn't have a huge selection left. The corset is a black low-rise thong with a very low-cut bra held together by black lace with purple flowers sewed in. It has another sheer piece that hangs over my shoulders like a see-through dress that the wings attach to. And there are two garter belts that snap into the panties. The wings are really what sold it for me. They are stunning. Large, black lace with purple flowers and gems sewed in. It also came with a crown too, so there's that.

I meet him at the stairs leading up to the offices. "What's up?"

"How are you?" He smiles.

Curious why he's asking, my head falls to the side. "Good... why?"

"Just making sure." He places his hand on my lower back and guides me to the floor. "Do you like?" He twirls around.

"I do. I think you did a great job picking out the decorations."

"It wasn't all me. Liz obviously had her say. I think she's more excited about tonight than we are."

She had rented out a room in Infernus months ago when we were still just talking about doing a themed night. It was Liz's idea, since the themed parties were working out so well at Vixen.

"I doubt that." I smile, laying my hand on his arm.

He places his hand over mine and brings it to his lips.

One of the things I love most about this place is that we don't have to hide who we are. Everyone knows we're in a relationship and have been really supportive. A few women thought they could try to step into our relationship and started flirting with the guys when they found out. Before I could correct them, Callum did. They tried to argue with him about how it wasn't fair that I got to have four of them, but they only got me and how I was being selfish. Callum quickly put them in their place, then gave them excellent referrals for another job somewhere else. I was concerned they would run their mouth, but one of the first things Callum did when he agreed to take over was to make everyone sign updated NDAs. The ones on file were for discussing customers, but he changed it to customers and coworkers.

"Do you want to give the speech tonight?" he asks.

I glance at my watch, not realizing what time it is. "I think it would be better if it came from you. You've really owned tonight from the beginning."

He pumps his eyebrows at me before he whistles to get everyone's attention. People stop what they are doing, climb down from ladders, and walk out from behind the bar, filling the main floor.

Wanting to give him space, I pat this butt twice, then take two steps to the left.

"Right." He clasps his hands together and holds them in front of his chest like he's praying. "Tonight is our first themed night."

The room erupts in applause, and his infectious smile spreads across his face.

"I want to thank every one of you for coming in early today after a late-night last night to help flip this place around into the spooky spectacular event that it is. It looks absolutely amazing and Ev and I haven't even finished touring all the rooms to make sure they're ready, but I have the utmost confidence in this team."

Everyone claps again.

He glances at his watch. "We have about four hours left before doors open and guests start arriving. We are catering dinner from Bo La Vie for all of you as a thank you. Emmett will drop it off in about two hours. Once you're complete with your final assignments and Ev or I check it off, you're welcome to leave or stay for some dinner. Not mandatory, of course, but," he pauses and looks at me. "I told Emmett to go all out with the food, so who knows what he's bringing?"

Everyone looks around excitedly.

"Memberships are up over the last several months, and with the email blasts and advertising we've done for tonight... we expect it to be a full house. Rooms are on two-hour rental blocks with thirty minutes in between for cleaning and sanitizing. We usually have three per crew, but we've bumped it to five and we'll have three total crews tonight instead of the typical one. We have also staggered the reservation times in fifteen-minute intervals to help as well. Guests staying in Eden and Infernus were charged a premium for tonight, and those rooms will not be turned. Remember to talk about our elite memberships and the benefits of those levels. I would love to get some conversion on premium memberships tonight. Whoever signs up the most premium memberships will get a thousand-dollar bonus and get an extra day of vacation."

Everyone starts excitedly chatting.

Knox looks at me and holds his arm out. "Thank Everlee for that brilliant idea."

Heat flushes my cheeks.

Knox claps his hands. "Ok team. Everlee and I will walk around, helping where needed so you all can get home or get to the changing rooms and change into your outfits for tonight. Remember, if you are on Infernus level, the darker the costume, the better. And be ready to scare the shit out of people, but no touching. We have a few chainsaws without the blades tucked behind some decorations. If you want to chase people, chase them. But again, no touching. When they booked the rooms for this evening, they were told what it may entail, so they are all prepared to be scared. If you're in Eden... well, good luck. It's going to be hard figuring out how to do light and happy, but scary." He laughs. "All kidding aside. The decorations up there are truly phenomenal! And last, the book nook. We have extra cozy blankets and socks in there for people who just want to read. I didn't think it was going to be that popular, but damn it if Everlee wasn't right. We need to keep a close eye on those rooms and have stationed the fourth cleaning crew for the book nook exclusively. If there is a long wait for those rooms, we may have to rent them out in blocks. Tonight will be a test, so be prepared for it to be clunky. If it is, it's ok. We'll learn and get through it. Just try to do the best you can." He looks at me and winks. "Is there anything else you want to add, Ev?"

Taking a step forward, I clasp my hands behind my back. "Not much. Just want to reiterate how proud of you we are and how excited for tonight I am. This place looks absolutely amazing, and it's thanks to all of you."

The crowd breaks up and Knox and I head back up to the office for a bit and run through some finances and projections for tonight. It's going to be a busy night. Potentially the biggest night we've had times two, which is equal parts nerve wrecking and exciting. I'm going to be on such a high that I likely won't be able to sleep at all, which will work out nicely for all the plans I have for tonight... rather, tomorrow morning. I just hope the guys are up for it.

EVERLEE - MISCOMMUNICATION

MY HANDS CLAMP TIGHTER onto the railing from the second-floor balcony as excitement dances through me. The main floor is buzzing with people and the demonstrations are standing room only. We've had ten percent of our members convert to Eden and Infernus tiers, with a few getting both levels. My head is still spinning with how great this night, hell, these last few months have gone. The only problem is that I'm scared it's going to lose some of its exclusivity feeling. I'm learning quickly that there's a fine line between the two. We increased new member dues last month, and I'm going to have to convince Knox to do it again.

"This is wild, isn't it?" Knox asks, grabbing me around the waist and spinning me in a circle. A high-pitched squeal shoots out of my mouth. I'd been so focused on the people below, I hadn't heard him walk up behind me.

"It's unbelievable."

"There are so many people. Definitely need to celebrate." He beams with pride.

"Yea... about that..." I drag out.

He stares at me and chuckles. "Look. I already know what you're going to say. I can see the wheels spinnin' in your head and I'm on board."

"You are?" I ask, shocked. I was ready to move through my entire speech about profitability and exclusivity and trends and charts and everything else.

"Yea. Why wouldn't I be on board? I mean, it may get a little messy, but..." he shrugs.

"I'm going to need you to share what you think I'm thinking about because the last time we did this, and I thought we were on the same page, I had to return a five-foot-tall oyster shaped statue."

"What? I still think it would have been a great addition to the décor."

"It had golden sequins."

He holds his finger up in the air. "I didn't know it was sequins. It just said gold."

"Knox."

He rolls his eyes. "Fine. That wasn't my best idea, but when you agreed... I was really excited."

"Which makes sense why you would think that since I was actually talking about doing a complete deep clean with a repaint on the interior."

"I hate we had to shut down for a week, but it looks better in here."

"So what did you think I was going to say right now?"

"That you wanted to use the fruit roll ups on our cocks tonight."

"What?"

"So you weren't thinking that?"

"No. Well. Not at this second."

"So you don't want to use them on us?"

"I do. I had plans for that tonight, but... how did you know?"

"Girl. I know more about you than you do." He winks, causing my stomach to flutter.

"Perv."

"What? It's the truth. So, if you weren't talking about that, then what were you thinking about?"

Nerves get the better of me because I don't want there to be a tension between us tonight. "We'll talk about it tomorrow."

"Talk about what tomorrow?" A hand claps on my back.

When I turn around, I find Emmett wearing a Dracula costume with a wig on and fangs in his mouth.

"Dracula. Classic."

"What? I thought he was a foodie and so am I."

Some sort of snort-chuckle flies out of my mouth and I clamp my hand over my lips. "Dracula? A foodie?"

"Ok, fine. He liked to play with his food and so do I. I was trying to not get all morbid."

"I love you," I say, pressing my lips to his.

With a moan, he deepens the kiss, his hand gripping my waist and drawing me towards him, as he spins us around and pins me against the wall. "I want to suck your blood," he says with a European accent. He presses his teeth to my neck and I immediately have to squeeze my legs together.

"Enough. Break it up, you two. I don't come to your place of business and start kissing on you, Emmett," Knox says, wiggling his arms between us. "Have some respect for the lady."

Emmett's eyes bounce back and forth between the two of us before he smiles and releases me. "You're right. I'm sorry."

I glance at my watch. "Guys should be here within the hour." And that hour can't get here quick enough. Between all of my plans for tonight with the guys and watching all the other couples move around... I. Am. Ready!

"Do you need help setting up for tonight? You can tell me which room is ours and I can put our stuff in it," Emmett asks, trying to spoil the surprise.

"Nice try, buddy." I push him away and he lets me.

"I need your help with something, E."

"What do you need help with?" I ask.

He smiles at me. "You have plans and so do I. I found something down in storage when we were doing the deep clean that I think we're all going to like a lot. And I think it will be a most excellent addition to one of our rooms."

"What is it?"

"Evey baby. I'm not going to tell you. You'll just have to find out later."

My eyes narrow to thin slits and he just laughs at me.

"I'm at your service, my liege."

"Damn it! You two better not mess up what I have planned."

"We'd never dream of it," Knox smiles and I flip him the bird just before they disappear into the office.

Change of plans. I pull out my phone and text Brady and ask him to meet me in the employee bathroom with my costume now.

JAX- A WOLF AND A DRAGON WALK INTO A SEX CLUB...

CALLUM AND I ARE in the car, driving over to Allure. Vixen just had another record night and Emmett's caramel apple vodka martini was a hit. Low has really taken to managing the bar in Emmett's absence, which is a good thing for him. He's not running himself ragged anymore and can focus on his restaurant.

The closer we get to Allure, the more my stomach knots. I don't know if it's more nerves or excitement, but I'm so ready to take all of Emmett in every way. He's been so patient with me as I explore this new side of our relationship. Every time we've been together since the beach, he's been so slow and thoughtful. Never pushing. But damn it. I want him to push. I want him to just be rough. I haven't felt him inside of me yet, in any way, and damn if I want to.

I've learned a new term. Frotting. It's what we do when I'm not fucking his ass. We lay on one another and rub our penises together, mostly because our moments start with flirting, then kissing, and we just don't stop. Everlee bought us a gift, because she's been absolutely over the moon with us exploring this new side. It's a silicone shaped device she says simulates her pussy when we both fuck her. We can lube our cocks up and fuck this toy if we don't want to use our hands or our bodies for friction.

My cock twitches at the thought.

Tonight.

Tonight is the night I'm going to suck Emmett's cock until he comes down my throat.

I rub my hands on my legs; the friction creating a soothing sensation.

"You ok there?" Callum asks, shaking my shoulder.

"Yea."

"You've been quiet. Are you nervous about tonight?"

"Not really. I mean, maybe a little. I just don't want it to be... bad."

Callum laughs. "Brother. I don't think you can."

The knots in my stomach twist tighter. Callum and I have talked about this a few times and he's been super supportive, but it's still weird as fuck. He told me he's thought for a while that I may be bi, but didn't want to say anything or push. He thinks it's part of the reason I joined the SEALs, so I could prove to myself that I wasn't. I don't know if that's why or not. I had so much anger when I was younger, and confusion. Confusion about who I was, who I wanted to be. I didn't have an issue with possibly loving another man, because I knew Emmett liked other men every once in a while, and that was fine. Love is love. It was just that I liked Emmett like that. It kind of snuck up on me from nowhere, and I was terrified. Terrified if I allowed myself to feel those things, it would ruin our family.

So I did what most people do in awkward situations.

I ran.

I ran off to the SEALs and fought hard. Worked hard. I became one of the best damn SEALs there was. Quick and effective. I felt nothing. No emotion. Just a brotherhood. Until I would come back for a visit and see Emmett, and then all the confusion would resurface. Again, I would ignore it. Push it down until I could forget about it.

Until Everlee.

Damn her.

She came in and found my little wound and ripped the damn band-aid off, exposing all my feelings. I let myself be loved by her and, in return, fell in love with her. It still felt… incomplete, though. There was a lot of guilt festering inside of me because I didn't want her thinking she wasn't enough. But the closer I grew to her, the closer I felt to Emmett. Each time we would fuck her together, it was like those feelings I'd pushed down were inching closer to the surface. She's not jealous of Emmett and me, and encourages it when she can, creating a safe space in our relationship to let us explore. She tells me it's perfectly normal to love more than one person. She loves us four, so why can't I love two?

"You good?" Callum asks.

"Yea," I laugh, running my hand through my hair. "Man, what are you even dressing up as?"

"I'm not dressing up."

"You know how excited Ev was about dressing up."

"I know. And I want to do that for her. But I don't like to dress up. I like her in costumes, but I don't like to be in one."

"That's fucked up."

"What are you dressing up as?"

I pull the wolf's mask out of the bag in the backseat. "She had a dream last night about me being a wolf, so I thought I'd make it come to life."

Callum laughs. "Well, you know what they say about wolves?"

"What?"

"They can hear better, see better, and eat better."

"It's hard to eat her better. I'm already a champ at that."

We both laugh.

"So you aren't dressing up for real? Had I known that, I would have gotten you a mask or something."

"I found a blue and gold jacket, so I'll wear that."

"Wow," I say deadpan.

"I don't wear a lot of colors... so this is scary for me."

"I can't with you."

Callum flashes the badge at the gate for Allure and the arm swings up. As we pull into our parking space, my body tingles.

When we walk inside, the place is packed. I shouldn't be surprised. Everlee and Knox have been talking about it for the last week. They were concerned about the shortage of staff given the number of reservations, not to mention the additional members who sporadically show up.

The woman at the front is dressed in a cat-woman outfit, complete with a shiny latex one piece and cat ears perched on top of her head. When we walk in, she starts to speak to us, then realizes who we are and waves us through, unlocking the set of internal doors. We usually use the back door, but we got here a little earlier than expected, so we want to surprise Everlee.

On the table just inside the door is a bowl of leftover candies and a few miscellaneous masks. They usually have simple black and white ones, but they've added a few others for the theme tonight- a cat, a clown, a wolf, and a dragon remain. I grab the dragon mask, because even though it's larger than the others, it matches his blue and gold suit. Almost like it was meant to be. "Wear this." I shove the mask into his chest.

He grabs it and smiles at me. "A dragon?"

"Matches your personality. Dominating, ruthless, fiery."

"Fine," he huffs, slipping it over his head. "Happy?"

"That's my middle name, brother."

"Bullshit."

"Now let's find our girl."

EVERLEE - WHEN DREAMS COME TO LIFE

ADJUSTING THE FAIRY MASK on my face, I walk around the club, glancing at my watch. It's been almost an hour since I've seen Emmett or Knox. They were up to something. I could tell by the shit-eating grin on Knox's face and Emmett was too eager to help. If they mess up the plans for tonight... I grumble before I laugh. There weren't a lot of plans. I just wanted to dress up for them because I know how much they love me in costumes. And fruit roll-ups. I've been seeing the trend float around on my socials and thought it could be fun for both Jax and me.

The hairs on the back of my neck prickle. Someone's watching me. When I turn around, I see a man in a blue and gold suit wearing a dragon mask, sitting in the corner of the bar playing with his drink, staring at me. My face flushes and I'm frozen in my spot. He feels familiar, but it's so hard to tell with his mask on. I know it's not Knox, because he still isn't drinking a ton, and Emmett is a vampire, and Callum and Jax shouldn't be here yet.

Fuck!

No.

I shake my head to clear it.

No.

For a brief second, like a microsecond, like the smallest of the small seconds, I thought it may be Dick, but he can't fill out a suit like that man can.

A hand brushes across my lower back, followed by muffled words I can't make out.

When I turn to find the man, there's no one there, just the backs of several people walking away.

Weird.

I look back at the bar, and the man in the dragon mask is gone. Turning quickly, I try to find him, but it's like he vanished.

What in the hell?

When another hand brushes along my back, I spin on my heel with breakneck speed. If someone's fucking with me, they picked the wrong person.

Emmett.

"You ok?" He looks at me and laughs, then pauses. "Goddamn Ev." He wraps his hand around my waist and pulls me in, brushing his lips against my neck. "I vant to suck your blood," he says with a thick European accent.

His teeth clamp on my neck, causing goosebumps to spread across my skin. "E." I laugh and playfully punch his chest. His tongue swipes across my neck before he clamps down a little harder, then releases.

"Sorry. You looked worried earlier, but when I saw you, I lost control. Everything ok?"

"Yea. All's good." I didn't want to tell him about dragon man yet because he'd go into full protection mode. "Have you heard from Callum or Jax?"

"Not yet." He glances at his watch. "They should close soon and be here within the hour. Are you ready for tonight?"

"So ready. You?"

"So ready," he mocks and I slap his chest, but he catches my hand. "Seriously. Thank you. I'm not saying that Jax and I wouldn't have gotten to where we are now without you, but... you showed him it was ok to love and be loved."

His sudden sincerity causes a ball to form in my throat and makes my stomach tighten. "E," I whisper out.

He grabs my other wrist and holds them pinned to his chest. "Sorry. Didn't mean to make you emotional. I just wanted you to know... I love you so much it hurts, and I'm so thankful to you for so many things."

"I love you too." Leaning in, I give him the most awkward kiss ever, because his fangs are halfway out of his mouth, so I'm kissing plastic. "Well, that was awkward as fuck."

We're both laughing when he stops and looks up at the second level balcony by our office and his eyes go wide as a low chuckle vibrates in his chest.

When I turn and look, I fall back into Emmett, knees weak and dizzy. "Fucking hell." A tear falls from my eye.

Knox is standing on the second level with his paintball mask on wearing black cargo pants and a black cotton shirt with the sleeves rolled up, exposing his muscles and tattoos. He looks like a mean son of a bitch. I'm panting and Emmett is standing behind me with his hands on my shoulders.

"Ass," he mumbles under his breath. "I didn't realize we were trying to be sexy."

I turn quickly to look at him. "You're a sexy vampire, my love, and you can suck my blood whenever you want... and my pussy." I kiss him on the cheek, much less awkward than before.

When I look back at Knox, he grabs onto the railing and fucking leaps over it, landing on the main floor in a superhero pose, knees bent, hand on the ground, looking up at me.

Wet dream.

Body buzzing and completely on fire, I walk over and stand in front of him. He stands without speaking and curves his neck in an S shape like a snake slithering up to meet its prey eye to eye. He leans forward and growls in my ear. A puff of air escapes and I'm pretty sure I'm leaking down my leg.

"Fucking hell."

He grabs my hand and spins me around, then pulls me towards him. His cock presses into my back as his hands slide around my body, over my hips, and between my legs.

"Who the fuck are you right now?"

"Your worst nightmare," he growls.

"Doubt it. More like my best nightmare," I mumble under my breath.

"Walk." He thrusts his hips into mine.

"Where are we going?"

"To play in the ropes, little fae."

Little fae. His words remind me of the dream I had last night.

Knox and Emmett walk me to the large circular room with the elevators in it that lead to Eden or Infernus.

Moments later, we're walking through the doors of Eden. It's still as breathtakingly beautiful as the first time I saw it with its golds, whites, and greens. Sometimes, before we open, I bring my paperwork and a blanket up here and sit under the large tree and work.

"Knox..." If he is trying to ruin my surprise, so help me!

"I'm taking over your surprise tonight, love," he says in a deep, growly voice.

"Are you shitting me?"

"I'd never." He breaks character only for a second when he answers with a bounce in his voice, before he corrects and repeats with his deep voice. "I'd never."

Most nights we would be out of place in our attire at Eden, but it seems others are getting into the Halloween spirit as well. A lot of fae running around, and a few dragons.

Dragons.

Speaking of, the blue and golden dragon is back and sitting at the bar watching me. The hairs on my arm stand as his head cocks to the side, watching me watch him. He gets up and saunters over to me, taking his time. With each step he takes, my pulse picks up, pounding harder in my chest- through my body. With a shaky hand, I reach out and interlock my fingers with Knox's.

"Little fae," the dragon calls, voice low and gravelly. When I see his eyes, the tension falls from my shoulders.

Callum.

"Where's Jax?" I ask, looking around him, expecting Jax to be here too.

Callum nods his head behind me. When I turn, I see a man with a werewolf mask on and I'm floored. Pieces of my dream from last night mess with my head, blurring the lines of reality. Obviously, I'm not a fae and the guys aren't supernatural, but it's like they're fucking with me. Callum is wearing a blue and gold suit with a dragon face, Emmett is dressed up as a vampire, Jax as a wolf, and Knox as a SEAL. Sure, it isn't a selkie, but seriously. What is happening?

Knox pushes the door open to our room, and I freeze.

EVERLEE - BEST NIGHTMARE

Shock freezes me in my spot for a moment while I stare at the room. I'm ashamed to say I haven't been in it much since we took over management because I don't go to most of the private rooms unless I need to. I'm regretting this now because I'm creeped the fuck out. Like seriously. Someone is playing a joke on me, although I don't know how that would be possible. It's not like they can see inside of my dreams.

The room is stark white. White floors, walls, and a white bed on the far left of the room. On the right is a white X attached to the wheel. There are several other differences from my dream, however, like the bed is here, versus the table covered by a white sheet and the shelf with glasses.

"Are you ok?" Emmett asks.

"It's just... this reminds me of my dream."

"We were talking about it last night, renovating this room. It's kind of... blah. Maybe that's why?" Emmett offers.

"We did?"

"Both you and Knox were going on about how it feels so sterile and would be the perfect place to kill someone. That's when I cut the drinks off."

"Well, drunk us weren't wrong." It also makes sense why I was able to get this room when all the other rooms had been booked for months. It's just plain. "What's that?" I point at some object in the middle of the floor covered in a sheet.

Knox claps his hands excitedly. "Something I had E bring up. I found it in storage and thought we should try it out before we figure out which room to put it in."

"Or no room at all. Put it on the main floor," Emmett suggests.

"What is it?"

"Oh love," Knox coos. "It's a medieval tongue chair."

"Come again?"

"You will. Again and again and again." He nods his head at Emmett, who whips the sheet off dramatically.

"What the fuck?" This was in my dream. What did I have to drink last night? Or today. Shit. Maybe this is still a dream. It has to be right? The guys are dressed up. They never dress up.

"It's a chair. You sit on it and we lay underneath and eat your pussy until you're coming down our throats." He points to the little circular pad held up by chains to the underside of the seat. "And it comes with a little headrest."

"I..."

Callum, now without his mask, walks up from behind and wraps his arms around me. His face is pressed next to mine, locking me in place. "I think," he whispers, unhooking my wings, "you should sit down." He hands them to someone, and as his fingers graze my skin, he slowly pulls my mesh top off my shoulders, his lips leaving a trail of kisses along my exposed neck. "You've had a long night." My top slips past my breasts then continues to slide down, so I'm standing in front of my men in nothing but my bra and panties.

"I really wanted to wear my costume for you all."

"You did."

"For longer than two minutes," I huff.

"You can wear it again, but I can't promise you'll wear it any longer next time," Callum says, roughly grabbing my breasts from behind. "Now move." He pushes me along with his hips, stepping when I step so his chest stays connected to my back.

When we get to the chair, he spins me around and pushes me down.

"This suit is making you more... aggressive."

His eyes twinkle at me.

"I like it."

"I know. Now shut your mouth unless I tell you to open it."

A tingling sensation sweeps across my skin, causing my hairs to stand on end. His single index finger presses under my chin and tilts my head up to look at him, with his eyes wide and waiting for a response. "Yes, sir," I hurry out in a pant.

"Good girl." My stomach clenches at his praise as I watch him walk over to our overnight bag on the bed. "Do you remember our safe word?"

I nod, then quickly correct. "Yes, sir. Cupid." We've never changed it.

He smiles, then pulls something out of the bag.

I want to ask what it is, but don't. It would break the rules and even though I want to see what his punishment looks like, I also want to be his good girl. Their good girl.

Emmett and Jax huddle to the right side of the room, bulges pressing at the seam of their pants. Knox stands behind me, with his mask still on and his hands clasped behind his back. This was not how tonight was supposed to go. I had plans. Sweet and messy plans. Plans that didn't involve me sitting in a tongue chair.

He slides the leather strap between his fingers, then lets it pop tightly like a folded belt.

My stomach clenches as I suck on my bottom lip.

He walks over and presses his thumb on my lip and drags it from my teeth. "No."

My heart is hammering a hole in my chest as I stare up at him. He usually watches the guys with me, filling in where needed, but tonight, he's not. He's taking what he wants first.

His hand slides down my neck and around my shoulder as he walks behind me. His touch lingers on my arm, leaving a tingling sensation as he places the leather cuff around my wrist, and then repeats the action on the other side.

"Eyes on me, baby girl," Callum says, walking in front of me. "Knox." He nods his head to the bed.

I start to look, but Callum shifts ever so slightly, reminding me to keep my eyes on him.

"Good girl."

I've never wanted to move my eyes more than I do right now. When someone tells you that you can't do something, every fiber of your being rebels, urging you to defy their words.

Callum stands with his legs pressed between mine and his hand around my throat, while his fingers rub along the back of my neck. "Are you going to be a good little fae for us tonight?"

My eyes were already on him, but when he calls me little fae, I feel them snap to him.

His eyes grow wide, waiting for an answer.

Swallowing the knot that has inconveniently lodged itself in my throat, I whisper out, "Yes, sir."

"Yes. Yes, you are. You will not come until we let you. You will not moan, you will not make a sound, unless we give you permission."

"Moan?" I cry out. They know me. That is my thing. It's as involuntary as breathing.

"Jax," Callum commands.

My eyes flick to the side to see him walking over with a deliciously evil smile spread across his face. He pulls out a flogger from behind his back and my legs clench together.

"Oh no, darling. Your legs stay open," Callum says, pulling my legs open at the same time Knox walks over with two leather cuffs.

He falls to his knees and straps my ankles to each leg of the chair.

Knox is still wearing his mask, so it's hard to make out his eyes, but when he tilts his head up to look at me, I glare at him. I can tell by the little shake of his chest that he's chuckling.

When Knox and Callum step away, Jax takes their spot and gently runs the flogger up my leg along the inside of my knee and flicks it at my pussy.

I moan out as the sting bites, but only for a second. The thin layer of fabric on my panties does little to help the pain.

"Again," Callum commands. "No noises, no moaning."

Jax flicks his wrist again and the leather tips sting. My stomach clenches tightly as I focus on not making a noise.

"Very good," Callum praises, then looks at Emmett and nods his head.

I'm getting the impression that this was all planned out and has been for some time. They are communicating with glances and head nods and know exactly what each other mean. I'm going to fucking get my fruit roll-up flavored cock though, even if that means I get no sleep tonight! It was the one thing I wanted to do. Well, that and orgasms, and judging by the mood in the room, that seems to be all they have planned for tonight.

It's been a couple of days since we've all been together at the same time, so it seems to be long overdue.

Emmett moves behind me and I can feel him sliding into position under the chair. When I try to look down, the flogger lifts my chin back up. "Eyes on me, little fae," Jax commands.

My eyes pulse again. I don't know why it's such a turn on. I'm not even wearing my wings anymore, but I am wearing my bra and panties. How is Emmett going to lick my pussy?

As if hearing my thoughts, Knox walks over with a pair of scissors in his hand and slides the bottom blade up my stomach, between my breasts, and cuts through the fabric. My breast bounce under the release of pressure. "Oh, so perfect," Knox moans, grabbing one breast in his hand. "I'm going to fuck you later," he says, leaning forward, lips barely brushing my nipple.

After another moment of holding and talking to my breast, he releases it and moves the scissors down to my panties. He slides the blade in the top and pushes down slowly, pulling out the panties enough so he doesn't stab me, but not far enough that the back of the blade doesn't touch me. As he pushes the scissors down further, his eyes, well, I assume his eyes, because I feel them even though I can't see them, lock on mine. The cool blade slides over my clit and fuck if I don't goddamn moan. I don't miss the smirk on Jax's face as his eyes stay glued on the scissors, slowly cutting through the thin bit of fabric that covers my lady bits. Not a lot to cut off, but Knox is taking his time, no doubt because of my moment of weakness, and he seems to enjoy teasing me right now.

He angles the cut sideways to the inside of my leg, then cuts across to the other, so the panties fall to the side. He grabs the fabric on the right and tugs, causing the panties to feel like dental floss across my asshole. I yelp out for a second, jumping as high in the chair as I can with my ankles cuffed around the legs.

"Oops," he sighs awkwardly. "It looked way more suave in my head."

Letting the fire between my ass cheeks cool, I touch the side of his mask. "It's ok."

The chains rattle underneath me and a moment later, a hot, wet tongue is running along my entrance. "Oh, damn."

"Jax," Callum commands.

He uses the flogger and slaps it across my breast. I yelp out in pain and receive another pop of the flogger on the other breast. I know he's holding back, but the leather ends still sting. Red lines form on my chest, so I glare at him.

"You can use your safe word." He smiles, twirling the flogger in his hand.

"I don't think she will. She's fucking drenched," Emmett says before pressing his tongue back in. I lurch forward in the seat, but say nothing.

"Of course she is," Jax says, letting the flogger dangle right at my pussy before he drags it up my torso and swirls it around my breasts. He presses it under my chin and lifts my head so I'm watching him.

A puff of air blows out of my nose as my stomach clamps down. My orgasm pushes closer to the edge while Emmett's tongue is working like a dream, swirling and pressing in all the right spots.

"E, you may want to stop," Jax suggests, but Emmett doesn't. "E!" Jax commands.

My head presses into the back of the seat as my hips try to move and my fingers grip onto the handles. There are little ridges on the underside of the chair's arms, no doubt from the many women who gripped it just as I am right now.

"Emmett!" Callum commands. Emmett's tongue slows to a stop, but he doesn't move.

The muscles in my body relax and I hunch over.

"Damn it," I whimper.

"Ev," Callum tilts his head to the side. "You only speak when I give you permission. If you can't follow commands, then I will fill your mouth with something so you can't speak."

"Don't threaten me with a good time." I know I wasn't supposed to speak, but damn it, I'd take the punishment.

Knox's fist flies to his mouth so he can bite it, only to hit the outside of his mask. "Damn it."

"Idiot," Jax mumbles. "Just take it off."

"No. I want to fuck her with it on."

My eyes pulse wide as excitement zaps through my body like a live wire.

"You know my one rule?" Jax asks, stepping closer to me, the flogger lightly brushing across my breasts.

I nod. They aren't supposed to come until I do. It is his one steadfast rule that no one breaks, no matter what.

"Well, tonight, I'm breaking it. You aren't coming until we *all* do."

My neck muscles lose their strength and my head bobbles like it's attached to a foam noodle.

"But when you do come, it will be the most powerful orgasm you've ever had. I want you to squirt so much you waterboard us."

Even if I was allowed to speak right now, I wouldn't be able to.

Callum places his hand on Knox's shoulder. "Knox. Fuck her mouth. Make her gag on your cock until you are coming down her throat."

Knox looks at Jax, foot partially in the air. I love Knox... so deep in my bones. He's not innocent. The weight of his experiences is unimaginable, yet he chooses to embrace innocence each day, and that brings a smile to my face. Part of me thinks that it's because he wants to push all the other feelings away and not face them, and the other part wonders if he does it for those around him. Jax needs an outlet, so Knox allows himself to be the punching bag in some ways. Selfless- always looking out for others, no matter the cost to himself.

Jax nods in my direction, and Knox waits half a second before he moves towards me. His hands clenched into tight fists, causing the muscles in his arms to tense up.

He's standing between my legs, so close I can smell his citrusy, musky scent. "Come here, baby girl." His hands run through my hair, grabbing at the root before he twirls my neck around in a circle.

"She's not a fucking vat of witch's brew," Jax comments.

"Shut the fuck up," Knox retorts.

My eyes grow wide as I draw in an excited shaky breath. Jax looks from me to Knox, back to me, face pulled taut, but Knox doesn't even turn around. "Ass," Jax smiles.

Knox releases my hair and unzips his pants, pushing them down only far enough to get his cock out. He fists it in his hand a few times. "Keep your hands on the arms of the chair. If you try to touch my cock, I will strap your arms down. Do you understand me?"

I don't know what's gotten into these men tonight, but hot diggity damn. "Yes, sir."

"Open your mouth." His hand tightens in my hair and he pulls my head back just enough so he can feed me his cock over my lip. Watching him in his mask, with both hands now gripped to the side of my head as he presses his cock in, causes my stomach to pulse.

He pushes it in slowly until he hits the back of my throat, while Emmett starts licking my pussy again.

KNOX - IT'S FUN TO BE DARK SOMETIMES

My teeth sink into my bottom lip, at the same time my grip tightens in her hair. Gah damn! I'm going to fucking explode in her mouth right now, if I can't think of something else. Anything else. Between this medieval tongue chair, Jax flogging her and Callum going all daddy dom on her, the energy in here is L.I.T! And me. I can't help it. This darker side is fun to play every once in a while. The dominance and control of it all. And her. She hasn't always been the best submissive. She has a little too much fight, but she's perfect.

Tonight, I can tell she's trying, but she's not trained. Which again, is ok, because she's *my* perfect submissive.

When I pull my cock out of her mouth, I pause, holding it in front of her lips and her eyes fall. I'm not trying to tease her. I'm just trying to last longer than three pumps. Her mouth is so fucking perfect and I have been thinking about this night, literally all day. I knew she wanted to keep this room a secret, but come on... I work at the club. Could

I have ignored the reservations list for tonight and scrolled past it? Yes. Yes, I could have, but obviously I'm not the bigger man.

Surprises make me nervous. I like to see what's coming so I can plan.

Anyway, I had found the tongue chair in storage downstairs the week we shut down when Ev wanted to do a deep clean. I've been hiding it ever since and it was killing me. Knowing that a toy I wanted to use on her was so close and I couldn't tell her about it. I told Emmett last night before Ev went to bed. I panicked, thinking I spoiled the surprise, but she was quite drunk. She was drinking her samples, plus mine less a sip or two.

"Knox?" Jax asks, putting his hand on my shoulder. "If you need me to fuck her mouth, I can."

Shrugging out of his touch, I blow him a kiss, then run my finger down Ev's cheek. "My perfect angel." Hyping myself up, I puff out my chest and feel my muscles flex under my shirt. "Open wide."

Her mouth feels so fucking good. I press until I hit the back of her throat and stop when it clenches around my cock. Gripping her hair tighter, I rock faster and faster until need takes over. Jax yells at Emmett in the background to stop because she's about to come. I can see it on her face and feel it in her mouth. She's sucking, trying to help me along, and I let her. I love when she gets like this. Wild and hungry for our cocks. She lets out a moan and a second later the flogger is between my legs and her chest, flicking at her. She clinches and I freeze.

"Fucking hell Jax. Do you want her to bite off my dick?"

He doesn't answer.

"Not cool dude. I'm playing flog our fae when your cock is deep down her throat. Like fucking Russian roulette."

"So dramatic. No more flogging."

"I'm not dramatic. Startled and irritated. We had a great rhythm, and I was about to come. We aren't edging me too. I'm a lot less fun to edge."

"Noted."

Ev licks her lips and looks at me with those fuck me eyes.

"Come to daddy," I say with an accent I've never heard come out of my mouth before, thrusting my hips out and running my fingers through her hair. She smiles and opens her mouth, tilting her head to the side. I swear if she were to wear pigtails with a white button-down collared shirt and a plaid skirt with a pencil...My stomach tightens as a tingle races up my spine.

Shit!

Needing to come down her throat, and not her chest, I slam my cock into her mouth, claiming her. My eyes roll into the back of my head and my thrusts become sloppy. Tears dot her cheeks, but my god she is beautiful.

"Fuck!" I yell, thrusting one more time, sending my cock to the back of her throat and exploding down it. She tries to swallow me down, but my cock gets in the way, sending it to the roof of her mouth. "That's it. Swallow me down." When I'm done, I drag my cock out but leave just the head in for her to give one last lick before she sucks. It's this little thing she does that drives me wild.

When I step back, I slip completely out of my pants and throw them out of the way. Everlee watches me, her eyes raking over me. I love the way she looks at me. Fuck, I love this woman! I want to claim her. I want her to be mine.

Ours.

Forever.

No question.

I tap Emmett on the leg. "My turn."

He slides out and I take my place. Have I laid down here a few times to get a feel for it after I found it? Yes. Yes, I have. I needed to be prepared.

Positioning my head on the headrest, I'm suddenly thrown back into a memory from last week when I was down here. It was a message from an unknown number.

Hey.

I ignored it, not sure who it could be from, but I didn't want to find out. Ten minutes later, I got another text.

Knox, it's your dad.

CALLUM - WHEN SHE'S TRYING TO FOLLOW THE RULES

EVERLEE IS LICKING HER lips, staring at me. "Such a good fucking girl. So hungry for our cocks, aren't you?"

She nods.

I could punish her for not speaking, but those eyes. She has a hold on me.

"Are you ready for my cock?"

"Yes, sir."

"Do you want to touch my cock?"

Her face lights up, and she smiles, "Yes, sir."

"You may grab my cock and do with it what you want."

"Thank you, sir."

My pulse quickens in my chest and my cock twitches.

She reaches across the short space between us and grabs it, bringing me to her mouth. Her hand clamps around the base, squeezing tighter than normal before she slowly sucks it into her mouth. Her teeth scrape just over the edges of it, a playful warning.

A warning?

Her eyes flick up to meet mine and she gives me a wink before she makes quick work of my cock. She moans out as her hips shift on the seat, riding, rather, trying to ride Knox's tongue. I don't know where this tongue chair came from or why Sammie didn't use it, but it's… interesting.

When he first told us about it, I had no idea what he was talking about. It didn't help that he also didn't know what it was or what it was used for. He came home raving about this U-shaped chair and how he was going to throw it out, but didn't because it looked old and thought it may be an antique. Some antique. I'm glad we researched it before we put it in our garage sale.

"Knox," I grit out between thrusts. Everlee isn't playing around right now, making it hard to speak. Fuck. Tingles are shooting up my spine. Too fucking quick. "Hold on, baby." I press on her forehead to help ease my cock out of her mouth.

She's panting and bucking in the seat.

"Knox!" I yell.

He comes to a sudden halt, leaving Everlee breathless in the chair.

"I was so close."

"I know. Too fucking close. You know the rule for tonight."

She groans out and tries to stomp her feet, but they're latched around the legs of the chair.

"She tastes so good," Knox whines. "I just want her to come on my face, down my throat. I want to be drowned in her come. Why won't you let me?"

"Here, I have something," Jax says, walking back over to the group with something in his hand.

Before I can stop myself, I'm laughing and Ev is glaring out at me, only making me laugh more.

"What the fuck is it?" She says with a tone equal parts disdain and acceptance.

One of the multitude of reasons I love her. She's always open to trying new things. We learned she was not a fan of o-ring ball gags, so we haven't used those since.

"He has a butt plug."

"Upsie-daisy," I say, pulling her up until she's bending over.

Emmett rubs her ass, humming to himself.

"You aren't brining a roast E," Jax chuckles.

"When you love something so much, and it's right in front of you... you have to rub it, hum to it, and simply appreciate it," he says, giving it a little pop, causing Ev to squeal.

Jax brings the lube over and they both begin to prep her ass before pressing the plug in. She lets out a gasp before a low guttural moan. Her orgasm is there on the edge, begging for release. We've never pushed her this hard or long without giving her release, and I know she's aching with need. I help guide her back to sitting and she lets out a few puffs of air and her eyes roll to the back of her head as she sits on the tongue chair.

"You're not allowed to come yet."

Her head lowers, but her eyes dart up at me, glowering.

"Oh, baby girl. With that look, I'll push it out for another hour."

Her eyes get big as panic tears across her face and I can't help but chuckle.

My hand glides through her hair, and grips at her scalp, jerking her head back with authority. "But I'm not that evil." I take her lips in a bruising kiss, pressing my tongue in and swirling it around. Her kiss is sweet, hungry. A moment later, her hand is sliding along my shaft, pumping up and down, causing me to moan into her mouth. She takes that as an invitation to pump faster, causing my orgasm to creep closer. As if sensing it, her grip tightens, and she pumps faster and faster. A second later, she's pushing me away from our kiss and pulling my cock to her mouth. She sucks it in hard and fast and it hits the back of her throat, then pulls it out and swirls her tongue around the head before sucking it in again. She's a woman who is trying to follow the rules and not come before us, so she's doing everything she can to make us come faster.

"Oh, goddamn." My muscles are clenching and releasing.

Her hands wrap around my balls and she tugs as she sucks in and holds it there as a tingle shoots down my spine and I unload down her throat. She presses her mouth on me a little further and I raise up on my toes as it almost becomes too much.

"Ev... Ev...," I cry out, dragging my cock out of her mouth.

She looks wild and hungry. "God, I love this woman."

"I want to suck both of you... for a minute, anyway." Ev points at both Jax and Emmett.

JAX - FRUIT ROLL-UPS

Nerves flutter through my stomach like a swarm of butterflies dancing through the air. I'm so fucking hard, and so is Emmett. She's sucked off both Knox and Jax, which leaves Emmett and me. We talked about tonight being the night I suck Emmett's cock for the first time, but Knox and Callum put together this little event too.

Ev points a finger at Emmett and me. "I want to suck both of you... for a minute, anyway." She winks and stares at me, so I give her a slight nod. It was the wink that said we're going to do this, are you ready? She's not pushing, rather asking for guidance. "But."

Emmett and I look from one another back to her without speaking.

"I want to do it my way, before all of this." She waves her hand in the air.

"You're done with the tongue chair?"

"For now. This padding with the butt plug in feels like torture and not the good kind. Definitely need to upgrade that."

"It's an antique, Everlee," Knox claps back playfully.

"Well, we need to find its partner in crime, the glory hole chair. If it doesn't exist, we'll build one. Get you a nice little knee pad chair with a hole you can stick your dick in, but we won't get any nice padding. Just concrete blocks." She laughs, then blows a kiss at Knox.

"I'll be back soon. I'm going to check on a few things," he huffs.

"I'm going to get us some drinks and some snacks for the evening," Callum offers.

Everlee looks back at me and pumps her eyes. They're giving us space. Me space.

Emmett and I undo the cuffs around her ankles and she immediately sticks her legs out, stretching them, sighing in relief.

"Now... where were we?" she asks. "Right. You two. On the bed." She points across the room.

My stomach is tensing and tightening repeatedly. She walks over to the door and grabs something out of the bowl.

"Ev?" I ask cautiously.

She whips her hair over her shoulder when she looks at me with a huge smile on her face. "It's Halloween, so what better way to suck a cock than with a sweet treat?" She holds up two fruit roll-ups.

"Ev?" My cheeks are hurting from smiling.

"I've wanted to try this for a while," she admits, climbing onto the bed.

She pushes Emmett and me back so we're laying side by side. His eyes rake across my face. He's looking for hesitation, or any hint I'm going to change my mind. But I'm not. I've been wanting to do this for a while. Tonight is the night.

She pulls our pants off and tosses them on the floor, then slowly starts unwrapping each fruit roll-up and twirls it around our lengths. It slips off at first, so she leans down and slowly takes each of us in her mouth, sucking it in one time until we're hitting the back of her throat. She licks her lips, letting out a low hum, then tries twisting the fruit roll-up around again.

"This is going to cause such a mess," Emmett says, looking down, abs flexed tight. Part of my cock is showing because the fruit roll-up doesn't cover it all, but at least it's colorful. I don't know if she purposefully got the rainbow-colored fruit roll-up for tonight, regardless, this will be the most interesting head I've ever received.

A voice crackles over the intercom, grabbing our attention. "This is your God speaking. No coming for our little fae until we're back in the room."

Knox.

"We know that I'm not one for rules."

"Everlee," I scold.

She scrunches her nose at me and laughs, then pumps her eyebrows. "Are we ready?"

We both nod, neither of us able to speak.

She lowers her head around my shaft and it feels weird at first, the heat of her mouth taking a minute to reach me. She bobs a couple of times then pops off, her lips glistening with a slightly darker shade of red. "It's delicious," she smiles, then adds, "And sticky." She looks at Emmett. "Do you want to try?"

He looks at me and I nod.

He sits up and wraps his hand around Everlee's head and takes her mouth in a passionate kiss, pressing his tongue deep. Fuck me. The way he kisses. My cock twitches, and I feel my arousal seeping from the tip.

I must have made a noise, because they stop kissing and Ev looks at the bead of arousal and swipes her finger across it, then holds it to Emmett's mouth. He grabs her hand and sucks her finger in, and I feel like I'm going to explode.

"That was just a taste," she says. "Now get down there and suck our man." She pushes his head towards me and smiles. She loves this. Loves us. And I love her.

Emmett's hand wraps around the base and slowly leans over. Just as his mouth is about to sink onto me, he looks up, eyes locking on mine. He smiles, then slides down, taking me in his mouth, eyes never breaking from mine. My hips buck up slightly, eager to fuck him deep. He pulls off and takes me again and again, getting faster and faster.

Moans start pulsing out and my hands grip his hair.

"Oh. E... Fuck. You feel so good. Oh... my..."

"Stop," Everlee says and just like that, he's pulling off.

My head falls back to the bed. I was so close. It takes everything I have not to fist my cock and finish myself off. If I didn't have a sugar quilt glued to it, I may have.

"Your turn Jax." She looks at me smiling and my eyes pulse wide.

"You suck on Emmett while he uses my mouth to suck your cock."

"Let's get to the edge of the bed," Emmett suggests. "You good on your knees, Ev?"

"Yea, hand me that pillow."

Handing Ev the pillow, I scoot to the edge of the bed with Emmett standing in front of me.

"We'll suck you together at first E, then I will move to Jax." She looks at me. "Good?"

Sucking my bottom lip into my mouth, I nod.

She's beaming. "Grab around his base and tease him a little. Lick the tip of his cock, then slowly suck him in. Watch the teeth, although the fruit roll-up will help."

She grabs around Emmett's shaft and sucks him in slowly, taking him all the way, before dragging him out again and repeating it.

She licks her lips. "I really am loving these fruit roll-ups."

"Kiss me."

"Anytime." She pushes up and presses her lips to mine. The sweetness of the fruit roll-up is still in her mouth. "I love you," I say when we pull off our kiss.

"I love you. Now suck our man's cock," she winks before sliding out of the way, but not too far. Her arm circles around the back of my calf for support.

Nerves firing through my body like loose electric wires, I wrap my hand around the base of Emmett's dick. It's not the first time I've held it, but this time feels different. He feels bigger. Hotter.

Leaning in slowly, I flick my eyes up to meet his. He's watching every move. Every breath. His eyes are burning with lust and fire, lighting me up from the inside out.

Wanting to savor and tease, I stick my tongue out and lick his tip. His knees buckle for a second and his hand falls to my shoulder. "Asshole," he mumbles, and I laugh.

"Not yet."

Everlee's hand reassuringly brushes up and down the back of my leg. A silent supporter, easing my nerves. I just want it to be good for him. We've talked about this so many times and now that it's here... I should have practiced on a banana or something. Don't know if that would have been better or just weird.

Here we go...

My mouth pushes around the tip of his cock and I can taste his arousal on the top of my tongue before the sweetness of the fruit roll-up envelopes my senses. My jaw feels tight for a second, but I relax it and push down further until he hits the back of my throat.

"Yes," Emmett encourages, drawing out the s, as his hand grips tightly onto my shoulder.

Dragging him out to the tip, I swirl my tongue around and suck him in again. I want to rip this fruit roll-up off and take him in my mouth. Him, his cock. Feel his rings.

His hand moves up and guides through my hair before he tugs. His moans... the way his body moves... it's intoxicating. No wonder Ev enjoys sucking us so much. We always think we're fucking her mouth, but really, her mouth is fucking us. She's in control. She has all the power.

I'm going to make Emmett fucking sing my name tonight.

When I press on his cock, a warm mouth sinks onto mine. A tingle shoots up my spine, and my head gets dizzy, overwhelmed by the sensations. She moves at my pace.

When I suck Emmett in, she sucks me in. When I'm pressed to the back of her throat, she grabs my balls. She's showing me what to do.

My hand slides up E's leg and cups his balls.

EMMETT - COCK IS LIKE A SOUFFLE

Fuck, it's not working.

Jax is sucking my cock.

Me. In his mouth.

I think I've just died and gone to heaven. Not heaven.
Hell.

I'm about to fucking unload in his mouth and he's only just started.

That cannot happen, but damn it... he looks so fucking good sucking my cock.

His mouth is like the perfect little oven. Nice and warm and my cock is like a souffle, only I'm about to pull the biggest no no and blow my load early. Hello collapsed souffle and collapsed cock. You never take the souffle out early and you never blow your load early.

And Ev. She's right there like a good girl waiting patiently on her knees, watching. She's moaning, but I don't stop her. Between us edging her, the butt plug in her ass, and her watching Jax suck me off... she's going to come. I know it. I'll deal with the wrath of Callum and Knox.

Oh fuck.

She's going down on him now.

He jerks on my cock when he realizes what she's doing. She's matching pace with him, following whatever he's doing. Why is that so erotic?

My left hand locks on her hair, and I gently shove her head on Jax's cock. She lets me and moans around him.

Fucking hell.

He just grabbed my balls.

Ohhhh... I feel like an angelic choir is singing behind me. Giving me the strength to stand while Jax sucks my cock and I control Ev sucking his.

Holy spirit, activate! Holy spirit, activate! Activate! Activate! If I could clap right now, I would, but my hands are glued in their hair and I'm not moving them at all.

Call me a marionettist because bam!

Ah shit. He just slurped. I heard him slurp around my cock.

He moves faster and so does Everlee. It's not surprising my hand is merely but an ornament in her hair. As usual, she takes control of the situation, bobbing on him faster and faster.

"Yes, Jax. Your mouth feels so fucking good wrapped around my dick. I'm so close to unloading in your mouth."

He hums around my cock, and I lose control. My hands grip in his head and I thrust my hips, pressing into his mouth.

He chokes as his eyes shoot up to mine, but he doesn't stop me.

I press again, hitting the back of his throat. I feel it clench.

His eyes are still laser focused on me.

"You want more?"

He winks.

He goddamn winks at me.

"Then more is what you'll get." My hands clamp tighter in his hair and I fuck his face, sending my shaft to the back of his throat one, two, three more times.

"Oh shit! Oh shit! Fuck!" My hot come is shooting down his throat, and he is swallowing it up and I'm seeing stars. My hands grab his shoulders to help keep me upright.

In a rush he pulls my cock out, quickly unwraps and tugs off the fruit roll-up, throwing it on the bed, then sucks my cock back into his mouth. He moans out as his tongue rolls across my cock rings, then he freezes, cock half parked in his mouth. He pushes me away and cries out.

"Damn baby girl," he groans.

She pulls off his cock and rocks back on her hind legs as Jax falls backwards onto the bed.

She's beautiful. A goddess. A dream. Passion and love consuming me, I reach down and help her stand, then tilt her back in my arms and kiss her... hard.

A second later, I stand her back up and she grabs onto my arm for support, a little wobbly from our kiss.

"You just wanted to taste him in my mouth," she jeers.

"I love you so much, Everlee. Do you know that?"

A blush tinges her cheeks. "What did you say?" she teases, searching for another I love you.

"I said you're a little shit." I give her a hard kiss on her forehead, then push her back on the bed.

"Now it's our turn." I lift her foot and start planting kisses on the inside by her ankle and slowly work by way up to the inside of her thigh. "You were drenched earlier." I lick up her sweet center and I'm rewarded with her arousal seeping out of her. "You're so fucking wet." I reposition my body and wrap my arms around her legs, and thrust my tongue in, licking and spearing her until she's a writhing mess in my arms and moaning out my name.

"E. You know the rules. No coming until they're in here."

"Fuck the rules E!" Ev shouts.

"E..." Jax reminds softly.

"Don't listen," she moans out and digs her hands into my hair, "to him. Fuck! Don't listen." She's so close.

Pulling back and wiping my hand across my face, I look at both of them. "What are you two? The angel and the devil? Don't do it. Yes, do it?"

"Well, this puts me in an awkward place," Jax teases. "I'm not used to being the angel."

The door opens and Knox and Callum walk back in, carrying a tray of chocolate-covered strawberries, some flutes of champagne, a few liter bottles of water and something else covered with a silver dome lid.

Everlee sets up on the bed and sees the dome Knox is carrying and starts screaming. "Did it already come in?" she asks, clapping her hands together.

If she's this excited, then... I don't know if this is going to be good.

EVERLEE - SPEECHLESS

OH MY GOD! MY pussy is literally pulsing with every slight gust of wind. I don't think I have ever needed to come so badly in my life. At this point, if I could just thrust my hips fast enough and hump the air, that would provide enough friction to get me off. I don't know how long this has been going on, but FFFUUUCCKKKK am I ready!

Emmett rocks back on his hind legs, his semi hard cock laying between them.

Flashbacks from a few minutes ago race through my head. *Jax with this mouth wrapped around Emmett's cock. The need and hunger he had at the end. And then when he ripped the fruit roll-up off. He was feral. I nearly came from that alone.*

The door opens, and Callum and Knox are walking in. Knox has a dome in his hand and my stomach does one thousand flips in a row. I ordered something special for tonight and found out yesterday that it wasn't supposed to be in until Monday. I was so bummed, which is why I had to pivot to the fruit roll-ups. It was something that I've been wanting to do for a while.

Emmett looks at me, then back at Knox. "Ev? Do you care to share what you're so excited about?"

"Oh, you'll find out, my love, in just a few minutes." He smiles cautiously at me, but I can nearly contain myself.

"Where would you like this, my lady?" Knox asks, bowing.

With a huge smile and nearly bouncing out of my skin, I point to the table beside the bed.

Jax leans towards it, but I hurry and climb over the top of him and reach for his arm.

"Ev. What are you doing?" he pauses and turns his head sideways to look at me. I'm sure I look like a flea on his back because he's so much larger than me.

"You aren't supposed to peek!" I shake his arm.

"What if I want to?"

"Jax!" I say, sitting up on his back so it looks like he's giving me a pony ride. "Don't you dare!"

"Or what?" Even though I can only see half of his face, I can see the smile curling on his lips and the fire in his eyes.

"I'll use it on you first."

Knox jumps up and down excitedly.

"Shit! If he's that happy, then it can't be good," Jax says, pulling his arm back.

"Depends on your definition of good." I lean over his back, so my chest brushes against his skin, and drop my arms around his neck. "Some would say biting and sucking is not good..." I whisper, inching up to bite and suck on his earlobe.

He lets out an appreciative moan and I start to rock my hips on his back, sliding up a little further.

"Some say this," I bite his neck and suck his skin into my mouth, letting it tent under my lips, "Isn't good."

A hand slides up my back, and I turn to see Emmett standing on the bed. My stomach tightens as excitement pulses through me. Is he going to fuck me while I'm on Jax's back?

Emmett sticks his fingers in my wet pussy and Jax must feel him there, because he gets tense, then looks over his shoulder.

I whisper in Jax's ear, "Now you're going to see what it feels like being fucked while on your knees."

A puff of air escapes from his throat.

Emmett scoots forward, and I can feel the tip of his hard cock at my entrance. So much for a long refractory period for him. He rubs his hands over my ass like he's waxing a car. This fucker is still teasing me.

He laughs, then blows a kiss at me when I shoot daggers at him over my shoulder.

He presses in and my head falls onto Jax's back as pleasure ripples through my body. The shaking of the bed pulls my attention back up. Knox has removed his clothes and jumped on the bed, crossing his ankles, interlacing his fingers behind his head. "I love watching you being fucked, my love."

A deep guttural moan echoes deep in my chest as Emmett slowly pushes all the way in, his piercings rubbing across my highly sensitive parts. "Oh, shit."

A second later, Callum sits naked on the side of the bed with something in his hand and a smile on his face.

"No," I whimper out.

"Yes," he smiles and clicks the button in his hand and suddenly my ass is vibrating.

Emmett lets out a string of groans and words as he thrusts hard into me, causing me to shift up Jax's back and causing him to groan out.

"Oh, they like that!" Knox says, munching on a fruit roll-up.

Oh shit!

Jax looks at Knox and huffs out a laugh, but doesn't speak. I smack him on the shoulder and start to warn Knox of where that's been, but Callum turns up the vibration in my ass and my tongue stops working as my mouth hangs open. My body is humming, hungry for release. Emmett picks up his thrusts, pounding into my ass, while his balls have to be smacking against Jax's ass, because he's also making groans.

"She's speechless," Knox says, laughing.

Oh God. I want to tell him he's eating a fruit roll-up that was wrapped around one of the guy's cocks and then sucked on until they came, but I literally cannot. My mouth is not working.

BAM!

My orgasm slams into me. The muscles in my body have clamped so tight, I'm terrified they're going to cramp. Can you pass out from having an orgasm? There is so much pressure that I just want to scream out.

"Fuck!" Emmett screams, pulling his cock out. "She's fucking squirting all over me."

I can't even turn to look because I'm frozen. Relishing in this bliss.

"Goddamn!" Knox has picked up the other fruit roll-up and is now munching on it.

Shit!

When my body relaxes, I collapse on Jax's back and Emmett presses his cock back in, thrusting a few times before he comes. Thankfully, Callum turns off the butt plug and Emmett takes it out.

My body feels like complete mush.

Once Emmett finishes, Jax collapses on to the bed. Eyes closed, I mumble out, "Knox... that fruit roll-up... was around their... cock."

"What the fuck!" Knox yells and I feel the bed shake as I presume he's jumping off. "You ass!" he yells and I open my eyes to see him pointing at Jax. "You saw me and smiled, you fucker!"

"Oops. It's not like you haven't tasted it before as much as we share and kiss our girl."

He looks from Jax to me, and huffs, "It would have at least been nice to know!"

Jax shrugs and a moment later, Emmett rolls off me and I roll off Jax.

"So what's in the dome?" Emmett asks.

"Something she's definitely going to use on Jax now," Knox retorts.

"Oh, stop!" Jax presses.

Callum grabs my ankles and pulls me towards the end of the bed, causing me to squeal. "My turn."

CALLUM - DADDY DOM

MOST OF MY LIFE, I have never put myself first. Actually, for as long as I can remember. Dad was gone and mom... well, even though she was physically there, she wasn't mentally there. We were lucky if she remembered to wake us up for school in the morning so we could catch the bus.

When I was eight, I had saved enough money from coins I'd found on the street to buy an alarm clock for Jax and I. We had a one-bedroom apartment, that was scarcely furnished. It had been at one time, but after Jax was born, she started selling off the furniture to buy his formula and diapers. I don't blame him for that, just stating a fact. By the time he started school, we had a worn-down couch, two mismatched chairs, and a mattress in the bedroom. We had a few blankets and a comforter which had so many holes in it we should have just thrown it away, but she refused. She said our dad bought it for her on their wedding day.

That's when she would lose it. When she thought about him and the way things were before he left. When he left, the only thing he took was a suitcase. He left it all behind. Us included. She never talked about him or who he was. Hell, I don't even know his name. A few years back, I did some digging and found our birth certificates and our dad was listed as UNKNOWN. It was a long shot.

I didn't tell Jax I was looking. I didn't want to get his hopes up. Part of him thinks our dad will miraculously show up on our doorstep one day and want to have a relationship with us. He's probably dead and gone. At least he is to me.

He abandoned us.

Abandoned me.

From the time he left, I stepped up. Taking care of a toddler when I was barely old enough was tough. We survived on peanut butter sandwiches and milk and would often try to sneak extra food at lunch in case we had nothing at the house. On occasion, when mom's friends visited, they would rummage through our pantry, leaving us without food for days. It wasn't until mom's mind cleared that she could buy groceries or give me a few dollars to do so.

I stopped putting myself first long ago. So long that taking care of others seems so natural. Everlee tries to push me a little. To take. We've had a few conversations about my past, but not many. I don't enjoy talking about it. To me, it's in the past. What's happened has happened and can't be changed. The past made me who I am today. Made me successful. I think it's why we all fell so naturally into sharing. Underneath it all, we're scared of getting hurt, of someone leaving us alone. Abandoned. We were protected in our cocoon of four and then Everlee.

She walked into our life with the red outfit, wings and all, and that was it. We were done for. When she left, it wasn't a surprise. We told her we weren't long-term material. She had to protect herself too, and I don't blame her for that. It wasn't until two weeks after that we realized we were being idiots. There was a spark between us. A fire that started off as glowing embers that turned into something more. We started planning ways we could bump into her, and then she walked into our club in that Easter outfit and that was all it took.

On the way to Mrs. Mary's event, we had talked on the plane and said we weren't letting her go again. We were going to make it work. She's a light for each of us. Slowly bringing out the parts that we've tried to keep hidden.

She's tearing down the walls we've spent our entire lives putting up.

She wants me to take more. To put myself first and that's what I'm trying to do. Well, as best as I can.

Knox yells something and jumps off the bed, bringing me back. "You ass!" he yells and points at Jax. "You saw me and smiled, you fucker!"

"Oops. It's not like you haven't tasted it before as much as we share and kiss our girl."

Knox looks at Everlee, then back to Jax. "It would have at least been nice to know!"

Jax shrugs and a moment later, Emmett rolls off Ev, and she rolls off Jax.

"So what's in the dome?" Emmett asks.

"Something she's definitely going to use on Jax now," Knox retorts.

"Oh, stop!" Jax presses.

Eager to sink my cock into her pretty little pussy, I grab her ankles and pull her towards the end of the bed, causing her to squeal. "My turn."

Her eyes pulse and a smile spreads across her face. "Callum."

"I'm daddy dom tonight." I yank her the rest of the way, so her ass is barely hanging off the edge of the bed. "Do you want to be my good girl?"

She nods, pressing her finger into her mouth.

"Now get up and walk over to the X."

"Yes, sir."

She stands up on the platform the X is on but doesn't move. She looks at me, waiting for her next instruction. A hint of fight remains, but she's getting better at playing the submissive.

"Everlee?" I ask, tilting my head to the side.

"Yes, daddy?" She smiles, rubbing her hands over her tits.

"Spread your legs."

Her eyelashes flutter, then she inches her legs apart slowly.

Stepping towards her, I push her backwards with my chest. "Are you going to be a good little girl for me tonight or not?"

"Yes, daddy."

The feel of her wet pussy against my cock takes my breath away for a moment.

Focus, Callum.

Leaning forward, I press my lips to her neck, then slowly plant kisses down her chest, under her breast, over her stomach, on her hip, then run my tongue over her clit one time. She lets out a moan and her head hits the circular board the X is attached to. I continue kissing down her leg until I'm at her ankle. Grabbing the cuff at the bottom of the X, I pull her leg towards it and hook it around her ankle before moving to the other side and hooking that one. Her skin feels hot under my fingertips as I slide them back up her leg.

"You're such a good girl." I grab both of her breasts and squeeze hard until she moans.

After a few minutes, I have both wrists strapped in as well, and she looks fucking fantastic.

The room is quiet and when I look behind me, I only see Knox on the bed, snacking on the strawberries we brought in for Everlee. When he catches me, his eyes pulse wide, and he shrugs his shoulders. Emmett and Jax must be in the shower, because I hear it running in the attached bathroom.

Watching Knox gives me an idea. I walk over to our bag and bring out a satin blindfold.

"Kinky," Knox hums, grabbing another strawberry, laying on his side, ankles crossed like he's a venetian god.

"Don't eat all of those."

He sighs, "I'm not. But they're so good."

When I get back to Everlee, she's wiggling a little, but not speaking.

"Are you ok?"

"Yes. My stomach just itches and I... can't... get it."

"Well, baby girl. I don't think swishing your butt around is going to help."

"I was trying."

With a light touch, I scratch her stomach, causing her to release sighs of enjoyment. "A little more to the right. Up a little. Down. Oh, right there. Now, over to the left." She lets out a moan. "Yes."

"You realize that you just had me scratch the same spot, right?"

"It felt different the second time."

"I love you."

"I love you, daddy." She winks.

"I'm going to blindfold you now. And then I'm going to feed you things."

Her eyes dart over to the tray on the bed that Knox has now curled himself around like a child hoarding all of their Halloween candy.

"No baby girl, eyes on me."

She looks back and scrunches her nose.

After slipping the blindfold on her, I take her breast in my mouth and her body moves in silent appreciation. I pinch both of her nipples, squeezing harder and harder until I see her face pull.

"Such a good girl."

She whimpers softly.

By the time I get back over to Knox, he's eaten half the tray. I pop him on the leg and he retracts it, pulling it to his chest. "I was going to save some."

My head tilts down.

"Ok, I was going to get more."

"Well, you can still get more."

He huffs, "Seriously?"

"You offered."

"Just to sound nice. I wasn't serious."

"Knox."

"Yes, daddy."

Before I can smack him again, he's rolling off the bed laughing as he walks to the door. He never took his pants off, so he just needs to slip on a shirt. Honestly, most of the people staying here are in their rooms for the rest of the night, so there's a slim chance he'd run into anyone, but just in case, I suppose.

Grabbing the half-eaten tray of strawberries off the bed and the bottle of champagne, I walk them over to a table to the left of the X and sit them down.

"Callum?" Everlee calls out.

"I'm here."

"I don't like that I can't see!" she huffs, the kind of sound that makes you just want to wrap her in your arms.

"I know. You know the safe word."

"I'm not using it for a flippin' blindfold, Callum. Give me a little more credit than that."

"Oh baby girl, I give you lots of credit." I step toward her and swipe my finger between her pussy, brushing over her clit.

She bites her bottom lip, pressing her head back. Her knees slightly buckle, but the cuffs around her wrists keep her upright.

"You know I have problems having orgasms while I stand. It's like it edges its fucking self."

A deep chuckle rumbles in my chest. "How horrible that must be!"

"Oh, shut it."

"How about you?" I say, rubbing the tip of the chocolate-covered strawberry over her lips. Her head jerks for a second until she realizes what it is, then slowly opens. "That's my good girl. Now bite."

She takes a tentative nibble and then another. "Oh, this is good."

"I know." I set the rest of the strawberry back on the tray, then run my hands up her body. She is mine. Tracing along her neck with my lips, I creep down to her chest, where I cradle her breasts in my hands, showering them with a blend of tender kisses and enticing nibbles. Dropping to my knees, I plant kisses on the inside of her thigh, across the apex of her legs to her other thigh.

"Callum. You tease."

"Are you wet?"

"How about you find out?"

Knowing that she's already stretched, I shove two fingers deep inside of her and she yells out a string of words.

"Hold on."

"To what? What are you doing?"

I unlock the wheel at the bottom and slowly turn her.

"What are you doing?" She yells out.

"Turning you."

"It turns?"

"No, that's the strawberry. I laced it with–"

"You drugged me?"

"I was kidding."

When she does a one-eighty and her head is at the bottom. I stop turning the wheel. The chains rattle a little as her body adjusts to being inverted.

"Callum," she whispers, voice shaky.

"You say the word and we stop."

"Not yet."

"That's my good girl."

Her lips are right there, calling out to me. I press mine to hers and kiss her deep until she laughs.

"What?"

"Do you think this is what that spidy fella feels when he's hanging upside down on the side of the building, kissing his girl?"

"Spidy fella?"

"You know it's late and I get slightly coo coo cachoo when I get tired. Plus," she shakes her head. "I'm upside down. All the blood has rushed to my head."

"Hmmm."

"Hmm, what? What's that hmm for?"

"We bought you a gift. I was going to wait to give it to you later, but now seems as good as time as any."

"Without them?"

"It's ok." I flip her back around for a second, so she doesn't pass out. One has to train and build up a tolerance to full inversion. I thought about getting those things for the doors and just hanging every once in a while, but I haven't done it yet. There's always next year.

I really should have moved the bag of goodies closer, so I don't have to keep walking back and forth.

When I get to the bag I shift through all the clothes and find it next to a black silk nighty Knox wanted to buy her. The guys and I may have gone a little overboard in Allure's new store. It was Lizzy's idea to add it, and wow. We can't keep things in stock.

Grabbing the purple flower vibrator, I walk back over to her and flip her around again, without warning. Partly because I was distracted by the pulsing flower and also because I just like to see her squirm.

"Callum!" she shouts. "What's that humming noise?"

"You'll find out soon."

"Callum."

"Man! Did you already give it to her?" Knox asks, walking back in with two trays of strawberries.

"Two?" I ask, chuckling.

"Two? Two what? I hate this fucking blindfold!"

"Upside down," Jax says, walking back in towel drying his hair with only a pair of boxers on, followed by Emmett.

"Is everyone in here?" Ev calls out.

"Yes," the room says in unison.

"Ready?" I ask the men, holding it up.

"Oh, yes," Knox says, grabbing a strawberry. As Jax reaches for one, he tries to push his hand away, only to step back in fear when Jax bucks his chest.

I set the flower vibrator on her pussy and Ev starts groaning and making other noises.

"Oh... you got me a flower?" She sighs, then cries out. "Oh damn. Oh damn. Ohhhhh dammmmn."

"I'm not jealous," Knox calls, angrily stuffing another strawberry in this mouth.

"How many of those have you eaten?" Emmett whispers, pulling his eyes off Everlee for only a second.

Knox just sticks his tongue out, then nods back to Everlee, who is a writhing mess. The chains are smacking the board as her orgasm tears into her. When she's at her peak, I snatch it off and toss it to one of the guys; I don't care who and flip her around. As soon as she's upright, I punch my cock into her and she cries out, screaming and arching her back.

"Boys. Feet."

Dragging my cock out slowly, I wait until I'm at the tip, then punch in again. Knox and Jax quickly undo the cuffs around Ev's ankles and immediately her legs shoot up and wrap around my waist.

Pulling her slightly off the X, I fuck her hard and fast. "Your pussy feels so good." The faster I fuck her, the more her breasts bounce. I want to bury my cock so deep inside of her, so I try. Claiming her.

"I want to see you. I want to see you," she pants out between thrusts.

I yank the mask off her head and toss it behind me. Her eyes find mine and she smiles. "Fill me with your come, daddy."

Faster and faster. Harder and harder.

My groans, her moans and the clanging of the chains are the soundtrack for the room. A few thrusts later, I'm filling her with my come. The release brings with it a wave of pleasure that courses through my body. It feels like someone has covered me with gasoline and lit me on fire. I burn for this woman. She is mine. Ours.

The guys have been mumbling the same sentiment. We always swore we would never marry, but this woman. It isn't simply enough to just tell her she is ours. I want the entire fucking world to know. I want to see a ring on her finger.

"What?" she asks, staring at me.

Shaking my head to clear it, I say, "Sorry. I just got lost in thought."

"Anything you care to share?" She quirks her eyebrow at me.

"Not right now." But soon. When I look over my shoulder, I see the guys looking at me with a quizzical brow. Can they hear my thoughts? Do they know what I'm thinking? Do they feel it too?

EVERLEE – DREAMS COLLIDE

HOLY SHIRTBALLS BATMAN! TONIGHT did not go exactly how I had pictured, but it was even better. The guys had bought some new toys, which I have to assume were courtesy of the new shop. There was one more that Callum mentioned later that hadn't come in. I was able to find out that it was a custom piece, so that excites me!

When I step out of the shower, the steam from inside pours out and the cool air stings my skin, causing my nipples to go hard. Knox slips out from behind me and grabs a towel, keeping it to himself for a moment while he appreciates my breasts. This man and my breasts.

He leans forward, wrapping the towel around my back and murmurs something about needing to warm up my nipples. He swirls his mouth around each one.

The cold air is still biting at my skin, so I wrap the towel around me and his head. I feel like I'm interrupting a private moment, with as much attention as he's giving them.

A knock at the door startles us both.

"You two ok in there?" Jax asks.

"Yes." My reply mixes with Knox's hum.

"Knox, get off her breasts so we can go!"

He pops his hand up and pulls it out from under the towel and looks at the door, which is still closed. "Does he have x-ray vision?"

He makes me laugh all the time.

"Let's get dressed. Our bed is calling me."

When I walk into the bedroom, I have a flashback to my dream that makes me chuckle.

Jogger Froggers.

The guys are dressed in joggers and tight shirts that stretch across their chest and hug their arms and I about come again... if that's even possible. After Callum released my arms from the St. Andrews cross, we had a group fuck, then Knox made me come twice more in the shower.

Jax hands me a pair of black joggers, a bra, and smirks when he hands me my shirt that's orange with a large pumpkin on the front. He gave me shit for buying it *because I already had one similar to it*. But what he fails to understand is while it may look the same, this one is way softer. Like velvet wrapped in satin, wrapped in clouds. Super soft. I slip on the joggers, then grab the shirt, leaving him holding my bra.

"Everlee..." he threatens with a low growl.

Taking a step towards him, I raise up on my tiptoes and kiss his hardened lips. "It's almost five in the morning. I'm walking out with you all to get in a car, to go home and climb into our bed. You can wear the bra if you want someone to wear it because it won't be me." I walk past him and seconds later feel a hand gripped around my waist, pulling me backwards, before he dips me back into a kiss.

"You're impossible."

"I like to think of it as I'm possibl...y your most favoritist person in the whole wide world."

"Something..."

Huffing, I push against his chest, but he doesn't let me out of his arms.

He kisses my forehead, then releases me.

"Let's go. It's been a long ass day," he says, stuffing my bra into the bag he's carrying and guiding us all to the door.

Something catches in the corner of my eye. When I walk over to the dresser, I bend down and pull out a thin golden bangle and stare at it. "What's this?" I ask the guys.

They all shrug. "Don't know. Someone must have left it in here from before."

The hair on the back of my neck prickles as I'm reminded of my dream. Samara's bracelets... No. Right? Can't be. This is just a coincidence...

"Are you ok?" Emmett asks. "Your face is all scrunched up."

I answer slowly, unsure. "Yea. This... bracelet... it just reminds me of my dream."

Knox wiggles his fingers in the air and sounds like a ghost. "Ooohhh."

"Stop. I'm sure it's nothing." I nod with uncertain certainty, walking towards the doors.

"I'll handle our checkout with the front and be home shortly," Knox says.

"I'll stay with," Emmett offers.

"I just knew you liked me!" Knox bats his one free hand playfully in the air. His other is holding the platter with the toy we never got to use, unfortunately.

"Knoxxy baby... can you package that back up and bring it home with you? Don't let Emmett see it, though."

Emmett snaps his head in my direction and glares at me.

"Emmett," I scold. "No peeking."

EVERLEE - BIG PLANS

THE LAST SEVERAL WEEKS have gone by in a complete blur. Both Vixen and Allure raked in record numbers for our Halloween weekend, and with the cooler weather coming and preparing for Thanksgiving in a few weeks, it has been chaos around the house. We haven't really had many group nights, since someone is always at a club or at the restaurant.

Bo's is doing really well and Emmett is redoing a few of the menu items so they feel more fall. As part of the change, he's working on making the bites and flights a permanent item on the menu. He only did it for Lizzy and me that one time, and then a few other high-end clients that were hosting parties. He's also working on a pumpkin soup offering, but he can't get the flavor the way he wants it, so of course, he refuses to release it. We have tried it and several variations several times and think they're all great, but...

For Thanksgiving, we're going to my parent's house, so we're closing all the businesses from Wednesday to Sunday. We were going to reopen on Sunday, but figured it was going to be a slow weekend anyway, with traveling. When we sent out a survey to Allure's members, only a few said they were going to be in town, so we thought we'd be nice and give the staff another paid holiday. We do that for all our businesses. I say our, because even though my name is technically only on Allure, the guys have really made me feel part of the team, taking my feedback and suggestions. For example, the bites and flights. Although that may have been more of a Lizzy thing.

My mother is so excited we're all coming down for Thanksgiving. She's made all sorts of plans and Beckett and Will are going to introduce us to their firehouse. Apparently, word got out at Beckett's firehouse that I'm in a poly relationship. The guys took it a lot better than I expected, so that's saying something. Honestly, they don't seem to be too concerned about it anymore.

When my phone rings, I look at the caller ID.

Mom.

"Hello?"

"Good morning, darling. How are you?"

"Good mom, how are you?"

"Fine. I'm just planning for dinner and wanted to know if the guys have any favorite side dishes they would like prepared. Also, if you could tell them that Mrs. Mary Mae said she could make it, and is looking forward to it."

Mrs. Mary Mae, their foster mother. They admitted they haven't visited her as much as they would like, but are trying to do better. Even though she's the mother they have known for most of their life, I think for them it always felt temporary, so they didn't let themselves get attached.

"I'll ask them about the dishes and let you know. I can tell you they will probably say whatever you plan on fixing will be fine."

"Oh, those boys. You know, darlin'... there's a lot of pressure on me this year."

"Why?" I laugh.

"Emmett Monroe is coming to my house to eat."

"Mom. It's just Emmett."

"Honey. You don't understand. When I told the ladies in bridge club about *the* Emmett Monroe coming over for dinner... they were all fanning themselves and teasing about how their ovens wouldn't be working, so they'd need to eat with us. I say teasing, until Thanksgiving comes and they're all banging down my door wanting to get in." She's laughing, but there is an undercurrent of nerves behind it.

"Mom. It will all be great. I'll follow up with the guys and let you know. I love you."

"I love you too. Oh. Beckett says to tell you samesies... whatever that means. You two always ragging on another." She laughs again. "Two weeks."

Mom is so worried about everything being perfect for the guys and Emmett. Geez. She's likely to give herself a heart attack with all that worry. I've never paid much attention to Emmett or his growing notoriety in the restaurant world. The last several months have been a whirlwind for him. He's had several- well, more than several articles posted about Bo La Vie's success and the chef behind it all. To me, he's always been just Emmett. He doesn't let the fame go to his head. If anything, it makes him slightly intolerable because he has to be even more perfect than he already is. I've gone to Bo's a few times to help him out when I'm not at Allure. The thing with these men and their—our—businesses is that it doesn't feel like work. I mean, sure, it does sometimes. That's only natural, but it's just fun and I love pitching in when and where I can help. Since I'm nowhere near the chef Emmett is, nor do I know how to run a kitchen, I usually help him with his books or finances. I'm good at numbers, spreadsheets, and ideas.

Things really couldn't be any better for us.

The guys are sitting around the bar in the kitchen enjoying their coffee and tea and eating the freshly baked cinnamon roll bread that, surprisingly enough, Knox made. Emmett has been trying to teach him the basics of cooking. Like boiling water. Seriously though, Emmett has been working with him a little. Mostly so he doesn't burn the house down when unsupervised. They offered to wait for me, but I told them to start. I had to finish getting ready.

Big plans today!

I'm meeting Lizzy at Le Rousso's, our local kink shop. We've partnered with the owner, and between the two shops, we're able to buy items in bulk for a discount. In addition to the fact, Madame Rousso is teaching us a ton about the industry.

"Good morning, love," Emmett says, using his foot to push out a stool between him and Callum.

"Good morning, my loves." I blow kisses to each of them.

Callum scoops out some of the roll, puts it on a plate, and slides it over to me, while Jax brings me my coffee.

"You guys sure know how to spoil a woman."

"You make it easy," Callum says, lifting my hand to brush his lips across my knuckles.

"Do you get to try any of the toys at the sex shop today?" Knox asks. "Because I'm just saying, if you do, then I should probably be there as well... since we're partners in all."

"No. You know we don't use them."

"You should," Jax chimes, walking his plate over to the sink and washing it. "How else will you know if it's good?"

"You make a fair point."

Knox's eyes grow wide.

"But we still aren't." I laugh. "What are you guys up to today?"

"Nothing much," Callum chimes.

I've been around him long enough to know that he's trying to play casual, even though there's something else going on. "Callum?"

"What?" he asks, crossing his legs and turning away from me.

"What are you hiding?"

"Nothing." He looks over his shoulder and casts the largest Cheshire grin I've ever seen.

Glaring at him, I take another bite of food. He won't budge. I could literally torture him for the answer, but he won't break. I think Jax and Knox must have taught him a few things from their time in the SEALs.

He laughs, "Nothing. Seriously. The guys and I may just go around and hit a few stores."

"Are you going to buy me anything today?"

"Wouldn't you like to know?" Callum teases, turning back around to look at me.

"Yes. Yes, I would. That's why I asked." I laugh.

"Well, you won't find out until later."

"Later?" I pump my eyebrows.

"I have a quick errand to run," Knox chimes, eyes darting between us all.

"Where is it? We can all go together," Emmett offers.

"Oh, uh. No. Not this time. I need to do something on my own, but I can meet you all somewhere after."

Everyone in the kitchen stops moving and turns their bodies to look at Knox. He's been off the last month, really the last few weeks. I heard Jax and Emmett talking a few nights ago about how they were concerned he was drinking again and going out to bars, but I don't think that's it. He barely touches the drinks when we're around and he hasn't been going out a ton when I'm not around. We spend nearly every minute of every day together. When I told the guys that, they believed me. They said he only gets in those drinking moods when he's sad or working through some stuff, but everything has been great between us all. But he has been off. There is something weighing on him even if he won't share it with us yet. I've tried a few times, but he shuts me down, so I don't push. Not yet, anyway. When he's ready, he'll tell us... hopefully.

"Ok then. Well, I don't know how long I'll be out today. I'll be home in the early afternoon. I think I'm going to grab some lunch with Lizzy. Hopefully, she doesn't get us kicked out of wherever we're eating."

"Where are you going?" Jax asks, then quickly continues, "I ask, not so we can join you, but so I can be sure we don't show up. Lunch with Lizzy is not my idea of a relaxing or fun afternoon."

"I know you like her and she knows it, too. Once you can admit it, then everyone would be a lot happier."

He winks at me, causing my stomach to tighten. "She's more tolerable now than she used to be."

"She's like a fine wine," I offer, smiling. I finish up my breakfast and walk my plate to the sink. Emmett is standing there and takes it from me, places it in the sink, then wraps me in his arms.

"She is a very fine wine." He kisses my temple. "I hope you have a great day today and tell her I said hello. I will also need to talk with her about some wedding plans if she has time today or this week. Nothing too important."

I give them each a kiss and head out.

EVERLEE – WHEN YOUR LIFE FLASHES IN FRONT OF YOUR EYES

AS I'M PULLING OUT of the driveway, I stop at the edge and start to text Lizzy to tell her I'm on my way, but my brother's picture pops up instead. It looks like his face is smooshed up against the inside of my phone, causing me to laugh as I put him on speaker. "When did you change my picture of you?"

"I don't know what you're talking about."

"Beck?" I pull onto the road, just as a flurry of leaves fall onto my windshield and across the road. I love this time of year, when the streets are blanketed in a mosaic of red, orange, and gold leaves.

"I may have had some help from Knox."

"That little shit!"

Beck's laughter vibrates through the phone, making me smile.

"What can I do for you, brother?"

"Just wanted to talk to you, sister, and see how things were going."

"I don't believe that, but we can pretend." He rarely called just to shoot the shit. He has an agenda, but I'll play along. "Things are so amazing right now. I'm so happy, Beck. It's baffling to think where I was this time last year... ya know?"

"Yea, wondering about douche face."

I laugh. "Yes."

"And now look at you. Fucking over achiever. Instead of bringing one man home for the holidays, you're bringing four." He laughs. "Speaking of which, mother is so freaking excited. She literally hasn't stopped talking about it for the last two weeks. About how happy she is for you, how excited she is that Emmett's coming, and how jealous all the girls are at bridge club. They obviously don't know that you're seeing all the guys. She just told them they're your friends you met last Easter and that they grew up with Mrs. Mary Mae. She, of course, tries to play it up that she's going to get you to date one of them."

"I hate she has to lie for me."

"Don't. I think it gives her a thrill." He laughs again. "I have seriously never seen her like this."

"How's dad with all of it? I know he says he's ok as long as I'm happy and he's been nice and accepting to the guys when they've spoken on the phone. I just don't know, you know. He's polite, but quiet."

"He seems good. I don't know if he fully understands the why behind it, but you're his little girl, so he will always try to look after you."

"Yea. He was fairly adamant that he didn't like Rich."

"Rich?" Beckett scoffs, "We're using his name? I like dick-face or douche for brains a lot better."

"You can call him whatever you want. I've moved on from him. I literally feel nothing for him. No hate, no dislike. Nothing. That's how I know I'm truly over him."

"How could you not be with your four hunks?" He pauses for a minute, then continues, "So, what are you doing? It sounds like you're in a tunnel."

"I'm driving to meet Lizzy. We're looking at some new toys a supplier is bringing in, and then going to have lunch with her."

"Without your guys? Is that allowed?"

"Yes." I laugh. "We don't spend every minute together. We have our own lives."

"Just most minutes... of every day... naked and in bed."

"Do you really want to talk about my sex life? Because we can."

"No!" he shouts.

"I didn't think so. So, what's up? Why did you call?"

"Can't a brother just want to call and catch up with his very best and most favorite sister?"

"I'm your *only* sister."

"So?"

There is a quiver in his voice. Excitement? Nerves? Something. "Is everything ok? Is there something going on you aren't telling me? Are mom and dad ok?"

"They are fine, but yes... there is something I want to tell you."

"You? Fuck, are you ok, Beck?"

He laughs. "Yes. I am fine, too. More than fine." There's a long pause before he blurts out. "I'm going to ask Will to marry me. At Thanksgiving. When you all are here!"

"What!? Are you serious? Beck! That is so great. Oh, my gosh. Wait. You didn't tell the guys first, did you?"

"Your guys? Before telling you? What kind of brother do you think I am?"

"Beck. You aren't answering the question."

"Ok. Fine. No, I didn't tell them in so many words."

"But they knew before me?" I try not to sound like a petulant child.

"No. Not technically."

"Technically?" I yell into the air.

"No. When I was talking to Knox, it was more of an idea. He was very encouraging."

"I'm going to beat him," I tease. "I love how close you are with my guys, but Beck. Don't make me jealous of them finding out things first," I whine. The closeness Beck has with my guys makes me so happy. So thrilled. The kind of happy that almost makes your heart hurt because you don't think it could be so full.

"It was all maybes when I was talking to them. You're the very first person who I've told that I'm actually going to do it. I bought the ring and everything."

"You did?"

"Yes. I'm actually sitting in my car looking at it. I don't know how I'm going to wait for two more weeks. Ev. I'm so happy and so excited."

I chuckle. "Isn't it amazing how much has changed in a year for both of us? This time last year, you were bouncing around from one dick to another and hated the idea of commitment. Now look at you?" I laugh again. "Becks. I'm really so happy and excited for you and Will. You're going to make the two most handsome groomsmen ever."

He gasps. "Above your men."

I laugh, but my stomach clenches. "I don't think they will be groomsman. It would be hard for us to marry."

"But you would want to? I know you always talked about it with douche face but then you stopped talking about it, saying how it wasn't that important to you anymore. Were you just saying that because of your situation? If you could, would you want to?"

Pulling to a stop at the light, I look at all the couples walking along the sidewalks hand in hand, or pushing strollers and my heart strings pull a little. "Yes. I would. I want everything with these men, but I also knew going into it they don't want marriage or kids. How would any of that work?"

Beck doesn't speak.

"Beck?" I ask, driving down the road again.

"Sorry. I'm here. All I'm saying is that maybe you should talk to the guys again... maybe things have changed."

"Do you know something I don't?"

He laughs, "No. All I'm saying is that when you first met them, it was supposed to be temporary. Now you live with them, run a business with them. All those things changed. Maybe their thoughts on marriage and kids did too."

"Maybe. Are you trying to help prepare me and or them for Thanksgiving with mom? Is she going to be pushing this?"

He laughs loudly. "When is she not? I think part of the reason she's so excited is because you have four men. She thinks she's going to get more kids now. Hell, she's even started talking about surrogacy with Will and I."

"She is on that grandma train hard."

He mocks in an elderly woman's voice, "Well, Beckett, I'm not getting any younger and I want to be able to play with my grandbabies."

"Oh lord. Ok. I will warn the guys. If you can talk to dad, or I can, and get him to talk some sense into mom before Thanksgiving. We can't talk about marriage and babies the entire time. Well, not mine. But we can talk about yours the entire time!" I squeal. "I'm really so excited for you. This has been the absolute best year." I pull to a stop at a large intersection.

"It has. Listen, I have to go. Give the guys and Lizzy my love."

"Same to you and Will. I'll see you in a few weeks! I love you!" I squeal again for good measure.

Silence fills the air as I press the disconnect button and stare at the cars passing. It truly is amazing how much has changed in a year. I used to dread going to my parent's house at the holidays because I knew there was going to be tension. Rich and my brother didn't get along. It was like the fake kind of happy where it just felt super awkward. Dad was quiet, but polite and mom was just all over the place, but not like in a happy way. Like an

I - n e e d - t o - k e e p - m y - self-busy-so-I-don't-have-to-deal-with-my-daughters-douchie-boyfriend kind of busy. This year... This year is going to be so different. There's going to be so much happiness and joy. My parents are excited. I'm excited. Beckett's excited. Hell, he's talking to the guys about important things before me, which both parts suck and is amazing. They have a real brotherly bond, which is what I always wanted for the men in my life.

I grip the steering wheel at three and nine and follow the car in front of me into the intersection.

I hear the tires screeching and then look to my left, and my heart drops like a stone in my chest.

Fuck!

Everything moves in slow motion. My body is being lifted into the air, as the car slowly rolls over and the belt digs into my hips as I hang weightless upside down. Shattered pieces of glass float in front of me as tires screech and metal bending echo around me.

The ground is getting closer and my heart is racing.

Oh God. I'm going to die.

Darkness.

CALLUM - GUY TIME

There's been something on my mind for a while now and I feel like it's on the guys as well. With Everlee having plans today with Lizzy, I thought it would be the best time to talk to the guys about it. I hoped Knox could be here, but he had other plans, which is fine. But I want to check in with Jax about that, too. In the past, whenever Knox has pulled away, I know Jax has kept a watchful eye on him. And while this feels different from the past, there's something going on that he doesn't want to share with us. Which is fine, I just want to make sure he's ok. Even though he's an adult and a fully capable man, I still worry about him. He's always been like a little brother to Jax and me, so I just worry...

Inside the little tavern by the tracks, the aroma of sizzling food and the sound of laughter greets us. It's loud in here, which is fine. The sounds of cheering and commentary from the football game provide a convenient cover for our conversation. We settle into a cozy booth tucked away in the back corner, and within moments, our server greets us with a warm smile.

"Hey! Names Candy, what can I get you men to drink?" She smiles and I don't miss the fact she checks all our hands for rings before she leans over and points at the drink menu.

Did she have to lean over? No, but she wanted us to admire her breasts. Unfortunately for her, they do nothing for me.

"I don't need to look at it, thanks. I'll have a Maker's on the rocks, please." I'd order an old-fashioned, but no one makes them like Emmett and I have regrettably turned into one of *those* people.

"Make it two," Emmett chimes.

"Three," Jax says, holding up a finger.

"Easy. I like it."

"Can we also get a basket of the fried pickles?" Emmett asks.

"Darling." Jax puts his hand on Emmett's.

"Love bug," Emmett coos. "I just love them so much, but not as much as I love you." He winks playfully.

Candy looks around the table, and her flirtatious smile falls before she walks away.

"Darling? Love bug?" I chuckle when she's far enough away.

Jax cuts his eyes, smirking. "I didn't feel like dealing with her flirtations all of lunch. She was likely going to come back with her shirt pulled down to her navel."

"So that is part of the reason I wanted to have this lunch today."

They both look at me skeptically.

"Look. I know we've had rules in the past and things we said we weren't going to do, but-"

"Yes," Jax says.

"Yes, what?" I ask, confused. I hadn't asked a question.

"Yes. We need to change the rules. No sense in you beating around the question. We want to marry Everlee, or have a union, or a binding ceremony. Call it whatever you want to."

Emmett nods, tapping his fingers on the table.

Before he can speak, Candy is back with our drinks. "Here you go. Your order for the pickles is in. Is there anything else I can get you?"

We place our orders for lunch and when she walks away, we all turn to one another again, but don't speak for a second.

"I'm with Jax," Emmett says. "I know we had the rules, but she's it. She completes us. She's already part business owner with us and she loves and accepts us. It's easy, it's perfect. She's perfect."

"I'd love to wear a ring, so women will stop hitting on me," Jax says.

I can't help but laugh. "Brother. They will hit on you even more because now you're taken."

"No."

"I'd hit on you," Emmett says, nudging his shoulder into Jax.

"You do that anyway." Jax's eyes twinkle when he looks at Emmett.

Usually going into fall makes me sad. The weather gets colder, people stay inside more, the landscape looks bare and twiggy and it reminds me of all the holidays.

All the family holidays.

During school, everyone would complain about having to travel to see all of their grandparents and family for Thanksgiving and Christmas. Or they'd complain about all the toys or clothes they got but didn't like. It was just a reminder that we didn't have family, clothes, or toys to complain about. Mrs. Mary would do her best, buying us each a new outfit, socks, underwear and a new toy each year, but it was a lot on her for all the kids she watched over. At her most, she had ten kids, and that was a lot. She did her best to provide for us with the meals. The church would bring by a lot of food for us on those holidays, but she would always make her turkey. She would get up when it was still dark outside to bake it and would baby that thing all day long until she sat it on the table for dinner.

We didn't have everything, but we had enough.

But now.... Now we have everything. We have Everlee. She is our everything.

"So, do you think Knox will be on board?"

"I'm pretty sure he would leave us before he let her go," Jax laughs.

"So we're doing this? We're going to propose to her?" I ask.

We all sit quietly, staring at one another while the weight and excitement of the words linger in the air. The server brings the basket of fried pickles and brings us each a glass of water before walking away.

"When do we want to propose?" Emmett asks.

"Is it silly that I think we should ask her parents?" I look between the guys.

"Not at all," Jax says. "I think she would appreciate that."

"Should we go look for rings today?" Emmett leans forward in his seat, dipping a pickle into the ranch before popping it into his mouth. His eyes roll into the back of his head. "I really love these."

"Let's just double check with Knox first. He would want to be involved in this from the start."

"I know. I was mostly kidding. I'm just excited because I've been wanting to talk to you all about this for a while, but didn't know how to bring it up. I just... I love her so much and I know that makes me sound like a pussy... but fine. I don't care." Emmett stabs a pickle into the ranch, getting it on his fingers.

"Easy killer. That ranch did nothing to you." Jax pats his hand. "We already knew you were a pussy, so..."

"Oh, fuck off." Emmett shoves Jax over in the seat.

It may be silly, but my heart feels so full right now. Watching Jax and Emmett and knowing that the guys are on board to propose to Everlee. This is going to be the best holiday season I've ever had. Finally, things feel like they are going my way.

When everyone stops laughing, we all look at one another and, almost sensing what's weighing on my mind, Jax asks, "So Knox?"

"Do we know what's going on?" Emmett asks.

Even though he says we, he means Jax. Jax knows Knox on a deeper level than any of us do. The time they spent together in the SEALs forged an untouchable and unbreakable bond between them.

Jax looks between both of us and sighs. "I don't think he's getting into any sort of trouble. Not like last time. But something's going on. He's been... not distant... but something, seems to be weighing on his mind."

"Should we ask?"

"Not yet. When he's ready, he'll tell us."

Emmett's phone rings and he pulls it out and laughs. "This can't be good."

"What?"

"Lizzy." He answers the phone and puts it on the table, pressing the speaker button. "Hello, love."

"Love?" she shouts into the phone. Fortunately, the volume isn't up very high and it's too noisy in the bar for anyone to hear her. "You keep my woman from me? Her and I had a date today! I'd say you were at home, but judging by the noise in the background, it sounds like you're at a bar and I swear if she forgot about me, so help her! Everlee! Are you there? Can you hear me, you little wench? Ignoring my phone calls!"

"Lizzy. Lizzy. Stop talking," I command, looking at the guys as we all scoot to the edge of our seats.

"What?" she huffs.

"She's not with you?" Jax asks, concerned threaded through his voice.

"No!" she stops talking as realization sets in. When she speaks again, all notes of playfulness have dropped from her voice. "Wait. She's not with you?"

We all look at each other again. "Lizzy. She's not with us. She left our house this morning." Checking my watch only causes the nerves in my stomach to feel like lead weights. "That was almost three hours ago."

"Three? Fuck!" Lizzy shouts. "When she didn't show up, and she wasn't answering my calls, I thought y'all were... oh God. Where is she? What if something happened?"

"We're on it," I say, looking at Jax, who already has his phone out, calling Brady. "We'll find her car and then her. Keep your phone on you."

"I am. I'm coming to your place."

"Ok," I say just before Emmett hangs up. We slide out of the table as the server is bringing our food.

"Everything ok?" she asks looking confused.

"Yes. We have to go." Emmett and Jax don't wait for me as I pull two hundreds out of my wallet and hand it to her. "This should cover everything. You all can eat the food, or box it up and donate it to a homeless person or someone in need. Thank you." She stares at me without speaking and as I walk out of the bar, I feel her eyes on the back of my head.

By the time I walk out of the front door, Jax is in the driver's seat, pulled to the front curb with Emmett in the back. Judging by the look on Jax's face, it's not good.

I'm barely in the car before he's driving off.

KNOX - FACTS

THE OLD WOODEN DOOR of the restaurant creaks when I pull it open and I can't help but pause for a second before I step into the dimly lit room. It's quiet and dark. A large sign perched on the front desk tells us to seat ourself.

I pause by the stand, looking into the small room. There are about ten tables in the center, four booths along the left side of the wall, with a bar that runs down the right side. Instead of liquor bottles filling the shelves behind it, there are several pictures in frames.

"Knox!" The deep voice of the man in the corner catches my attention. He's pushing to stand from the booth as he waves at me.

I take a deep breath, shoving my hands in my pockets and slowly make my way over to the table. The man looks to be in his early fifties, wearing jeans and a red and white plaid shirt with the sleeves rolled up to his elbows, revealing several tattoos on his arm. He has a tight jawline, short silver hair, and green eyes like mine.

"Wyatt," I say, walking up to the man. My brain cannot process what I'm looking at.

"Hey, son. Sit down." The man gestures to the seat in the booth across from him before he sits back down.

"Don't call me son," I hiss.

He looks at me, then nods. "You're right. I'm sorry. I shouldn't have." He looks around nervously, patting the wrinkles out of the napkin on the table. "Thank you for meeting with me."

An older server walks up with a tray on her hip. "What can I get you, Knox?"

Startled she knows my name, I stare at her without speaking.

"Oh, I'm sorry, baby. Wyatt here has been talking about you for weeks now. I feel like I know you already."

Wyatt clears his throat and shakes his head like he's embarrassed.

"Do you have a menu?"

"We're a dry bar."

"That's fine. What do you serve? You know what... just get me a lemonade."

"Excellent choice! We have several kinds. Do you want regular, peach, or today's special has a little kick of jalapeno?"

"Regular is fine. Thank you."

"Sure thing, sweetie."

She walks away and I look back at Wyatt. My dad.

No, not my dad. The man who contributed his seed to the woman who birthed me then abandoned me.

We stare at one another, neither of us speaking, I'm sure for very different reasons. I thought I would be ok with this... with seeing him. But having him here in front of me. I'm angry. Which is funny. For years, I wanted nothing more than to have him back in my life. For him to reach out to me and tell me he messed up and regretted his decision to walk away.

When I got a text from a random number weeks ago, I couldn't believe it. I thought it was a joke. Thought Jax was trying to screw with me, but then I knew he wouldn't do something like this. That would be a line Jax wouldn't cross.

"So. How are you doing?" he asks with a shaky voice.

"Good." I'm fucking wonderful. I have an amazing girl and a group of guys I love deeply who make me happier than should be humanly possible. That's what I feel, but he doesn't deserve that. He doesn't deserve to get to know about the best parts of me. He left me. The rage is just simmering under my skin, and I can feel it getting hotter and hotter the longer I sit here. "Look I... I don't know if I can do this." When I start to stand, the server brings my lemonade over.

"Bathrooms in the corner, sweetie, if that's what you're looking for."

"I-" I freeze. Words stuck in my throat. "Thanks." I weave through the tables scattered around the floor to the large neon sign that says bathrooms. My head is in a complete daze and I feel numb. When I walk inside, I push the door closed and lock it, pressing my back up against it for a minute.

Damn it!

I want to scream. I want to yell. The palms of my hands press into my eyes, like I can press the tears back in.

He doesn't deserve them.

Taking two deep breaths, I stare at the ceiling, trying to keep my cool. I won't leave. I'm not like him. He wanted to talk so I will hear him out, but he will not get a relationship from me. He had a chance years ago and walked away from it.

Taking another two quick breaths, I walk over to the sink and stare in the mirror before washing my hands.

You can do this. You're motherfucking Knox Fisher and you can do anything.

When I walk out of the bathroom, Wyatt is rubbing the condensation off the side of his glass with his foot nervously tapping on the floor. I slide into the booth and pick up my lemonade, taking a big sip.

"Look," I say, then pause before continuing. "I can't have you pretending like everything is fine between us. Like we're two friends just meeting up together after a long time."

He nods, but doesn't speak.

"You left. You..." my hands rake through my hair. "You fucking left me." My voice cracks,

"I was sent-"

"No. I'm not talking about that. I'm talking about after. I came to see you. I came..." I growl out in frustration, feeling my throat get tight again. Taking a deep breath, I try to regain control of my emotions. "I came, and you left. You left me a fucking note," I whisper shout, pressing my palms into the table.

"You're right. I'm sorry. That was a shitty thing for me to do. I just... Look. It's not an excuse, but when I got out of prison, I wasn't in the right head space. I was angry, and I felt like a loser. What kind of man abandons his son-"

"So you-" I start, but he holds up his hand.

"So I did what I was ashamed of doing to begin with. I know what you're going to say. And you're right. Yes. Like I said. I didn't have my head on right and I'm sorry."

"You shouldn't have gone to prison. It was bullshit."

"Well, I shouldn't have lost my temper like I did. That man would still be alive if I hadn't."

"He was beating up on a woman."

"You're right. Look," his voice drops in defeat. "I've come to terms with what happened to me. I was a coward when I left you that note and even though I walked away from you, I never stopped thinking about you. And then I was at the dentist one afternoon and picked up a food magazine and I saw your face in a picture and I swear... I cried right there in the office. The ladies didn't know what was going on. It was a sign."

"I'm in a magazine?"

"Yea with Emmett Monroe. Is he your friend?"

"Yea."

"Well..." he hesitates and swallows, staring at me. "If you don't want to share, that's ok, but I would love to hear about you. About your life and all."

My insides are pulling in opposite directions, nearly making me sick. I want to tell him. I want to share everything with him, mostly to make him regret leaving me, but the other part of me doesn't want to share any of that with him. He shouldn't be able to be gone my entire life and then just pick up the pieces after.

Shaking my head, I say, "I don't think I'm ready to share that yet."

He nods. "I understand. I get it. My therapist said you may not be ready."

"Your therapist?"

"Yea. I see her once a week. It started off as mandatory when I got out, and I hated it, but now. It's great. We've been together," he quickly corrects, "not like that. Just in a professional sense, for a long time. She has a little boy now, and he's about the age you were when I was sent away. So that's brought up a lot of stuff recently for me to work through. Just seeing all I missed out on." His fingers pinch the bridge between his nose. "I'm so sorry I wasn't there, Knox."

My chest tightens, but I try not to react. I can't.

"What do you do? For work?" I ask.

He pats the table a few times and looks at me. "I'm a woodworker. Work on custom pieces. I live in a cabin on the lake about an hour or so from here. Lots of space and it's real quiet. After I got out, I bounced around from job to job. Really just trying to do anything to get by and stumbled into Ben's shop. He made custom furniture, but he was getting older and it was getting hard for him to move some of the pieces around or sand for long hours. So he let me help him for a couple of hours each day. I really liked it and we talked. He knew my entire life story because I didn't want to hold anything back. Days turned to weeks turned to months turned to years. He passed away last year, and he left everything to me. Said I was the son he never had. I love it. Working with my hands. Watching the wood grains pop. Near the end of Ben's life, he started watching those videos online and wanted to work with resin, so we started dabbling in that more recently. Well, I say we even though it's just me, now. But I feel him there with me every day. Always critiquing my sanding or shaving or something." He laughs and his eyes drift off for a minute, like he's thinking about a memory or something.

"I–" my phone rings and cuts me off.

Callum.

I press the end button and set it on the chair beside me. I'll call him back in a few minutes.

"I–" My phone vibrates and cuts me off.

A message from Jax. Three numbers on the screen. 911. My heart stops beating. Someone's in trouble.

"I'm sorry. I need to go."

"Everything ok?"

"No. I don't know. Listen. Thanks for today." I slide out of the booth and drop a fifty on the table.

"Knox," he calls after me, but I dart out of the restaurant.

Moving with precision and hyper focused, I find my car, climb in and call Jax.

When he answers, there's no joking, no teasing. Just facts.

Fact. Everlee has been involved in a serious car crash.

Fact. She's at the hospital in surgery.

Fact. It doesn't look good.

Feeling numb, I disconnect the call and speed towards the hospital. She is my life. I cannot and will not lose her. I've lost too many people in my life and she will not be one of them.

She won't.

CALLUM - NEWS

THIS SHOULDN'T BE TAKING so long. She's been in surgery for hours now.

Hours!

Fucking Everlee! Why does she have to be so stubborn and independent? Would she be here if she would just let Brady drive her? I know she isn't the type of girl to be driven around, but damn it!

Although based on the what the cop said, there was nothing Brady could have done any differently. Eye-witness accounts corroborate the wreckage. The car that hit Everlee was speeding and ran through the red light, smashing directly into the side of her door. Everlee's car barely clipped the car in front of her before she went airborne, then rolled several times. There's not enough left of the car to save or fix. Cop even said it was a miracle she was still alive when they got to the scene, which I think was meant to be reassuring, but had the opposite effect. They had to use the fucking jaws of life to pry the door apart to get her out.

The wooden handle on the chair creaks under the strain of my hand, so I quickly release it. The waiting room is on the smaller side, only fifteen seats and there's only two other people in the room other than us. One is napping with his head pinned in the corner and the other is a woman who has her nose buried in a puzzle book.

Fucking puzzle book. Maybe I should get Everlee one for when she wakes up. She won't be leaving here anytime soon and she will get bored. I pull out my phone to add that to the list I've started for Brady. Comfy socks, her favorite silk pajamas, her e-reader and charged, and now puzzle books.

The loud clang of the door handles smacking against the wall catches my attention and Jax is on his feet before I can even process what's going on.

"Where is she? Where's Everlee?" Knox demands, eyes darting around the room.

The man who was asleep in the corner nearly jumps completely out of his seat before his eyes land on Knox glaring at him, but Knox doesn't care. His only focus is on Everlee.

Jax has his arm around Knox's shoulder and is ushering him to the side of the room. Knox needs Jax. Jax is probably the only one that can handle Knox when he's like this. We always get the fun-loving Knox, but right now... we have warrior Knox. Fighter Knox. The Knox that would do anything to make sure she's safe. This Knox would burn down the entire world for her.

There's nothing I can do except watch. Watch and intercede if I need to. Intercede. I laugh at myself. I'm a larger man. A strong man. But Knox... he's a trained killer. Something we forget. He's the most dangerous of all of us because others wouldn't expect it or see it coming. No... Knox is lethal and right now... God help the person who did this to Everlee.

Lizzy looks at me nervously. This is the first time she's seen this side of Knox, and to be fair, we haven't seen it very much. "It's ok. He's ok."

She nods. I know she wishes Tony were here, but he's in California meeting with a client. He's getting on the next flight out, but that's not for a few more hours.

Emmett pats the chair between us and she moves across the room to sit with us. "Knox loves her so much. He's just worried."

"I get it. I feel the same way he's acting," she mumbles, gripping the tattered tissue in her hands. Her eyes are red and she's been crying for most of the last two hours. Jax was consoling her for a while, giving her a shoulder to cry on. I think in some ways they find connection and peace with one another.

Emmett's hand pats her knee. "Have you talked to her parents or Beckett yet?"

She shakes her head. "I don't want to talk to them until I have news to give. They're going to ask questions I don't have answers to."

"Smart." He nods his head.

"Her dad has a heart condition and... her mom... I can't... and Becks..." she starts crying again. "I'm sorry." She throws her hands in the air. "I just... I can't... I can't lose her. She's my life. My rock. My sister."

"You aren't going to lose her. They have lots of doctors in there working on her and fixing her. She's going to be ok. She is stubborn as shit... you know that," Emmett tries to reassure.

"She is a stubborn bitch," Lizzy agrees, trying to laugh through her tears before pressing her palms into her eyes. "I shouldn't have called her a bitch." A new wave of tears stream down her face.

"She would want you to call her a bitch... only you can do that. It's like a term of endearment between you two. You know that, and she knows that."

Another minute passes, and she has calmed down just as Knox and Jax walk over to sit in the seats in front of us. Knox nods at me, then shrugs. His way of telling me he's calmed down. For reassurance, I glance at Jax and he tosses me a wink and my body relaxes.

A calmness sweeps over the room as we all just sit quietly... waiting... begging silently for an update.

The doors open and a doctor walks through and the entire room tenses. She's just above average height for a woman and has wisps of dark hair poking out around her scrub cap.

"Family for McKinley. Everlee McKinley."

"Here!" we all say in unison, standing.

The doctor takes a step back in surprise. "Ok." She walks over.

Watching her take the ten steps to close the distance makes it feel like time has stopped moving. My brain watches her hands, her eyes, the way she walks... trying to analyze every detail, every micro expression on her face looking for any hint, any clue of the news she's about to share. Looking for a hint, she's about to tear our world apart...

Knox is beside me and I glance at Jax, who gives me a quick nod, and then to Emmett, who does the same. Jax has Knox, Emmett has Lizzy. Everyone is accounted for and taken care of.

The doctor looks between Knox and me, unsure who she needs to speak to.

"How is she? How's Everlee?" I ask, offering her a person.

"Everlee's out of surgery and is in the ICU. She had some internal bleeding that we were able to get under control and had some lacerations from broken glass across her face, but it missed her eyes, which is good." She pauses for a second and her voice drops. "There was some swelling in her brain, so we've put her in a medically induced coma for now to help the swelling go down."

"Coma?" Lizzy mumbles, turning into Emmett's arms. He rubs the back of her head for a moment until she looks back at the doctor. "But she's going to be ok?"

"We're going to continue to monitor her, but she's a fighter." She pauses for a moment. "If there aren't any other questions, the nurse will be down in a few minutes once we get her situated. Only two at a time, though. Rooms are small."

She nods and looks at everyone before leaving.

We all take a collective sigh of relief.

"I'd like to see her first," Knox asks and everyone nods.

Jax looks at Lizzy, and she nods at him. "You can go first."

"You sure?"

"Yea," she holds Emmett's arm.

Knox and Jax will go first, followed by Emmett and Lizzy, and then me. Pulling out my phone, I fire off the text to Brady, letting him know what the doctor said, as well as the items for Ev and a food order for the group. It's going to be a long night, because I don't imagine anyone will leave her side.

EMMETT - 669

LIZZY'S ARM TIGHTENS AROUND mine. I'm not used to seeing this vulnerable version of her and it's freaking me out a little. We all sit down and wait for the nurse to come out and get us. Knox and Jax are going to visit her first, which will be good for Knox. He needs to see her. I don't know why, but he's dealing with something. Hopefully Jax can get it out of him later tonight.

Sitting down, I grab Lizzy's hand. "Do you think we should call Ev's family?"

"Yes... but..." Her eyes grow wide and I can see the vein in her neck pulsing rapidly.

"I'll do it," I offer. "I'll call Beckett."

"You will?" she asks, relieved.

"Yea." I drag out my phone and dial his number, taking a deep breath.

On the third ring, he answers, "Look. If you're calling to give me shit because I told her first, then you'll just have to deal with it. I'm not apologizing. I figured she'd tell you, which is why I didn't call."

What is he talking about? "What?" I ask, completely confused.

"Will??" Beckett says his name like it would jog my memory."

"Will?"

"She didn't tell you?" he asks, shocked, then laughs at something going on in the background. He must be at the firehouse working. It's so hard to keep up with his schedule.

"That's why I'm calling."

The moment he hears the tone of my voice, the humor vanishes, and he asks with concern, "What's wrong, E?"

"She's alive-"

"Emmett. What the fuck?" he snaps into the phone, causing me to flinch.

"She was in an accident this morning. She's ok," I rush out.

"What happened? Give me all the details."

"She was on her way to meet Lizzy and got in a crash."

"I talked to her this morning," his voice falters a little. "What? When?"

"She was driving through an intersection. A car ran the red light and hit her. They were speeding. It sent Everlee airborne and her car rolled several times."

A crash echoes in the background and all I can envision is Beckett's legs giving out as he falls to the floor. A minute later, I hear voices rushing over to him and know he's ok, so I continue.

"They had to use the jaws of life to pry the car apart to get her out. She was fighting consciousness at the scene and the police officer that came to talk to us said she's a fighter. She just got out of surgery and is doing well. We haven't been able to see her yet."

"Surgery? How bad?"

"She had some internal bleeding, but they were able to get it under control. No broken bones. A few cuts on her face, but eyes are clear." I pause for a second and he picks up on it.

"Emmett, what else?"

"There was some swelling in her brain, so they've put her in a medically induced coma to help. Overall, the doctor seems very positive."

"Hell yea, she is. She's my sister. Stubborn as shit." He sniffles a few times, then lets out a low growl.

"Yes, she is." I smile.

"Why the fuck didn't you call me earlier?"

"Becks. We thought it best not to worry you until we had information."

He takes a breath. "Yea. Good call. Sorry."

Silence lingers on the phone between us for a few minutes.

"She's ok though?"

"I think so." The doors open and a nurse in light blue scrubs walks out with a smile on her face. "Hold on one sec. The nurse just walked out."

"Family of McKinley," she asks, looking at us. When we nod, she continues, "She's in room 669. Only two visitors at a time."

Everyone laughs, and the nurse looks confused.

"What? What happened?" Beckett asks through the phone.

"She's in room 669." I don't know why, but I'm smiling. We're all smiling and I'm fairly certain the nurse thinks we've all lost our mind.

"Visiting hours end at eight tonight." She looks at her watch. "So that gives you all a few hours with her."

Knox and Jax walk out of the room with the nurse. Lizzy squeezes my shoulder and nods towards the phone, so I put it on speaker.

"Hey Becks," she whispers.

"Liz," he sighs with relief.

"Hey. Sorry, I was a chickenshit and made Emmett call you. I just..." She takes a few deep breaths and looks towards the ceiling, trying not to cry. "I just... I was scared. I'm not anymore though. She got room 669, which is a sign. A sign she's going to be ok."

"Yes, she is. She's a McKinley." He waits a second then asks, "You haven't called mom and dad yet, have you?"

"No. We called you first. Thought it may be better coming from someone in person," I offer.

"You're just as much of a chickenshit as Lizzy is. It's ok. You can admit it." He laughs, then quietens down.

There are voices talking to Beckett on the other side of the phone. He comes back on and says, "Cap said I could take the rest of the shift off. I'm going to go home now and talk to mom and dad. You call me with updates?"

"Every single update. Call or text."

"When she wakes up, I want to see her."

"We'll call you and your parents immediately."

"Emmett..." Beckett pauses.

"Thank you all for being there with her."

"No place we'd rather be."

"I know." He's quiet. "I don't know how she got so lucky. I mean, she was due after all the assholes she had before. I'm just glad it was you all."

"Love you, man."

"Same."

"What the fuck am I? Chopped liver?" Lizzy laughs even though I can see her eyes want to cry. Like she feels guilty, she's laughing, but I know she's trying to process.

"Never, Lizzy Loo. I love you too."

"I love you Becks," she says and her eyes tear up again. "Ugh. I think they spray like onion juice in this room or something."

Smiling, I hold the phone up to my ear. "Knox and Jax just walked up. I think Lizzy and I are next. We can video chat, but I don't know what we'll be walking into. It may look worse than it is."

"I've seen bad E. I'll be ok."

"I was thinking about your parents."

"Right. I'll talk to them, but I imagine they'd want to see her. I'll try to set expectations, though I imagine it'll be hard. Words can't really do a lot of that justice."

"Ok. One of us will text or call with updates."

"Thanks."

My body relaxes as I lean back in the seat, letting out a deep breath and feeling my heart rate gradually slow down.

It's going to be ok.

Our firecracker is going to be ok.

KNOX - BROKEN

WITH EACH STERILE WHITE door we pass, the harder my heart pumps in my chest. This is my fault. My fucking fault. If I'd just been with her, this wouldn't have happened.

We should have been together.

She wanted to go by herself with Lizzy, and I let it happen so I could meet with Wyatt. Had I not been so selfish, I would have made her let me come with her and this wouldn't have happened.

"You good, brother?" Jax whispers, looking over at me.

My eyes cut in his direction and I snap out, "Yea."

He cocks his head at me. I know he's worried. It's why he was the first one up when I barged into the room, and why Lizzy let him come up with me instead of her. They think I'm going to lash out. I'm not. I'm controlled. Admittedly, I came in the room a little intense, but I was worried. Am worried. And angry. Angry at myself.

"Sorry. I'm good... it's just... my fault."

"How is this your fault?" His brow pinches in confusion.

With a moment of hesitation, I choose to keep the information about my dad to myself, and before Jax can press any farther, we're stopping in front of a door.

Her door.

We look at each other and try to build up the courage to push it open.

The nurse is standing at the door with her hand on the handle. "If you've never seen someone on a ventilator before, it can be a lot to take in. Like the doctor said earlier, she has some cuts and scrapes across her face and she had surgery to stop the internal bleeding. So..."

We both nod, because neither of us knows what to say.

The nurse pushes the door open and I feel like someone has punched me in the gut. I've seen dismembered bodies, scrapes, gashes, and several other wounds. I've been in the medic bays while they work on my friends, but none of that. None of that. Prepared me for this.

She- our Everlee- is laying in a stark white bed, with blankets tossed over her legs and tubes running out of her mouth. Her face has several bandages and she's just lying there... lifeless.

Our firecracker.

Our spitfire.

My feet move me forward even though I feel numb. When I pick up her hand, I expect her to squeeze it back, but it doesn't move. My heart is literally breaking into a thousand pieces. I've never felt this kind of pain before.

Jax is across from me, holding her other hand, staring at her.

"Talk to her. She won't respond, but studies show that talking to her can help."

"Evey baby." I wait for the Knoxxy baby, but I know it won't come. The image of her bouncing along with her bright smiling face exacerbates the pain. Tears trickle down my face as I just stare at her.

Jax's hand clamps on my arm. "She's going to be ok. She'll get through this."

"I know." I hastily wipe my face on my shoulder, the fabric brushing against my cheek. "I just... I hate seeing her like this... This isn't our Everlee."

"I know. She's a fighter, and the doc didn't give us any reason to be concerned."

Her arm dangles in the air as I bring her hand up to my mouth to kiss it. Her heart monitor lets out a little bleep, catching both of our attention, and this feeling of peace washes over me.

She's here. She feels me.

I don't know how long we sit in the room in silence, but we do. Just watching the machine pump air into her chest. Watching, hoping for any sign.

"We've been in here for a while and probably need to let the others up."

"Do we have to?" I pout.

Jax smiles. "For a little, but we can come back first thing tomorrow morning."

"I can't leave Jax." I quickly add, "The hospital. I'm not going home."

"Ok." He doesn't push, and I appreciate that. I get it. We can't be in the room with her and the chairs downstairs aren't comfortable, but... I don't like the idea of being that far from her. It's only a fifteen-minute car ride, but still...

Jax leans over, his movements careful, and tenderly plants a kiss on the unbandaged portion of her forehead. He quietly steps out of the room, allowing me a moment to be alone with her.

I lean over and kiss her cheek, just beside her ear, and whisper, "You better wake up. I'm sorry I wasn't there with you today. My... my dad found me and reached out. We've been chatting over texts the last few weeks and we finally met... in person. I was kind of a dick to him, but still Ev. My dad. I want to tell you about him and who knows... maybe one day you can meet him. I love you big." When I kiss her again, I wish for something, even the smallest bleep, but there's nothing.

Back straight, I take a few deep breaths and blink my eyes fast a few times before I meet Jax in the hallway.

EMMETT – BUILDING BONDS

··

IT'S BEEN ALMOST FORTY minutes since they've been gone and we're running out of time. Hopefully Jax isn't having to pry Knox away from her... my heart thumps hard as worry pierces me like a knife. What if something happened?

Before my head falls down that rabbit hole, the doors are opening and Jax and Knox are walking in. Their faces are just... somber.

When I stand, I immediately reach down, offering my hand to Lizzy as she rises. I glance back at Callum, and assure him, "I'll be back soon, so you can go up."

He nods, and Lizzy and I head past the guys after Jax quickly points out where the elevators are and gives a small warning of what we're walking into. He sounded ok, but that's Jax. Hard exterior.

When we get in the elevator, I pull my phone out of my pocket and fire off a quick text to Beckett, letting him know we're going up. He texted about twenty minutes ago saying he'd told their parents and that they're waiting on my video chat so they can see her.

Lizzy's hands are fidgeting in front of her waist, and I know she's trying not to cry again. I think it's more the idea of what could have happened at this point. I just keep repeating to myself that she's fine. She's in a hospital, she made it through surgery. All is going to be fine in time. One minute, one hour, one day at a time.

We push the door open and Lizzy grabs onto my arm. "Emmett…"

"It's ok."

"She looks so… frail." Lizzy walks over and grabs her hand, so I stand on the other side of the bed and brush the hair off her face. I know how she hates it tickling her forehead.

"Ev. You listen here. You need to heal up quickly because you're making me manage these men of yours. I know we've talked about this before… but four men… that's a lot for me. Especially when they are like this… all over protective and shit. I know if you saw them, you'd be turned on right now, you little horn dog. Oh shit," she looks at me, then breathes a sigh of relief. "I forgot you were going to call her parents and didn't know if you had dialed them."

"No, Lizzy. I've learned my lesson around you." I can't help but laugh, which makes her smile.

"Ok. We'll finish this conversation soon. E's going to call your parents and brother right now, so be on your best behavior. I don't need you stirring up any drama while we're on the call." She kisses her hand, then gives me a nod.

I dial Beckett and he picks up on the second ring. Will and her parents are in the background.

"Hello Mr. and Mrs. McKinley. Will."

"Emmett darling, you can call us mom and dad," Everlee's mom says, fiddling with the tissue in her hand. Her eyes are red and her cheeks still look wet with tears.

"I'm in the room with Everlee. She's on a ventilator, so it may look a little shocking. Doctors or nurses haven't given any other news, so I'm going to take that as good news." I pause for a minute to see if there are questions.

When no one speaks, I turn the camera around. I can hear Everlee's mom gasp while their dad consoles her.

"Again, she had a few scrapes on her face from the glass, and they had to do surgery to stop her internal bleeding. They have her in a medically induced coma to help her brain heal."

"Everlee, baby. This is your mother."

I move the phone closer to Everlee.

"Thank you, Emmett. Now listen here, baby. You have us all really worried, so I need you to just get better. I know this accident wasn't your fault, but still... heal up real fast now. Beckett, say something to your sister."

"Hey sis. So you know I'm not one for speeches and talking about my feelings, so the fact you're in this situation is pretty selfish."

"Beckett!" Donna slaps him on the shoulder.

"Oww. Now you're making mom slap me. Nothing? You got no response. I mean, I guess I could say anything I want to you right now and you can't defend yourself. Like that one time, mom thought it was me that broke the lamp in the living room with the baseball, but really it was you. You promised if I didn't tell, you'd eat all my vegetables for a month."

"Is that why? I thought she was just going through a growth spurt or something."

"Or that one time that boy-"

"Hey Becks!" Lizzy pokes her head into the video. "She may be resting right now, but I will still come through the phone and beat your ass if you don't shut up."

Beckett rolls back, laughing, and Everlee's parents are smiling. Leave it to these two to bring some sort of normalcy to this situation.

"I was just wanting to see who was going to break first. Ev or you," Beck defends.

"Shitty brother. What do you see him, Will?" she points, smiling at him. A moment later, the laughter dies down and we're back to staring at Everlee.

"So visiting hours are between eight and eight. I'm going to pass the phone off to Lizzy and let her stay up here a little while longer. Callum still hasn't seen her yet, and I don't want them to kick us out before he does."

"Are you going to stay at the hospital?" Everlee's dad asks.

"I don't know what we're doing yet. I imagine we'll split up. Some will go home and the others will stay here, just in case."

"You won't be able to visit her, though?"

"No. Not until eight tomorrow morning."

"You all should go home and sleep in your beds, because I'm sure once they move her out of the ICU, you won't be leaving her side."

"No, we won't. There have already been conversations about how much we have to pay someone to let us stay in her room tonight. Unfortunately, it's tiny." I move the camera around to show them.

"Oh, wow."

"We've already paid the money to get her the largest room they have once she's out of the ICU. They reserve it for VIPs, but it's not being used right now."

"Well, she is a VIP," Donna says.

"Yes, she is."

"Oh, if I was there with you, I would just squeeze you."

"Donna," their dad warns.

"Mother."

I laugh, "It's ok. You can squeeze away."

"Did you hear that, boys?" When the laughter dies down, we all stare at one another again.

After a few minutes, Donna asks, "Will you please call with any updates?"

"Of course. I will call tomorrow morning when we visit?"

"That would be lovely. Beckett, can you get him my number?"

"Yes, mother."

"Everlee, we love you baby," Donna says.

"Love you, darling," her father says.

"Like you a lot," Beckett says before getting slapped in the arm by Donna. "Ow, fine. I love you. I love you so much the sun and moon are nothing without you here."

"Beckett. Why can't you just be simple?"

"Because I'm gay."

"Don't put me or all gays in that category," Will chimes for the first time.

"I see where your loyalties lie, traitor."

"Just saying. You're a whole lot of extra."

"Good seeing you all. And I will call first thing tomorrow morning or if we hear any updates before that."

"Thank you, sweetie."

"Bye McKinley's!" Lizzy waves before I disconnect. She looks at me and grabs Ev's hand, kissing it. "Well, that went better than I thought it would."

"Yea. I thought it went pretty good." I plant a kiss on Ev's forehead. "She looks so peaceful like this."

"I don't like it. I need loud, obnoxious in your face."

"Are you talking about yourself?"

"Har har har. Are you going to let him talk to me like this Ev?" Lizzy leans over and lies on the edge of the bed, careful to avoid any wires.

"Can I trust you won't climb into bed if I leave you unattended?"

"No promises." She winks.

"Be good," I say before I walk out.

"No promises."

When I walk into the hall, the nurse steps around the desk. "There's about twenty minutes left before visiting hours are over."

"Thanks. I'm getting Callum now."

"Perfect. I'll talk with him before he leaves."

CALLUM - ADMISSIONS

THE DISTANCE FROM THE waiting room to Ev's room isn't far, but it feels like it's miles. When Emmett and Lizzy went to visit her, Jax and Knox filled me in on what to expect. Tubes and breathing machines, bandages and silence.

When I push the door open, I hear Lizzy singing a song, while she's bent over with her head on the bed next to Ev's shoulder.

She stops when she sees me and sits up. "I can leave if you want some alone time with her?" she offers.

"No. You can stay. What were you singing?"

"I was just humming... nothing in particular. When we first started having sleepovers, I would get scared sometimes. I don't know why, really. It's silly looking back now on it. Or when my parents were going through their divorce. It really bothered me and so she would just hold my hand and sing to me. She'd always forget the words to whatever song it was, so she just got to a point where she hummed random notes."

"That's really special."

"Yea. She is." She sits up and rubs Ev's arm. "I know how you like your time with your men, so I'm going to leave you two alone. No kinky stuff. I know how you are Ev." She kisses her hand several times, then stands to leave.

"I was going to have Brady bring us some food here until I realized we have to leave at eight. So he took it home and has it waiting on us if you want to come over."

"Thanks. Tony should be home soon."

"Are you ok to drive? I can have one of the guys take you home."

"I'm ok. Thank you, though."

"Will you at least call me when you get home, then?"

She sighs, "Yes, dad." She looks back at Ev. "I know you have daddy on lockdown, so don't worry."

Lizzy leaves the room, and it's just me and Ev.

I take the seat Lizzy was in and grab her hand. "Well, you've done it. You've made us realize, if we already didn't know it before, that our world revolves around you. You are the center of our universe, Ev. It's almost like you knew what we were talking about at lunch and you wanted to drive out any doubts. Damn you, Everlee. Damn you for making me love you so much. For making us love you so much. You know. This wasn't supposed to happen. You were supposed to be a quick fuck. Although if I'm being honest with myself, I knew you would never be that. From the first second your eyes locked onto mine at that club, this... this feeling came over me. Like I wanted to claim you as mine, which is baffling because I had literally only just seen you for the first time. Well, maybe. It's kind of crazy we grew up so close to one another. Perhaps we've seen each other before and just never remembered." The machine beeps two times back to back, quickly catching me off guard. "Yea? You agree? Ev... I don't want to do life without you in it. You came in saying you were a rule breaker and I should have listened. At least I would have been better prepared for falling in love with you." I lay my head on the bed where Lizzys was, praying for a movement of the hand like you see in those movies, but there's nothing. Nothing but the machine breathing for her and the steady beeps of the machine.

I don't know how much time passes, but when the door opens, I push away from the bed. A nurse. "I'm just here to check her vitals and things. You have a few minutes left."

"What if I just hide in the corner when they come back to check?" I laugh.

She looks at me nervously.

"I was just kidding."

She nods, but doesn't speak as she looks over the numbers and checks… well, I don't know exactly what she's checking.

The door opens again. "Mr. McCall?"

"Yes?" I give Ev's hand a kiss, then lay it gently on the bed.

"She's in excellent hands," the nurse tries to reassure. "So it doesn't seem that Everlee is married. Do you know if she has a medical power of attorney?"

"No. I'm fairly certain she doesn't." We haven't talked about it at least. Maybe we should add that to the list of things to have the lawyer draw up.

"Ok. Do you have her parents' contact? That's who it would revert to in case of emergency."

"Yes. I can get that for you." I pull out my phone and text Beckett. "Just waiting on a text back," I say, waving my phone in the air. "When will she be able to move out of the ICU?"

"It really varies on the injuries and how she responds to treatment. Could be a few days, or even a week or more. It's hard to say."

My phone dings and I give her the information.

"Tomorrow morning at eight?"

She nods. "We can also just call you with updates, if it's easier."

"No, thanks. We'll be here."

"All of you?"

"Yes. All of us?"

"You didn't say? Are you her brother?"

"We didn't say. And no. We aren't her brothers."

"Friends?" She was searching for information.

I smile at her and wave at the other women who are trying to peek around the corner. "Have a good night and see you tomorrow."

When I'm walking away, I hear their whispers about who we are. One woman mentioned boyfriends, but the others quickly shoot her down and told her that only happens in books.

KNOX - WRONG KIND OF BOUQUET

It's been three days when they move her to the VIP room, which is much larger than her ICU room. It's painted a soft shade of green, adorned with artwork on the walls and boasts a spacious walk-in closet and bathroom, along with a large wall mounted TV. The far side of the room is all windows, which allows the natural light to pour in. It's been dreary and rainy the last two days as a storm moved through, but today the sun has come out. Maybe it's a sign that Everlee will wake up.

It's been hard leaving her every night, but we were all there at eight in the morning with donuts and muffins for the staff. When they found out who Emmett was, some of the women lost it a little. I mean seriously, what's so special about a chef? I know how to kill a guy a dozen different ways and make it look like an accident.

The clubs open tonight and Lizzy volunteered to help look over Allure while Low is handling Vixen. Emmett's head chef has been stepping in more since the beach and has been running things while we've been here. When we told the businesses they moved her into VIP, they all asked what room, even though we told them no visitors. The room isn't that large, but I imagine she'll get flowers. Seems like the thing people do, plus I know Everlee would love to see that when she wakes up, so I may have ordered a few dozen already.

The doc just left a few minutes ago and said she could wake up in a minute or hour now, so we're all glued to the edge of our seats, watching her and waiting.

My dad has texted a few times, checking in on me. I didn't tell him what was wrong because I'm not ready to share my life or Everlee with him yet and fortunately he's been understanding. He accepted what little I was offering and said he hoped everything was ok and that he was thinking about me. He asked if we could meet up again for lunch, but I haven't gotten back to him yet. Between Everlee and the little bit I have to do at Vixen, I just haven't had time. Lizzy has been great. The management that Sammie put in place before she left has been fantastic. They've allowed Everlee and me to get up to speed and really dig in to drive the business forward.

Lizzy's there now, checking in the shipment of new toys. It's something her and Everlee have been really excited about- getting the shop up and running. She's going through and cataloging the new items and getting them on the website. I think it helps for her to keep her mind busy. She's been here the last couple of days with us. Tony's been popping in and out, bringing us food or coffee.

Nights have been the worst. I miss her so freaking much. Her laugh. Her chuckle. The warmth of her body.

Fuck it.

I walk over to her bed, slide her hand out of the way, and climb in.

"Knox," Callum warns.

"I'm not touching anything. I'm on my side with half my ass cheek hanging off the edge of the bed."

"More than half," Jax chimes.

"I feel like that was supposed to be a dig at how large and lovely my ass is, but I'm choosing to ignore it."

Jax scoffs and rolls his eyes. He's just jealous.

Callum's phone rings, pulling our attention.

He glances at it and his brows furrow. "This can't be good."

He presses the speaker button. "Lizzy? Is everything ok?"

"Look." She pauses. "You can't be mad at me. How was I supposed to know?"

"Know what Lizzy?" he asks slowly, looking around the room at the rest of us to see if we have any clue as to what she's talking about.

"The bouquet."

"What bouquet?"

"Wait." She's clicking around in the background. "You haven't gotten them yet?"

"Gotten what? A bouquet of flowers? No. Why would we be ma-"

"Praise baby Jesus!" She hangs up the phone.

"What was that about?" Callum asks us.

"You never know with that one," Jax says.

There's a soft knock on the door and a nurse walks in, cheeks ten shades of red. This can't be good...

"Umm... I have... ummm... these..." her voice is shaky, and she has turned an even darker shade of red.

"Oh... my... God," I say, slowly sitting up from the bed. I'm closer to the nurse so I can see what she's holding. "Sit those down there." I point to the closest thing to her, which is the tray beside Everlee's bed.

"Is that?" Jax starts, then stops.

"Yes."

"Fucking Lizzy," he growls, and I burst out into a fit of laughter.

Callum's phone rings again. "It's almost like she knows..." Callum presses the speaker phone.

"Damn it! I tried to stop them. I'm so sorry."

"Lizzy. You sent a bouquet of rose vibrators to Everlee... at a hospital."

"Fuck! I know! I know! Why do you think I was trying to stop it? I was trying to multi-task here with loading up all the images to Allure's store and it was taking too long. Side note, upgrade the internet. Shit. If it was faster, this wouldn't have happened."

"How do you accidentally send a bouquet of vibrators..." Jax asks.

"Well, Allure obviously wanted to send her some flowers, so I was looking online and flipping back and forth between the two pages while things were loading and saw a bouquet of roses. I mean honestly, change the name. Why would you have so many vibrators, anyway?"

"They're lovely," I call across the room. "All the colors... if only we needed a dozen rose vibrators."

"Well, I was going to go all out and buy five dozen, so be glad I didn't do that," she pauses. "Well, I guess that makes sense why it was so much. You may want to call your credit card company about that."

"You used our credit card? How did you get that?" Jax bristles.

"Me..." a low voice rattles from beside me.

"Ev?" I look to my side and the room stops talking, well, except for Lizzy.

"EV!" Lizzy shouts, then hangs up.

I roll out of bed to give Everlee some space at the same time the guys are coming to a stop beside her.

"Let me see her! Let me see her!" Lizzy is shouting through the phone.

Callum turns the phone to face Ev.

"Everlee! You're awake," she coos softly, then abruptly shifts gears, "Thank the Gods because woo girl. I don't know how you do it... so much... man- men."

"I heard... vibrators..." Everlee is smiling, but it doesn't reach her eyes. They're still exhausted and I can tell she's trying to process where she is and what's going on.

"Hold on Liz." I grab Ev's hand. "You were in an accident. Everything is good. No broken bones."

Her hand grabs her side as she winces a little.

"They had to do some surgery. You had internal bleeding, but they were able to get under control." I start to tell her about the brain swelling and coma, but thought that could wait.

"Accident?"

"Yes. Someone ran a red light and crashed into you."

Her nose scrunches like she's trying to remember, then her face falls, "I don't remember."

"It's ok."

"Is our patient awake?" the doctor asks, walking in. She's putting a pen back into her pocket before her hands grab onto the stethoscope around her neck. "How long has she been awake?"

"Just a few minutes. We haven't even had a chance to come get you."

"Well, lucky I was making my rounds then." She slides the side table out of the way, then does a double take at the number of rose shaped vibrators.

"Long story," Jax offers and the doctor smirks.

"One simple mistake," Lizzy mumbles quietly through the phone.

The doctor is by Everlee's side, lifting her gown and checking her incisions. She moves around her body, examining her head, her reflexes and a variety of other things. I know there's a reason, but I don't care what it is. The only thing I care about is the doctor keeps nodding and smiling while saying positive things.

The doctor talks to us, mostly Everlee, for a few minutes, then leaves and the entire room lets out a collective sigh.

"I'm tired," she yawns.

"Do you need anything?" I ask, grabbing her hand.

"Nothing," she smiles, but before she can say anything else, her eyes are closed and she is sleeping.

"I'm calling Beckett," Emmett offers, pulling out his phone.

"Good call," I mumble, fighting the urge to crawl back into bed with her.

"She's going to be ok," Jax squeezes my shoulder.

His simple gesture unleashes something inside of me and my throat tightens.

"I need to go for a walk. I'll be back in a minute."

"You good?"

"Yea, J. All good."

As I walk out of the room, the sounds of chatter and footsteps gradually fade away, leaving behind a soothing white noise. A low hum. To my left is a little courtyard, so I push through the doors and I'm immediately hit with cool air. I take a seat on the bench under some sort of large potted tree and just... be.

Everlee's awake.

She's going to be ok.

EVERLEE - HOME SWEET HOME

IT'S BEEN JUST OVER a week since I've seen home. When the car pulls into the driveway, a sort of peace sweeps across my body as I stare at the brick exterior.

Home.

Callum pulls the car to a stop and puts his hand on my knee. "You ready, love?"

All the guys have been beyond great with me, waiting on me hand and foot. Helping me to the bathroom, making sure I have my medicine, my food. Everything.

Lizzy visited a few times, but she was keeping herself busy with Allure. Partly because that's just how she is when she's worried- she becomes a whirlwind of productivity, determined to prove her reliability. She's always a playful smartass, but when it matters, she's there. As a thank you, the guys told her they would pay for her and Tony's honeymoon wherever they–she- wanted to go. I advised them to set a limit to avoid spending a substantial amount of money. I was partially kidding. Lizzy would pick something nice, but not abuse the gift. Even though I know she's actively going to make them freak out. Well, maybe just Jax.

As she entered for her first visit after I woke up, she immediately spotted the bouquet of roses she had picked out for me, causing her to burst into laughter. She carefully selected a few from the bouquet, saving them for us, and in typical Lizzy fashion, offered the rest to the ladies at the nurses' station. I don't want to even imagine how that conversation went. I guess it's not every day your patient offers you a vibrator.

"What am I walking into?" I ask Callum when he helps me out of the car. Although I was capable of climbing out by myself, Callum insisted and quickly circled the car. I'm not trying to be a pain in the ass, so I waited for him. With the headaches gone and the cuts on my face mostly healed, I can finally focus on moving forward. I'm still a little sore around my mid-section, where the seatbelt pressed into me and still tender at my incision site.

When the doctor came to evaluate me this morning and finalize my release paperwork, she made a point of mentioning the impressive healing of my incision. It wasn't a very large cut, but it was mostly healed- well on the outside. I eagerly awaited my six-week follow-up, as it meant I could finally take a bath or relax in the hot tub without worrying about the risk of bacteria entering through micro cuts on my skin. Until then, I could only take showers. And that, I'm very excited about.

"I don't know what you're talking about," he smiles, then winks at me.

"Lizzy didn't come in today and Knox was itching to get out of the hospital once the doctor verbally signed me out. Those two together can only lead to no good."

He tosses his head back, laughing.

"Callum. I promise I will act surprised and not tell them you told, but I need to be prepared." I tug gently on the beard that's growing on his face. Through everything, I'd forgotten about no shave November until I woke up. I'd joked before that I wouldn't shave either, and I didn't realize at the time it wasn't a joke. Because of my hospital stay, I haven't shaved and now part of me wants to go all natural.

"Just hold my hand when we walk in."

"Big?"

"Not too big. Lizzy didn't want to overwhelm you." He scrunches his nose. "Which I think is saying a lot for her."

"You have no idea."

"Let's get you inside." He presses his key fob twice, so the horn blows.

I cut my eyes with a smirk.

"What? I'm a rule follower." He winks, then leans in and presses his lips against my cheek, inhaling my scent. I cringe, because I've only taken one shower in the last week. The guys have gladly given me sponge baths and massages, but still... there's something to be said about taking a shower at your house that just makes you feel extra clean. "Ready?"

"Yes."

He jiggles the handle for a second, then pushes the door open and waves his arm so I can lead him in. When I step through the door, I'm prepared to be assaulted with something... anything, but there's nothing.

Looking at Callum, he closes the door and winks at me. "Let's go to the living room so you can rest on the couch."

I nod in understanding. He takes my hand, kisses my knuckles and we walk towards the living room. As soon as I turn the corner, I hear a mangled combination of surprise and welcome home!

Lizzy turns towards the crowd, who all look confused. "Yea, that was my bad. I just got so excited I yelled the wrong thing."

"Shocking," Jax chimes from the back.

My guys, Brady, Lizzy, Tony, Betty, and Gerald, are standing in the living room in front of an oversized balloon arch. The room was overflowing with flowers they had brought home from the hospital.

"Were you surprised?" Knox walks over, grabbing my hands and bringing them both to his lips.

"Yes. It was very sweet, and you didn't have to do this."

He pulls me in for a hug. "Don't you ever do that to us again," he mumbles into my neck.

"Trust me. I don't plan on it."

"So you're agreeing to let Brady drive you everywhere, then?" Jax asks, walking up and gently pulling me from Knox's arms.

Scrunching my nose, I look up at him, arms tucked between us with my chin on his chest. "I don't think that's what I said."

He glares at me, then presses his lips to my forehead. "What am I going to do with you?"

"I don't know, but you better figure it out because you're stuck with me." I unfold my arms and wrap them around his wide body, and let him hold me for a second.

Emmett steps up behind me and taps me on the shoulder, causing Jax to grumble before he lets me go. I turn around and look at Emmett. "Hey, love."

"How do you feel?"

"With my hands," I smirk.

"Cute. I can see your humor is still intact."

"I'm feeling fine. Happy to be home and maybe just a little sore."

"Knox is so happy you're home."

"Just Knox?"

"Stop. We're all happy you're home, but Knox... good luck getting a second of privacy. You scared him. Scared us all, but he... he definitely took it the hardest."

"He told me he blamed himself. Which I don't understand."

"Yea, something's going on with him."

We both turn to look at Knox talking to Betty and Gerald in the corner. The light in his eyes seems to be back, which is good.

"Ok. Scootch ya bootch," Lizzy says, pushing Emmett out of the way. "My turn to hug my love muffin."

"Be gentle with her or you'll have four very protective men on you."

"I can take you all." Lizzy bats her hand before wrapping me gently in her arms. She whispers in my hair, "Are they still watching me?"

"Yes," I whisper back.

"At least they're looking at my best side. My ass, if that wasn't clear."

I let out a mangled sort of laughter.

"I missed you," she admits, still holding me closely. "And you scared me, Ev. Like scared me big. Don't do that again. I can't do life without you."

Trying to soothe her, I let my body relax and sink into her hug. "I'm not going anywhere, boo boo. It's going to take a lot more than some car t-boning me and flipping me over a couple of times."

She whispers back in all sincerity, "I'm sorry... I stopped listening after you said boning."

Laughing at her causes my side to tweak, and I accidentally suck in a breath as the pain catches me.

Lizzy pushes me away and holds her hands up, "I didn't do it!"

I smile at her, the corners of my mouth lifting in a reassuring gesture, and say, "I'm fine." My gaze shifts between the guys, noting their tense expressions as they anxiously look back and forth between Lizzy and me.

"I'm just so horny. Between worrying about you and running Allure, I've not had time to get my freak on."

"Well, now you can. I'm back home."

Her phone rings and she looks at me, eyes wide with panic.

"What's wrong?"

"I knew I forgot something." She pulls her phone out and looks at it, lips flattening into a thin, hard line. "It's for you."

Beckett.

I chuckle. "You forgot to call him when I got home, didn't you?"

"To be fair, there was a lot going on and you know how I do in these situations. My head gets all squirrely. It's why I need you in my life."

I give her a quick kiss on the cheek before I answer her call.

"That wench!" Beckett announces when he sees me on the screen.

"Oh, shut your trap!" she calls back, walking over to Betty.

"Hey sis," he says.

"Everlee, darling," my mother coos, coming into frame with my father. "How are you feeling?"

I walk the phone into the kitchen and climb into the bar seat. There's a whole spread of food that Emmett or someone must have set out. I pick up a grape and roll it between my fingers. "I'm doing good. Feeling ok. Still on some pain meds, but weaning myself off."

"What did the doctor say today?" Beckett asks, poking his head into the frame.

"She said I was healing nicely and was impressed with the look of my incision. It's not fully healed, so I can't get into the hot tub or bath yet, but showers are fine as long as I continue to keep dry. I don't need to wear a bandage over it anymore, but I still might. I feel like it gives me an extra layer of protection. It's still a little sore at the incision site, but not too bad."

"Scrapes on your face look like they are mostly gone."

"Yea. There's one here," I pull my hair back and show the scrape at my temple going into my hairline, "that's having a hard time healing. I think this cut was a little deeper."

"Are the guys taking good care of you? If not, I'll come up there and whip some ass," Beckett teases.

"I'd like to see you try, buddy," Knox retorts, walking to stand behind me with his hands on my shoulders. He starts gently massaging my neck, and my head lolls from side to side.

"Oh, you boys," Donna laughs before her face falls.

"What's wrong, mom?"

"Everlee. I have to tell you something, and I don't think you're going to like it."

Knox's hands freeze on my neck.

"What's wrong?" my heart beats a little faster.

"I know we had plans for Thanksgiving and you all were coming down next week, but I don't think it's a good idea for you to travel."

"Mom," I huff. "I feel fine."

"Everlee," she scolds. "You just got out of the hospital."

"And I feel mostly fine."

Mom looks over my shoulder at Knox, with an expression on her face that tells me they've already talked about it behind my back and decided without me.

"Don't look at him," I bark, irritated, because I know I'm fighting a losing battle.

"Evey baby," he coos.

"No. No Evey baby for you right now."

He lowers his head beside mine and presses his lips on the side of my head. "We all talked about it and agree..."

"Well, I'm super glad that you all agree, but I don't. I want to travel. I want to see my parents for Thanksgiving. We had it all planned out. First holiday..." Tears start streaming down my face. They don't get it.

For so long, I was worried I was going to have to pick between my family or the guys and after the beach... that changed. I could have it all. I could have the family holidays with everyone. And this was the first one. The first big holiday. It was all planned, and it was going to be so perfect. They rented the same house as last time and we were going to do walks around the lake. Beckett was going to give them a tour of the firehouse. It was all going to be perfect.

"Babe," Callum says, walking over.

"No. I don't need you all ganging up on me and making decisions that involve me without even letting me be a part of the conversation. No."

"We talked to your doctor about it too," Callum says with a tone of finality, running his hand down my arm to my hand.

I bat his hand off and growl before grabbing a cheese cube off the tray and shoving it into my mouth.

"Fine. Can you come here, then?"

"We're trying, but flights are all full."

"And I can't get the time off work," Beckett adds.

I lean back against Knox's chest, and he wraps his arms around me. "This sucks."

"I know, baby. But we'll definitely plan something for Christmas."

"So long as you don't get in any accidents," Beckett chimes.

"Too soon," I bite back and he shrugs.

"Beckett," Mom scolds, slapping his arm.

"Geez. It was just a joke. I thought we had moved to that part of her healing journey."

"Healing journey?" I chuckle.

"What? I didn't know what else to call it."

"Let's let her go enjoy her time with her friends," Mom says. "We'll be in touch about flights."

The call disconnects, so I hand Knox the phone so he can hand back to Lizzy. A few minutes later, Betty walks over with Gerald in tow.

"Now you listen here darlin'," she waves her finger at me. "You get the friends discount with Betty's Bitchin' Rides."

"You did it?" I smile when I hear the name.

"Sure did. I pulled a page out of your book and went into business on my own. Got me a car magnet with a nice pink lightning bolt around it and everything. Was going to dye my hair hot pink to celebrate, but Gerald here..."

He laughs, "Don't Gerald nothin'. I said if you wanted to, you could."

"You're leaving out the part where you said you wouldn't go out with me in public."

"I was just teasing you."

"Well, it didn't seem like it."

He picks up her hand and kisses her knuckles. "If you want to dye your hair hot pink, then who am I to stop you? I would follow you to the ends of the earth... just maybe not to dinner." He laughs again.

"Fine then. I don't need you to go to dinner. I got Lizzy Lou and Evey Bean to go with me." Her brows perk up like she's asking for confirmation.

"Of course." I smile.

"Boom! Doing it."

A sort of light buzz hums through my body as happiness fills me from head to toe.

"But seriously darlin'. You've got all these men, a driver, and me. You don't need to be driving anywhere."

I smile. I don't want to get into another conversation about how I'm independent and don't need to be driven around. That's something they all seem to forget is that even though I have all these people to drive me, I simply don't always want to be driven around. Sure, I can deal with it sometimes...but not all the time.

"I didn't mean to pry, but I heard you won't be going to see your parents and wanted to offer up my house if you all want somewhere to go for Thanksgiving. Although you have Emmett Monroe... so maybe we should just invite ourselves over for his cooking," she laughs.

"Honey," Gerald rubs her back.

"What... I's just sayin'..."

"I have no idea what we are doing yet, but regardless, you'll be welcome."

Betty turns to look at Gerald indignantly. "See."

I reach for the lemonade pitcher, but Knox is leaping across the counter and grabbing it before I can get to it and pouring me a glass. "You don't need to ask for anything," he sighs, frustrated with me. "Your independence is going to kill me!"

"You're going to kill me trying to baby me."

"Get used to it, honey," Betty chimes. "I'll let you two have your little lovers quarrel, because the makeup is the best part." She winks hard at me as they turn and walk out of the kitchen.

"No sexy time for you, though... for a while."

"Wrong. Doc said when I wasn't in pain." Knox just looks at me and I let out a loud sigh. "Are you all seriously going to twat block me?"

"Safety first, love bug." He runs his hands through my hair.

"Lest ye forget, I was gifted with an entire bouquet of rose vibrators. I'll be fine. Hell. I may even make you watch. Kerchow!" I karate chop the air.

"Damn you, woman."

"I love you, too."

"Yea, yea." He turns me around in the seat so I'm facing the counter and wraps his arms around the top of my chest and rests his chin on my head.

CALLUM - GUY TALK

STepping onto the deck on the roof, I am met with a crisp, cool breeze. The guys are already sitting in the hot tub with drinks in hand, and Teddy Swims playing on the speakers.

"Drinks over there." Emmett points to my left at the bar.

Grabbing it, I walk over and climb into the hot water and let it soothe away the tightness in my muscles.

"She down?" Jax asks.

"Yea. She's asleep in the Nest." I feel like the name keeps changing, but this one seems to fit nicely. "She expects to wake up tomorrow morning with all of us in there."

Jax mumbles, "She would actively have to prevent us from laying with her tonight."

"She ok?" Knox asks.

"Yea. I gave her half a pill for the pain. She didn't want any at all, because according to her you can't feel pain when you sleep, but we compromised on half."

"She's stubborn," Jax says, taking a sip of his drink.

"You're one to talk," Emmett laughs.

Jax splashes water in his face.

I don't think we realized how much our lives have changed since she walked into it. The house felt so empty last week without her here and now, even though she's not with us, the house just feels... happier.

"So," Knox says. "I feel like there are a couple of things we need to talk about."

We all look at Knox.

"Yea...I'd have to agree. Like what the fuck has been going on with you?" Jax blurts, and I nearly choke on my drink.

"Subtle," Emmett mumbles.

"I was talking about the little conversation you all had last week about our future... and also about Thanksgiving. Ev is super bummed we aren't having Thanksgiving with her parents. She said it's the first year."

"So we aren't going to talk about you at all, then?" Jax presses softly.

Knox sighs and looks at all of us, but no one speaks.

He grabs Jax's drink and tilts the rest of it back. "Fine. That day." The day that doesn't need to be named or described because it was such a shitty day. "I... was having lunch with Wyatt."

"Your dad?" Emmett nearly screams out in shock.

"What?" Jax asks, grabbing his empty glass back from Knox and sitting it behind him.

"I didn't want to say anything just yet. He's been texting me for several weeks. He came across a picture of me in a cooking magazine from the event we attended for Emmett several months ago. Said he regrets walking away from me and he's trying to make amends."

"That's amazing Knox. Why keep that from us?" I ask, shaking his shoulder.

His eyes fall on me and he shrugs. "He's not my family. You guys and Ev are."

"So. We can share," I wink.

"I don't know. I've always wanted a relationship with him, then he turned his back and left me... I guess I'm just scared."

Everyone is silent as the bubbles kick on again, filling the space between us.

"Ok, so now you know that... can we please talk about Ev and Thanksgiving?" Knox asks. He sinks under the water and pops back up, running his hand through his hair, slicking it back.

"We want to propose to Ev, and this whole thing that just happened, I feel like sort of solidified that. We need to figure out the legalities of it all, but we want her for now and always."

"And kids?" Knox asks, then speaks when no one says anything. "I want that... with her. I want at least ten, hell twenty."

"You want ten or twenty kids?

"Well, obviously kidding," he huffs.

"It wasn't obvious," Emmett chimes. "You may want to work on your delivery so she doesn't throat punch you."

"In all seriousness though... if she wants them, which I think she does... I want them too. I don't care which of us is the father, but I want little Everlee's running around. Could you imagine?"

Jax chuckles and motions his hand towards Knox. "Yes. Every day."

"Shut up! I don't act like a child."

Jax just quirks his eyebrow at him.

"Just because I think your room needs better decoration doesn't mean I'm a kid. In fact, I think it speaks to my maturity and my excellent eye for decoration. If Allure doesn't work out, I could be an interior designer."

"My room doesn't need life-sized posters of you in banana hammocks."

"Well, that's where I beg to differ. I think it really brightens up the space."

Emmett chimes in, "What I find probably the funniest is that you have had several posters, probably at least a dozen printed off so far, and none of them are the same. I have no idea how many pictures you took, but I think it's fucking hysterical."

"Don't encourage him," Jax warns.

"He's Knox. He doesn't need encouragement to do the shit he's going to do. But I say, keep doing you, bro. I love it."

Jax leaps out of his seat and lunges at Emmett, putting him in a headlock and driving him into the water. He pulls him back up a minute later, as Emmett sucks in a deep breath. "Take it back."

Emmette's eyes lock on Jax. "No."

Jax presses him under the water again, then lets out a yelp and Emmett breaches the water's surface, laughing.

"Dude, that was my dick. Low blow."

Emmett shrugs, not caring at all, and casually takes his seat with Jax glaring at him.

Knox waits a beat then says, "So... I'm aligned on the engagement, if you are all aligned that I plan on actively trying to put a baby in her."

"I'm down for that, because I'm not going to lie... I think I have a breeding kink," Emmett says. "I've never wanted to put a baby inside of someone so badly and the things it does to me, the way I feel when I come inside of her and know she's dripping with me, with us. Fuck, it's making me hard right now just thinking about it."

"I'm aligned," I say, finishing my drink and setting it behind me.

We all look at Jax, who huffs, "Well, yes. Obviously."

Silence floats in the space between us as realization sets in. Obviously, we're going to make sure that Everlee is aligned to everything, but... we're doing this. We're going to marry her and have kids. Something that we said we'd never do.

Damn Everlee and changing the rules again.

For a long time, I was scared I wasn't going to be good for them- the kids. Mrs. Mary was great for us, but aside from her, I didn't have a male role model, someone to show me how to be a father. I don't want to fail our children. But I'm slowly beginning to see now that I won't. They need love, support, encouragement, and I know our kids will have that in abundance.

"Ok, so Thanksgiving..." Knox says, breaking the silence.

"Yes. I say we have it here. Do we surprise her and get her family here?" I ask.

Knox pulls his lips. "So I may have already sent a note to Dufrey to see if we can borrow his plane for them..."

"What did he say?"

"I just sent the note a few hours ago and haven't checked yet for a response."

"Well, what are you waiting for?" Jax asks.

Knox stares at him, undoubtedly trying to figure out if he's being a smartass.

Jax laughs. "I'm serious. I would love if we could surprise her with her parents. She would be thrilled and I imagine they want to see her after her accident. Becks said they were trying to figure out how to get up here."

"Well, I think it's settled then. We get the plane or we caravan down and drive them up," Knox says.

"Thanksgiving is next week. I'll work on getting a turkey and putting together a dinner menu," Emmett says.

"I guess we should invite Lizzy and Tony, then," Jax adds.

"You pretend like you don't like her, but I saw you two at the hospital," I quip.

He rolls his eyes.

"She sort of just worms her way in and before you know it... you like her and you don't know how you got there." I laugh.

"Probably invite Betty and Gerald, too. They may already have plans, but it would be nice to offer," Emmett suggests.

"Ok. So we have our jobs. Knox, you are going to lock down transport. I will talk to Becks and let them know what we are thinking. They can stay in the guest house for as long as they want. Emmett, you work on food-"

"I will need to get a headcount fairly quickly so I know what to buy."

"Ok, we will get you that. And Jax, you will reach out to Lizzy and have her either reach out to Betty or get her number."

"Let's go broooo!" Knox shouts.

I look at him, hesitant to ask, but still do. "Do you want to invite Wyatt?"

He stares at me, and doesn't speak for a minute. "Not yet. I don't know if I'm ready for him to meet you all or Everlee yet."

"Makes sense. I wanted to offer just in case."

"Shit," Emmett chirps.

"What?"

"We have the gobble 'til you wobble party at Vixen this weekend. I haven't come up with a drink."

"It's ok," Jax offers.

"No. I need to. It's become a thing now."

"Well, you have two nights," I chuckle.

"I'm going into Allure tomorrow. Probably time I show my face there, even though I've heard reports that Lizzy has been crushing it."

"She probably bribed them all with something to say that," Jax teases.

"Whatever. She's been amazing this last week."

"She has. And so has Low. Maybe I will invite her over tomorrow afternoon and her and I can talk through drink ideas for Saturday. Plus, she's been wanting to see Ev."

"If we're all at work, then who's going to be here with Ev?"

"We're all pretty close, so we can take shifts, rotating in and out every hour or so until she goes to sleep. Fortunately, the medicine makes her drowsy, and the doc said sleep is the best medicine for her right now."

"I've been checking in on Loveuz, and obviously they close earlier, compared to the rest of our businesses, so I can float around wherever I'm needed."

"You can work at Allure then all night, so I can just stay home with our girl."

"Not going to happen," Jax retorts.

"Do I need to make a schedule?" I ask.

"You can, just so Everlee can mess it up. You know she won't stay home all night. Her ass is going to try to go into Allure or Vixen."

"What's wrong with Bo's?"

"She may go there too. Hell, she'll probably try to hit all of them up."

"Should we let her?" I ask. "Look, we know she's stubborn as hell. Knowing that, let's just make a plan. She will probably go to Bo's first, then..." Pausing to think about it and not coming up with an answer, "I don't know if she will go to Allure or Vixen next."

"Yea, that's a tough one. I'd say Allure, because she wants to see it, then Vixen. But she will also know once she goes to Allure, she won't want to leave... my guess is Vixen first, make her rounds then Allure," Jax suggests.

"Sounds like her," Emmett agrees.

"So, we will watch her while she's at our place... Emmett, then me, then Knox, then Jax will somehow get her to come home."

"Should I drug her so she's tired and wants to come home on her own?" I laugh, but there's a hint of seriousness to the question.

No one answers, because while we all think it's a great idea, no one actually wants to do it.

"Hopefully, she won't try to push herself," Knox offers, then we all laugh.

"Ok. We got a plan." I clap.

"Only for Ev to destroy it," Jax jokes.

"Let's go see our girl."

"Dibs on laying beside her." Knox shoots out of the water.

"Oh, no, you don't." Jax grabs his leg and pulls him back in.

Next thing I know, it's a mad dash out of the hot tub and down the flight of stairs.

EVERLEE - RELEASE

A THIN LAYER OF sweat covers my body, waking me up. I don't know what time it is and I don't want to wake the guys up, so I try not to move.

"Good morning," I hear whispered from my left.

Callum.

He's laying on his side, shirt off, tattoos on display with his arm bent up, with his head resting on his palm.

"What time is it?" I whisper.

"Nine." Another voice behind me whispers.

I cock my head up and see Emmett and Jax both laying on their stomach with their chin resting on their hands.

"Sleep good?" A voice behind me whispers as fingers trail up my spine.

Knox.

"So you're all awake?"

"We've been awake for a while, love."

"You stayed in bed?"

"You wanted to wake up with us beside you, and selfishly we love watching you sleep," Callum whispers, lifting my hand to kiss it. "How are you feeling?"

The guys have been so good with me, but Callum has been extra attentive to everything. I want to roll over and lay on him, but my left side is still sore, which makes it a little hard.

"What do you want to do today, baby girl?" Knox asks, letting his fingers play in my hair.

"You're giving me an option?"

"Within reason. We'll step in if we think you're pushing yourself."

"How about a shower, then some breakfast while I think about it?"

"That sounds like a good plan." Callum kisses my knuckles.

Ten minutes later, Callum and I are in his shower. I told him I didn't need help, but he didn't care and who am I to refuse looking at a gorgeous naked man in a shower?

"Tell me if the temperature is too hot," he says, reaching up to feel the water coming out of the showerhead.

"It's fine. I'm not going to break, you know?" I run my hands over his chest and around his pecks.

"Everlee," he mumbles.

"What?" I try to sound as innocent as possible.

"You know we can't have sex."

"Who said anything about sex?"

"Everlee," he scolds, as my hand inches further down his chest.

"You've been taking such good care of me, I want to repay the favor."

"Everlee."

"Fuck, Callum." I snap, only mildly irritated. "I know my name." My hand clasps around the base of his cock and slides to the tip and back down.

"This isn't a good idea."

"I know *you* think it's not a good idea." I unwrap my fingers and gently cup his balls.

"You just got out of surgery a little over a week ago and got out of a coma a few days less than that."

"My mouth didn't have surgery." I sink to my knees, trying not to wince as the incision site tweaks. "I'll be gentle. If you think I'm overdoing it, then just stop me."

"I'm trying to stop you now, and you aren't listening." I run my tongue up the length of his cock and over his tip, licking up the small bead of arousal.

"You could stop me."

"You know I'm a selfish ass."

It's funny that he often refers to himself as selfish, because the Callum I know is anything but. My Callum is thoughtful and caring. He's the one who gave me sponge baths every morning and night at the hospital. The man who walked me to the bathroom for the first couple of days and helped me wipe my ass. I mean, I'm not modest around these men, but that... that took our relationship to an entirely different level.

I suck him into my mouth, knowing that he's not going to stop me and let him hit the back of my throat. My eyes nearly roll into the back of my head. I've missed him. This. His taste. His feel. Even though I'm on my knees, I know he's doing this for me. Giving me a bit of normalcy.

"Fuck, Everlee." His hands latch into my hair, cradling me in place.

My hand wraps around his base and squeezes as I drag him back out.

"Your mouth feels so good wrapped around my cock."

I hum around him and swirl my tongue around his tip.

"But I can't." He pulls his cock out of my mouth and pulls me to standing. He laughs when he sees me frowning. "Everlee. If you loved me, you wouldn't put me in that kind of situation. Do you know what the guys would do to me if they knew what just happened? Fuck. If I had finished?" He runs his hands through his hair. "I shouldn't have let it go on for as long as I did."

"I want to."

"I know you do, babe." He brushes the wet pieces of hair that are sticking to my cheek behind my ear. "That's why I let you taste. I know it's more for you than for me. I mean, I love when you suck my cock. Your mouth is a drug, but..."

"Please." A tear trickles down my face.

I'm not crying because he won't let me suck his cock, but because I can't. Because I was in a wreck. A bad wreck. I was hit in the side and I rolled over and over and over. It's a miracle I survived. I was in a coma. I had surgery. Thoughts and images swirl around in my mind like a vicious tornado. I haven't stopped to think- stopped to process everything that's happened in the last week. While it doesn't seem like that long ago, in other ways, it feels like a lifetime.

I want intimacy. I want my guys. I want Thanksgiving.

Tears stream faster down my face as the raw emotions dig and scrape at me.

Callum wraps his arms around me and helps carry me to the floor in the corner. He pulls me between his legs, where I curl into a ball and bury my face in his chest.

"Let it out, love. Let it out." He rubs my back and I just cry. I cry so hard my body shakes. "You're safe now and you're fine."

How does he do that? He knows me so well. He knows what I need even before I need it and it's so frustrating. Balling my fist up, I pound it into his chest and continue to cry.

Fucking showers!

I don't know how much time passes, but my sobs stop. Callum's love and strength never falter, not even for a second. His arms are still wrapped tightly around me like a baby swaddled in a blanket. Something to be said about being wrapped up tight in times of vulnerability. It's like our body's innate sense of safety.

Pushing myself away from him, I tilt my head back to meet his gaze. "I'm sorry."

His head falls to the side. "Love. You have nothing to be sorry for."

"Sorry for trying to suck your cock."

"You never have to be sorry for that." He presses his lips to my forehead. "But with all things considered, maybe we shouldn't mention it to the guys. They wouldn't understand."

"How you could turn me down?" I laugh awkwardly, trying to make a joke, because we both know that's not what he's talking about.

After another minute passes, I look at him. "How did you know?"

"Know what?"

"That this hot mess express train was coming?"

"Babe. I can't tell you all my secrets, because then I could never find ways to impress you."

"I don't believe that."

"Let's just say I've dealt with trauma before..."

Is he talking about Jax? Emmett? Knox? All of them? I imagine they had moments similar to this when they were growing up. Did Callum ever have anyone to hold him while he cried? Something tells me no and that makes my heart break.

"I love you," I say, cupping his cheek in my hand.

"I love you, too, babe. More than you could ever know." He waits a minute, then stands, lifting me with him. "Let's get you washed up. I'm sure the boys are wondering where we are."

He stands me under the rainfall shower head and washes my hair and body, taking care not to rub too hard over my incision site. There's a pinkish line where it was and it's been itching like a bitch for the last couple of days. All I can hear is my mother's voice saying, *'That's how you know it's healing'.*

I'm so bummed we can't see them for Thanksgiving. This was going to be the first time they were going to meet my dad in person. I mean, sure, they've talked to him several times on the phone, but in person. All my men under one roof...

We'll have Christmas.

EVERLEE - A BIT OF NORMALCY

I DON'T GET IT. The guys are being super understanding. They've been letting me do what I want all day. After the shower, Callum and I walked downstairs to a breakfast set at the table. I don't think we've ever eaten there, except the one time they were eating off of me, but I don't think that quite counts. After breakfast, we all cuddled on the couch for a while and watched holiday romcoms.

Knox's idea, not mine.

Then the guys had to get ready for work. When I told them I wanted to come along, they all looked at each other... then agreed.

What?

I was fully prepared for an argument. For the *'you just got home Everlee'*, or the *'you need to stay home and rest'*. But no. They said ok.

And then they walked out of the room to get ready.

That was it.

I slapped myself to make sure I wasn't dreaming, because it sure as shit didn't feel real. After standing by myself in the living room for a few minutes, completely bewildered, I finally walked to my room to get dressed.

When I got downstairs, the guys were waiting for me, looking fine as hell.

"We're having an early dinner at Bo's tonight. You can stay after or come with one of us to Vixen or Allure." Callum holds out his arm to lead me to the car.

I hesitate getting in for a second and I know as soon as I stutter step, Callum senses it.

"Jax, can you drive?"

He glances at Callum, then nods. Freaking bro code. Not the hook up with girl's bro code, but the actual brother code. Where they are so in tune with one another that all they need to do is a glance.

Jax moves to the driver's side while Emmett takes the passenger seat. Callum slides into the second row, then me, followed by Knox. Callum double-checks that the seatbelt isn't digging into my lap, then gently presses his hip against mine. His arm and hand rest on my lap, creating a secure embrace with the upper part of his arm.

He's protecting me. Making me feel safe.

I interlace my fingers in his and grab Knox's hand and hold them both on my lap, while I rest my head on Callum's shoulder.

When we get to Bo's they valet the car and we quickly hustled inside. During the week I was in the hospital, winter came. It's freezing tonight. Not quite, but the wind. When it whips...

We step inside the main room and Lizzy is standing there wearing a long black pea coat, with her hair in a bun on top of her head. "Close the door. Close the door. It's colder than a witch's titties in a brass bra outside."

"Why is she here?" Jax groans from behind.

"Obviously, because you need me. And because Emmett offered a free meal here. So how could I say no?"

"Simple. Two letters. N-O."

"You're such a tease," she says, batting the air in front of Jax.

"But I wasn't kidding..."

"Ok." She does a big, slow wink.

"No winking."

"This guy!"

"Let's go to our table," Callum suggests.

The guys are acting really weird. So agreeable. And why is Lizzy here?

We walk upstairs and take our seats at the table. Callum takes his at the head, and for a moment, I want to ask him to sit beside me. He's becoming my security blanket that I don't want to let go of. He must sense my hesitation, because with his palms pressed on the table he begins to stand back up, but I subtly shake my head.

I take the seat at the other end and he tosses me a quick wink. Lizzy sits to my left beside Jax, while Emmett and Knox sit to my right.

"Here ye, here ye," Lizzy exclaims.

Emmett speaks. "Thanks for coming. As you know, Thanksgiving is coming up and we have our Gobble 'til you Wobble party at Vixen's this Saturday. We're a little behind on the special fall drink, so we need to brainstorm. We have tonight, because I need to run Low through it tomorrow so she can train the bartenders before Saturday."

"Let's do something with apples," Lizzy exclaims.

"We just did something at Halloween with apples," Jax notes.

"Right," she frowns. "I was just thinking something with apple cider and caramel. Maybe because the one at Halloween was so good."

"I'm thinking something with pumpkin," Emmett suggests.

"And vodka," Lizzy chimes.

"Why don't we just have a pumpkin spice latte?" Knox teases. The table looks at him, rolling their eyes. I lay my hand on his arm, "Seriously though... what if we do something like that? They are really popular, so maybe something with Kahlua or another coffee liquer?"

"Well, Kahlua, cream and vodka is a White Russian," Lizzy says, nearly bouncing out of her seat.

"So maybe like a pumpkin spiced white Russian?" Emmett says, mulling it over in his head.

Our server comes over and takes our drink orders. The guys get Old Fashioned's, but I just get a water.

"You aren't pregnant, are you?" Lizzy laughs.

"No. I'm just not sure if I'm going to take some meds tonight, so I'm trying to be responsible."

"Well, good on you, queen." She puts her hand on mine. "How are you doing? Are you healing ok?"

"Yea. I'm ok."

"You're looking a little dull." She waves her hand around my body. "No sexual healing?"

"She just had her insides messed around with," Jax huffs.

She leans in and whispers, "Use the new vibrator. Holy shit. It snatched my snatch, then snatched my soul."

"I love you, you know that?" I cup her cheek lovingly.

"Yes, but you can keep telling me," she says, pressing her cheek into my hand.

Our server comes back with our drinks and takes our menus. "Emmett's already ordered for the table."

When I look towards Emmett's seat, I find it empty.

"He said he had an idea, but really I think it was to get away from this one." Jax pumps his brows.

"You big 'ol love bug you. Did you miss me? Is that why you're acting out a little?" She leans towards him and wraps her arms around him. "I'm not going anywhere, pookie bear."

"Nope. Don't do that. Don't call me pookie bear. We don't have pet names or nicknames. Honestly, if we just didn't use names at all..."

Lizzy looks at me and thumbs over her shoulder, "This guy."

"So. Did Emmett tell you we finalized a menu for the wedding?"

"No. That's exciting. What are you going to do?"

"I'm not going to tell you."

"Seriously?"

"Well, yes, and no. I may change my mind."

"You just said it was finalized."

"Yes... that word. Well, we'll see."

A small shot glass is set in front of us. When I look up, I see Emmett excitedly flitting around the table, grinning from ear to ear.

"What is this?" I ask, holding up the glass to examine it.

"Our idea. I just mixed everything together."

"Pumpkin Spice White Russian?"

"Yes. Then I sprinkled some Pumpkin Seasoning on top for a little extra oomph."

We all wait until Emmett sits down, raise our glasses in the air then tip the drink back.

Lizzy is first with her moans. "Hello, daddy! Get in my belly! Wooo! Yes, King!"

"Do you like it?" he asks with a smile on his face.

"Mama like a lot. That is delightful. The right amount of cream." She tosses me a wink and I shake my head at her idiocy. "And the right about of pumpkin."

"Yea, this is good E," Jax says in approval.

"Second," Knox says.

"Ev?" He looks at me, waiting.

"Yes. I like very much."

"That may have been the quickest we have ever come up with a holiday drink," Callum says.

A few minutes later, french onion soup is being placed in front of us and my mouth waters.

EVERLEE – GOBBLE 'TIL YOU WOBBLE

STARING AT MYSELF IN the mirror, I pat the feathers down on my skirt. We have the Gobble 'til you Wobble party tonight and I know the guys aren't wild about me going. When we went out a few nights ago, I got tired pretty quickly. I'd made plans to hit Allure, then Vixen, but never made it to Vixen because I felt so drained. I feel stronger each day that passes. Lizzy is going to come over and Brady will drive us. I don't plan on doing much tonight, mostly just sitting in our booth and enjoying a few of Emmett's special drinks. I just need to feel a sense of normalcy.

The doorbell rings, and I give myself the once over. It's a simple outfit tonight- white fitted t-shirt, with a brown skirt with yellow, red and orange feathers on it with suspenders. It's about as sexy as a turkey can look.

Before I can get downstairs, I hear the tinkling of glasses in the kitchen. Lizzy obviously just rang the doorbell as a courtesy before she let herself in. I don't mind. I love how she feels comfortable enough here to just let herself in. She also knows the guys aren't here either. Emmett is at Bo's, Knox is at Allure and Jax and Callum are at Vixen, so there isn't anyone to stop her.

"Well, pluck my feathers and call me a chicken!" she says, running around the counter to look at me. "Very modest, yet sexy."

Lizzy, on the other hand, donned a tutu in a stunning array of colors - orange, red, and brown - paired with an extravagant bra embellished with feathers. Suddenly, I felt overdressed.

"Stop," she commands, picking up on my mood change. "You look great, love. You just went through a lot. Plus, I'd still fuck you!" she tosses her head back, laughing, "And I'm pretty sure the guys would too."

"Thanks."

"How are you feeling? Still up for going out?"

"Yes. I need to get out of this house. I can't promise I'll want to stay out all night, but at least a little."

"Well, then. We need to get this party started!" She grabs a few bottles and glasses off the bar in the corner and mixes us up a drink. I don't know what she's making and honestly, I don't care. I'm just thankful for the bit of normalcy that is Lizzy's craziness and pre-Vixen themed party drinks. Tonight isn't like the usual costume parties we usually host, but we still needed to have something since it is a holiday.

Lizzy slides a glass in front of me and I cautiously pull it to my nose and smell.

"Oh stop! You're going to love it. Emmett has inspired me to experiment a little with my drinks."

The cool glass presses against my lip as I slowly tilt up the glass. Scents of orange dance in my nose before the cool liquid hits my lips.

"You are really babying it aren't you," she grumbles, sitting her glass back down. "It's delicious!"

The liquid parts my lips and I hold it in my mouth for a second before I swallow. A mixture of orange and cherry and something else plays on my tongue.

"Vanilla vodka."

When I swallow, my body doesn't flinch. "Not too shabby."

"See! I told you!"

"You aren't trying to get a job as a bartender at Vixen, are you?"

"Fuck, no! I'd get fired within the first hour for drinking the drinks I make instead of serving them."

"Probably true."

"Definitely true."

Once I finish the drink, we quickly wash our glasses, then set them back on the bar. "Ready?"

We're in the second row of the Audi a few minutes later. Brady is driving us to Vixen, and there are still parts of my dream that are playing with me. It's been weeks now, but still... it's like déjà vu or something like that. A doctor would likely attribute my dream to the reorganization of everyday sights and sounds, but a part of me questions... I'm not saying it was real... but how else can anyone explain Callum wearing a blue and gold suit? He never wears anything that flashy! Coincidence?

"You know... Gobble 'til you Wobble is a fine name, but I still think they should have gone with mine... they were catchier."

"Cluckers and fuckers, or what was the other one? Wings and ding-a-lings?"

"Yes."

I can't help but chuckle when Lizzy huffs. "I don't know if those were the best..."

"That's malarky and you know it!"

"Malarky indeed."

She mumbles something to herself about the names again as she looks out of the window.

A few minutes later, we are pulling up at the side entrance and my stomach is suddenly tight with knots. I just hope the guys don't lose their shit. I know they want to protect me, but damn, let a girl breathe.

Lizzy, being the bestest best friend she is, grabs my hand before we walk into the side door. She must also think the guys are going to lose their shit when they see us. We barely make it in the door before a wall of muscle greets us.

Callum and Jax are both standing in the hall, arms crossed with scowls on their faces.

I glance over my shoulder and glare at Brady.

Traitor.

He simply shrugs his arms with a quirked brow.

"Listen," I start, holding up my hand. "I had to get out of the house. Brady drove us and we aren't staying late, nor do we plan to get wild."

Lizzy makes a sound, but I ignore her.

Their eyes softened a little, and their arms uncross. "Ev," Callum starts, then sighs. "Fine. Just be careful. I know you're a grown woman and we have no right to tell you what to do..." I can see the anguish on his face as he says each word. "Just please. We don't want you hurting yourself. It's only been a couple of weeks."

Before I can speak, I run and jump on him, "Thank you. You'll hardly even notice we're here."

"Impossible, Squirt," Jax chimes in.

"Hey-yo!" Lizzy chants, holding her hand in the air for a high five that Jax purposefully ignores. "Fine. I didn't want one anyway, you big oof."

He casts a side eye at her with a sly grin.

"At least you're dressed a little better."

"This is only because of the scar on my stomach."

Callum cups my cheeks in his hands. "Love, your scar is part of you, and I love it. While I'm not advocating for you to walk around here showing off our body to these men and women, you shouldn't let your scar make you feel any less attractive."

Jax jumps in, "In fact, it makes you more attractive. A little more badass. Some of these delicate flowers in here couldn't have gone through what you did. Your body- our body- scars, flaws, and all, is so sexy."

Lizzy creeps her head in beside mine and whispers, "Are you moist? Because I am."

"Fuck Lizzy," I growl.

She stands back up, and I turn to look at her. "What?" she asks, confused.

"Please go before I kick you both out." Jax waves his arm in the air, a playful smirk tugging at the corners of his lips.

"Thank you, Daddy," Lizzy calls over her shoulder, before laughing out loud.

"No," Jax snaps. "There are two of them. Fucking Knox and now her!" I hear him mumble to Callum behind me. I don't turn around to see what Callum says, but only hear his chuckle afterward.

"Well, that went better than expected," Lizzy says, her voice tinged with surprise and satisfaction as she loops her arm in mine as we head upstairs to our booth.

"It did. Almost too easy."

When we get upstairs, we walk to the bar and see Low working. She runs around the counter, arms flailing in the air like a wild woman running over to us. Lizzy holds her arms out to receive the hug, but Low passes right by her and takes me in her arms.

"That's fucked up," Lizzy huffs with humor in her voice.

Low pushes me back and looks over me. "How are you? You look good. Sorry, did I hurt you? I didn't even think."

"You hurt me," Lizzy snaps. "Well, my feelings."

Low turns around and gives her a quick hug, then looks back at me. "Are you ok? The guys were beside themself when they came back to work. They didn't want to be away from you. My goddess... when I heard what happened..."

"I'm fine. I'm getting better every day. There's a small scar on my stomach and the bruising is mostly gone. There are still a few places where it's a little yellow and greenish, but I'm good."

She leans in and gives me another hug. "So glad you're doing better and I'm super glad I got to see you tonight." She glances over her shoulder at the growing bar and scrunches her nose. "I have to get back. These holiday parties are getting too big. I swear I feel like each one is bigger than the last!"

"All that outstanding social media coverage! What? What? Who's in the house? Lizzy's in the house!"

"Girl, you are too much, but I love it!" Low says, smacking her ass, before running back around to the bar.

We squeeze in on the end and wait for Low to make a few drinks before she walks over to us. "Emmett's drink?"

"You know it."

"It's been super popular tonight. I swear people are coming here just to see what drink he comes up with next."

"Hey," a man says behind me.

Before I can turn around, Lizzy is already claiming her territory. "Move along buddy. She's already taken."

He has slicked back dark hair and stands just under six feet tall. His eyes travel up and down my body, then lands on my hand. "She doesn't have a ring."

"Dude. I wouldn't if I were you," Low says, sliding us our drinks.

"I can show you a good time tonight. Better than whichever idiot let you come to a bar by yourself."

Lizzy pulls her lips, then leans back on the bar, propping her arm on it. "Do you have any popcorn, Low?"

"What?"

"I just want popcorn to watch this show, because you friend are a persistent mother fucker who doesn't know when to stop."

"I just know what I want, and I want you." He leans in and places his hand on my shoulder.

"Wrong move, buddy," Lizzy chuckles.

"Wh-"

Before he can finish, I loop my arm around his, locking him in place, putting pressure on his elbow until I have him in full control, moving him away from the bar. "Do not, and I repeat, do not ever touch a woman without their permission. Or anyone, for that matter. They are not yours to touch as you please and, for God's sake, read the room. I'm not playing hard to get, so back the fuck off."

"You don't have to be such a biiiii–"

"Sorry. What were you saying?" I ask, tightening my arm a little more, causing him to raise on his tiptoes and groan out in agony.

"Sorry. Fuck. Sorry. Just let my arm go."

"Everything ok over here?" Jax asks, walking up with that possessive look in his eyes.

"No, man. Get this–"

"I wasn't talking to you, shit stain."

"I'm good babe. Just dealing with a prick."

"You." He looks at Jax, putting the pieces together. "Fuck me. I'm sorry, man. I didn't know she was with you."

"Don't apologize to me. Apologize to her," Jax says, looking at me and smiling.

"We all tried to warn him, but then, selfishly, I was placing bets with myself on who would kick his ass first. Ev or you," Lizzy chimes, knocking back the rest of her drink.

"I'm sorry," the man says, looking at me. "I'm sorry I didn't listen and I'll do better."

Pleased by his apology, I release his arm and he immediately cradles it against his chest, soothing the ache, before unleashing a sinister glare and walking away.

"Damn. I really did want popcorn. What are your thoughts about adding a machine or two?" Lizzy asks, turning to Jax.

"No."

"I'm beginning to think that is your favorite word. I barely had my question out before your lips were already forming the n."

"It was coming out of your mouth, so I took my chances I was going to hate it."

"You kid."

"I don't."

Lizzy swipes her hand across the air. "I like you. You're a little rough around the edges and have fuck off stamped across your forehead, but I like you."

"Thank God. I was dying to know how you felt," he says deadpan. He loops his arm around my waist and pulls me towards him. "Now to show everyone in here who you belong to." He presses his lips against mine and takes me in a passionate kiss, pinning me against the bar. His hips press against one of the only remaining bruises, a painful reminder of the seat belt digging into me while I was hanging upside down, but I try not to flinch. I miss his roughness. Desire swells in my stomach like an evil temptress, because the guys still have me on ice.

Which is completely fucked up.

And sweet at the same time.

But mostly fucked up.

When he releases me, a heat sweeps through my body and my head is dizzy. "I'll be in the office, watching you the rest of the night."

With a playful glint in my eye, I pump my eyebrows up in a teasing manner.

"Stop." His brows peak. "Don't get any wild ideas."

"Too late."

"Damn you," he sighs, and I don't ignore his clenched fists at his side.

I take some solace in the fact he's also craving a release.

Lizzy grabs my arm and pulls me to the dance floor. "Let's go."

"What are you doing?"

"Creating space. Want. Need. He wants to fuck you bad and your glow meter is in the shitter. Absence makes the heart grow fonder and what not." She looks at me, humor dropping from her face. "Are you feeling ok? Do you want to sit down?"

"I'm good for now. Let's get a couple of songs in, then we can sit down."

Lizzy watches me for a second, then nods. She wants me to sit down, but she doesn't force me, which I appreciate. I so desperately want things to go back to the way they were before the accident- the sex, the roughness, the dancing, and the sexy outfits. I want to walk around without people freaking out I'm going to break.

After a few dances, I move to our table and can't miss the sigh of relief from Lizzy.

"I'll get some more drinks, then head over," she calls over her shoulder, not waiting for an answer.

When I sit down, I feel my body relax and my muscles have a gentle ache to them. Not painful, just enough to be annoying.

"You ok?" Lizzy asks when she gets back, setting the drinks down.

"Gravy."

"Did you say that because you're a turkey?"

Confused, I look down at my outfit. "Right. Turkey. Haha. No."

Lizzy faces the camera in the room's corner and gives a wave and a thumbs up.

"What was that for?"

"Letting Jax know you're ok. I know his ass is in there, perched at the table, watching you like a hawk."

"You give him such a hard time."

"He makes it easy... and fun. Definitely fun."

I can't argue with her there.

We finish our drinks, do some people watching, dance for a few more songs, then head home. I thought I was ready to be out, but it's still exhausting.

EVERLEE – OPERATION FUCKSGIVING

I'VE BEEN HOME FOR over a week now and we haven't had sex once. My pussy is shriveling up. I can't say it's dry because that bitch is wetter than Niagara Falls. I mean, every time they walk by and she gets a hint of cock in the area, she's like a faucet, spritzing, hoping her pheromones will lure in an unsuspecting cock. Bitch has a mind of her own and I'm just along for the ride.

When I've tried to get handsy, the guys gently remind me I'm damaged, or was damaged. They'd never say those words exactly, but they shy away, scared they're going to hurt me.

No more!

Tomorrow is Thanksgiving, and Emmett is going to be busy cooking, so it has to be today. I'm going to seduce them with all of my power. Make them so hot that they won't be able to say no. And I have several hours to make it happen.

They had to run out to check on some things at the businesses and said they'll be back in a couple of hours. They offered for me to go with, but I could tell they were just being nice. Plus, I needed to stay here so I can enact operation Happy Fucksgiving. I'm not saying we need to go all out and have a good hard fuck, but a cock here or there wouldn't hurt.

I jump in the shower and shave- everything. I'm going to be like a freshly plucked turkey. Bare. Ready to be basted.

I have to stop with the analogies. Shit is getting weird. It's like Lizzy crawled into my head and is just sitting there throwing out all these random ass things.

Step One. Shave and shower.

Step Two. Clean off the dining room table.

Step Three. Decorate the table with a variety of fall vegetables and two of the mini pumpkin pies Emmett made. He has an entire shelf in the fridge for mini pumpkin pies. I asked why he made so many and he said it was because of the recipe. He won't miss two. Or the whipped cream.

Step Four. Climb onto the table and serve myself up for them to feast on.

Once I get out of the shower and dry my hair, I check my watch. Just over an hour. The silk robe Knox bought me a few weeks ago is hanging on the back of my door, so I grab it and slip it on. It's black with large light pink flowers weaved throughout. I rub my hands down its smooth texture and can feel my body warmth seeping through the cool fabric.

Excitement pulses through me as I hurry down the stairs to the kitchen. The guys have to be ready to bust, needing release. I know I do. I've been tempted to use a vibrator or the green monster, but I haven't. Not yet, but if these men keep pushing me, then I'll use it on myself and make them watch. Maybe tie them to a chair so they can't touch themselves.

Suddenly, my head is being filled with images of my guys lined up naked, tied to chairs in a row, while I'm masturbating in front of them. Oh fucksicles.

Focus Everlee.

Goddamn, though.

FUCK, I AM HORNY!

It's fine. I'm fine. Everything's fine.

I'm going to decorate the table, perch myself on top and not take no for an answer.

Setting the decorative plates, chargers, silverware and glasses to the side, I wipe off the table and visualize where and what I want to place back on the table. Trying to keep in the theme of fall, I run outside and grab our pumpkins that we decorated for Halloween. We've been meaning to donate them to a local farm or zoo for the animals to play with, but we haven't made it there yet.

I arrange them on the table, three in the bottom left corner and two at the top of the table same side. Needing something else, I run into the living room and grab the fall leaves and flowers garland and run it along the edge of the table between the pumpkins. There are still some empty spots, so I use the apples I just removed to fill them in. It still looks pretty empty. In my head it was going to be overflowing with fall things, but I'm now realizing I didn't put enough thought into this.

There's a fall fleece blanket in the living room that would go nicely on the table, take up some space, and provide a soft place to lay, so I grab it, pulling it down the center. Checking my phone, I see I have about twenty minutes left. At least I assume. They weren't too sure on how long they were going to be out, and estimated a few hours.

Adding the final touches to the table, I grab a pumpkin pie out of the fridge and set it on the table with some whipped cream. My mind keeps bouncing between how I want to use the pumpkin pie. At first, I was going to have two sitting on my breasts, but that was going to be a balancing act that would likely spell disaster. Then I thought about having them under each breast, so my nipple is like the cherry on top. But I'm fairly confident it would be like one of those things were the idea looks amazing, but in reality it's a super fail. Knowing me and my knack for screwing things up, I should just take the simple route and dip my finger in it seductively, because nothing could go wrong there.

I hope.

Ten minutes.

The cool air hits my skin when I slip out of my robe and place it on the banister. My hand brushes over the small scar that's forming on my stomach, and I press in just a little to see if it's tender. No pain. Good. I place my phone on the island and climb onto the table to wait.

Let's go!

Excitement bubbles under my skin, causing my stomach to clench, and my heart to pound. In T-minus ten minutes, hopefully, I'll be getting sexually ravaged.

CALLUM – SHOPPING

Nerves course through me, feeling like needles pressing under my skin as we approach the brick building. There was no sign. No indication this was actually a business. All we had was an address written on a piece of paper. This company only works on word of mouth and you'll never find them online.

We lied to Ev this morning, which I hated. But we couldn't tell her the truth and figured if we told her we had to run to the businesses really quick she wouldn't want to come. Only because no one would be there and it was more of a run in, run out sort of situation. She's itching to get back to work, and I imagine after the holiday it will be damn near impossible to stop her when she decides to go back. Even though she wants to right now, she knows her body isn't up for it yet.

When we open the door, a soft bell chimes in the store, alerting them to our presence. It's a small room with a long wooden counter on the right, with mirror paneled walls on the left. The floor is a cream-colored plush carpet that sinks when you step on it, making you feel like you're walking on clouds. The room is simple, but sophisticated.

A woman standing near the back lifts her head to look at us. She's wearing an all-black form fitting dress with her hair wrapped into a tight bun on top of her head, with black high heels on.

"Gentlemen," she coos with a high-pitched voice, as she approaches us. "What can I do for you today?" Her cheeks flush the closer she gets to us.

"We have an appointment with Laurent."

"Oh." Her face falls, and she stops walking. "All of you?"

"Callum," a voice booms, walking from around the corner. A man wearing black pants, a white button down with a hunter green silk vest, has a smile spread wide on his face. "Excellent, you brought your friends."

"Yes."

"Please come this way. I have everything ready for you," he says, waving us towards him.

"Excellent. We're on a bit of a time crunch."

"No worries, my friend. We will get you taken care of. Would you care for some champagne?"

"No, thank you," we all say in unison.

"Very well, if you change your mind, let me know and I will have Tina bring us some. I've booked a private room for you all."

"Thank you, Laurent. Sophie has said wonderful things about you."

"Oh, Sophie..." he says something in French, but I can't understand him, but judging by the look on his face, it seems to be good things.

He punches in a series of numbers on a keypad, then pushes the door open. The room is dim, no natural sunlight, but there are several glass tables stationed around the room with bright lights shining down on them. He waits for us to all walk in before he closes the door. It clicks locked behind us, sealing us in. I imagine a security measure.

"Don't worry, in case of fire or emergency, it will unlock," he offers, as if reading my mind. We walk to stand behind the center table. "I've taken all of your wishes into consideration and picked several options for you to look at."

The guys filter out, each taking a table and looking through the rings sitting on top. We talked about some ideas which I sent to Laurent a few days ago when we made the appointment.

We all agreed that we want a diamond cut as unique as Everlee, but that we also wanted a five stone ring, symbolizing the five of us, but clean and not gaudy. Which seems like conflicting requests, so I'm excited to see what Laurent has for us.

Sophie had heard about Everlee somehow and called to check on her. She was napping when Sophie called and when we were talking, it came up we wanted to propose. Sophie is excited for us and recommended Laurent. He splits his time between his two locations–here in the states and in Paris. He happened to be here for another three weeks, so the timing couldn't have been more perfect.

"If you don't find what you're looking for, I'd be happy to have my designers create something, custom. Do you have a timeline?"

"We'd like to propose soon."

"We?" His brow furrows as he studies us, then nods. "Yes. Very well. This makes sense now," he says, waving his finger in the air.

"Guys," Knox calls us over to the far left table. "I really like this one."

Laurent walks around the other side and smiles. "Yes, this is one we actually just designed. It's a beautiful piece."

"May I?" Knox asked, pointing at the ring.

"But of course."

Knox carefully picks it up, holding it like a newborn chick.

He slips it on his pinky about halfway up. "Do we know what size she is?"

Laurent and I start to speak at the same time, but Laurent motions for me to talk first.

"Yes. Size six." I shrug. "I may have measured her finger when she was sleeping one night."

Laurent continues, "Yes. I was going to say that Callum sent me her measurements and these are actually all a size six. Well, there may be one that is a little larger."

"So we can take the ring today if we find one?" Knox's eyes sparkle with excitement.

"Yes."

Jax walks over to the other table and retrieves a ring, carrying it over. "This is one I was looking at."

"Another good choice. Similar to this one, however, the side diamonds are a little larger, so it may look... bulky on her hand."

"Yea Jax, her fingers aren't as big as yours," Knox says, staring at the one on his pinky, moving it under the light to watch it sparkle.

Jax walks over and holds his beside Knox's, then agrees. "Yea, I like yours better."

Taking Knox's hand, I pull it up so I can look at it on his finger and, for a second, my stomach tightens. This is what it will look like on her finger. Well, close to it. For a man, Knox has some dainty fingers.

"Yes, a thousand times yes, I will marry you Callum," Knox fans his face with his other hand and tosses his foot up.

"Shut the fu-" Jax stops, looking at Laurent. "Just shut up."

Laurent laughs.

"Emmett?" I ask. He's been quiet since we walked in. I don't think he's changing his mind, but something seems to weigh on him.

"Yea?"

"Do you like it?"

"Yes."

"Did you even look at it?" Jax asks.

"I did. It's beautiful. Honestly, we could buy her a ring pop and she would love it and it would look just as great on her." He looks at Laurent, "No offense. I don't care about the ring. Only what it symbolizes. I care about her and have no opinion about this, only that I'm happy we're doing it."

Knox bounces up and down even more. "That's three. Cal? You're it."

Pulling his hand towards me again, I stare at the ring. It's beautiful. Platinum band, thin, but not too thin, the center diamond is an Asscher cut, and there are two emerald cut diamonds on both sides. It's not oversized and doesn't look gaudy. It meets all the checkboxes I sent him.

"I like it, but..."

Knox's face falls.

"It just feels too easy. It looks perfect."

Laurent chuckles, "My friend. This is why Sophie sent you to me. I make it easy peasy." He swipes his hands like he's wiping crumbs off of them. "You sent me very specific things you were looking for and I deliver. We don't need to spend hours digging through rings."

"I guess so."

"He knows so!" Knox says, bouncing in his shoes again.

Looking for one last confirmation, I look at Jax and Emmett, getting their nods, then look at Knox, who looks like he just won the freaking lottery.

"Ok. Let's do it."

Laurent claps his hands. "Beautiful!" He walks over to Knox. "May I take this from you?"

Knox pouts, but slips it off his finger.

"He has to box it up," Jax says, lightly popping him on the back of the head.

"We're doing this!" Knox literally jumps into the air, then jumps on Jax's back.

"Get off of me, you little koala."

"Not going to do it! Not even your resting fuck off face could ruin my mood."

"Don't tempt me with trying."

"Jaxie boo boo."

Jax shoves his elbow around, then swings his arm and pulls Knox to the floor. If he finished the move, he could lay him out on the ground, but Knox is wearing a suit, so Jax stops.

Why is Knox wearing a suit? Because we're on the way to the airport after this to pick up Everlee's parents, Will and Beckett.

Ev is going to be so surprised and I can't wait to see the look on her face.

KNOX - MEETING THE PARENTS

My hands rub over the tops of my pants for the hundredth time. Thank the good lords I'm not driving. I'm a nervous wreck. It's not like we haven't talked to him before or even seen him through video chat, because we have- me especially. I've probably talked to him more this week than Ev has, but still... that doesn't change the fact that we are meeting him. Face to face.

We also decided after we left Laurent that we're going to ask him for Ev's hand in marriage while they're here. We don't know when we're going to propose, but it has to be soon. I feel like a rocket has fired itself up my ass.

I'm going to explode.

My phone dings, so I pull it out of my pocket.

Beckett.

"They just landed and are taxiing to the hangar."

We pull up to the gates leading to the hangars and see a small plane coming to a near stop at the end of the runway.

"That's them." Jax points.

Callum punches the code in at the gate and we wait for it to slide open.

We were able to get them here with Michael Dufrey's plane, then get them tickets on a commercial flight on the way home. Will and Beckett are leaving on the first flight Friday morning, to get back in time for their shift, and Ev's parents are leaving on Sunday.

A few minutes later, Will, Beckett, and her parents are walking down the stairs of the plane.

I pat my hands on my pants one more time for good measure.

"Get over here, you little shit!" Beckett says, dropping his bag and Will's hand running over to me.

"Becky boo!" I run to him and jump in his arms.

"Had I known we were reenacting famous romance scenes, I would have prepared something," Emmett says, walking up to us.

I climb off Beckett and pat my jacket down.

"Are you wearing a suit... to meet my dad?"

"Shut your face," I snipe back, with a smile.

"He wants to make a good impression," Jax says, leaning in for a hug.

"Two things. One, you just hugged him. You never hug me."

"Obviously, I like him better than you."

I bat my hand in the air. "And two... well damn, I forgot what the second thing was because you made me so flustered about the hug."

"Dad." Beckett waves his arm. "These are the guys."

Oh God. For a second, I'd let myself forget. My hands fumble over my jacket as I pat it down for the millionth time at this point. The other guys are dressed in jeans and sweaters. But not me. I freaked out. I freaked the fuck out. Jax yanked the tie out of my hand and tossed it to the side and would have smacked me across the face had Ev not walked in before we left.

Naturally, she thought it was weird I was wearing a suit. Jax made up a lie about me meeting with some vendor, which was a stupid fucking lie because it made her want to come. So then we had to continue the fabrication of falsehoods and tell her it was a quick meeting and the guy may not even show up and we had to go. I mean really, if she stopped to think about it for two seconds, she would have seen through it and maybe she did and just didn't want to call us out.

"Mr. McKinley." I hold out my hand when he walks over.

"Knox. A suit? Looking sharp. And call me Dave."

"Oh boys!" Donna calls walking around with her arms open wide, dropping all formality and giving each of us a hug. "Thank you so much for taking care of our baby."

"I thought I was the baby," Beckett chimes, grabbing Donna's purse off the ground.

"Oh, hush Beckett." She swipes her hand in the air, walking over to me and wrapping her arms around me.

Catching Beckett's eye, I stick my tongue out before giving Donna a hug. I've missed that guy.

Will walks around and gives each of us a handshake, still reserved, although I guess it's needed to balance Beckett.

"I thought Ev would be here," Beckett says, helping load stuff into the back of the car.

"She still doesn't know." I grab the bag from his hand and fit it on top of the suitcase, and just as I'm about to close the trunk, the flight attendants come out carrying boxes and ceramic dishes.

My curious gaze falls on Beckett and then to Emmett, who is frozen in his tracks.

Beckett chuckles. "Mother had to bring some of her things. She didn't want them all going bad."

Another attendant walks down the stairs with another box. Head doing some rough and dirty calculations, tells me we don't have enough space.

"Oh, right. I almost forgot! I brought some things for dinner tomorrow. I already had them and didn't want them to go to waste."

Emmett smiles, "No. Of course not." His eyes meet mine for a second and I can see his wheels turning. It's always been his kitchen and this week it's about to be Donna's. Emmett's going to have problems letting go. When she was here last time, it wasn't that big of a deal because she wanted to go to different restaurants, but now... a deep chuckle waits in the shadows of my gut.

Maybe we should propose to Ev before Emmett loses his shit with Donna in his kitchen.

Trying to make room in the back, I shift her parent's suitcase, and Will and Beckett's duffle to one side. Because of the third row being up, there isn't enough space in the trunk for the last big box so that will have to go on someone's lap.

Beckett, Will, and I climb into the third row, where I purposefully sit in the middle. One to screw with Beckett because I haven't seen him in several months and need to make up for it since my time with him is limited and two, because I like to sit in the middle, so I can see out the front window. Callum and Jax take the front seats, even though Jax offered it to Dave. Emmett climbs in the second row, while her parents climb in after.

"Emmett, dear, would you mind holding this for a second?" She asks, sliding the box across the seat.

"Sure, Donna." He's smiling, but I can read him like an open book. He's looking in the box, trying to figure out how to tell the mother of the woman he loves, that he's not going to let her cook after she just hauled half her kitchen here on a plane to do just that.

Donna and Dave climb in, closing the door behind them.

One big happy family in the car.

EVERLEE – FUCKING SURPRISES

PERHAPS I SHOULD HAVE texted them to see if they were running late or on time, before I climbed onto the table and got into position. The blanket is at least providing some relief from the hard surface, but I definitely could use another layer. I won't admit I'm still sore, because I don't want the guys to freak out and not stick their dicks in me. I've had enough and I need cock!

The whipped cream that I prematurely sprayed on my breasts has slid into a nice pile on the table. I've got most of it up with my finger, but thought it best I wait until the last-

A car door closes outside.

They're here!

I nearly jump off the table in excitement, grab the can of whipped cream and spray it over my right breast, then chuck it across the room and out of the way. In all this time waiting, I decided the side welcome would be best because I can't wait to see their faces when they walk into the door.

The door opens.

"Everlee?" Callum calls out.

Excitement is bubbling under my skin and the muscles in my cheeks are pulsing, "In here!" I call out.

"We've got a surprise for you," he says, his voice drawing nearer.

"I've got a surprise for you, too." My heart is pounding out of my chest and my pussy is getting ready to be pummeled. I pick the pumpkin pie up in my hand, then sit it back down, then pick it up again. In all this time, I should have figured out what to do with this damn pie.

"Surp-" Callum stops dead in his tracks, like he's walked into an invisible barrier.

"Hey Darl- oh dear!" my mom screams, batting the air in front of her eyes like a hoard of bats are attacking her face.

Knox slides in a moment later with jazz hands. "Surprise!" His eyes fall on me. "Oh, shit!"

"What? What?" I hear Beckett yelling in the background with a smile on his face. A moment later, his head appears behind Callum's shoulder and he just screams. Not like a manly scream, but like a goat scream. High pitched and scary.

"What the fuck?" I yell out, regaining movement. In my embarrassment, my fingers become weak and the pie slips and clatters to the floor.

"Oh dear," Mom says again, still trying to process.

"What is it?" my father's voice bellows from behind the wall of people forming.

My eyes grow wide as panic hits me wave after wave, making my stomach turn as bile rises in my throat. "No! No! No! No!"

Callum and Knox spring into action, swiftly turning and extending their arms to shield my father from peeking around the corner.

I scramble off the back of the table, pulling the blanket to wrap it around me.

"Probably shouldn't have surprised her..." Knox says deadpan.

Beckett peaks through his fingers and lets out another scream.

"Beckett, I know you're gay, but there is nothing wrong with the female body," our mother chimes.

If I wasn't so completely and utterly mortified right now, I would have laughed at both what she said and the way she delivered it so matter-of-factly.

"Gross, mom!" he snaps back.

"You know I used to surprise your father like this... it's how you were conceived." She pats his cheek.

"Gross, mom!" we both yell in unison.

"Do you all have a river close by?" Beckett turns to ask Callum.

"Not super close. Why?" His brow furrows in confusion at Beckett's question.

"Because. I need to go bathe in the water whilst I sing spiritual hymns to cleanse me of the sins I've just seen and heard."

"Stop being dramatic babe," Will says walking up and grabbing his hand.

"Hey Will." I wave meekly, still from a crouched position behind the table.

"Hey Ev. Glad you're feeling better." He tugs on Beckett's arm. "We're going to take our stuff next door and get settled."

"Probably a good idea," Callum agrees, hand still pressed firmly to the wall.

"Yea. Perhaps we should too," mother chimes. She turns around then stops, looking at me, "Surprise!" She throws her hands out to the side and kicks her foot behind her before she disappears. My father's voice filters through the halls, but I can't make out exactly what he's saying, since he's talking in hushed tones.

Once the door closes, I push off my feet a little to peek out of the window and see mom leading dad across the small walkway between the houses.

Completely flustered, I push all the way up and grab an apple, throwing it at Callum, hitting him in the side. "What the hell?"

"Ow," he pulls his leg up and uses his hand to block in case another apple flies at him. "What was that for?"

Knox walks around the corner, followed by the other three guys, so I quickly grab three more apples and fire them off.

The guys are laughing as they easily dodge the apples.

"Babe," Jax coos, holding his hands out as he walks over to me. He flinches when I rear my arm up, ready to throw another one at him. "These apples did nothing to you."

"You're right." I drop it and reach to grab his cock and gasp when I feel it quickly hardening in his pants.

"It's not my fault. You're standing naked in the kitchen with whipped cream sliding down your body."

I'd forgotten about it and quickly glance down to see it's now at my stomach. My eyes flicker up quickly to see Jax's have darkened as he closes the distance between us.

"No, you don't." I weakly push against his chest, but he bats my arms away like they're nothing. "It's your fault."

"My fault?" His voice lowers, and he steps towards me.

"Well, not just yours. All of yours," I mutter out, getting flustered again.

"How so?"

"You've been denying me sex."

They all laugh in unison, stepping forward a few paces to close the gap between us.

"You want our cocks?" Jax says, lifting me to sit on the table.

"I did." I lie unconvincingly.

He steps between my legs and pulls his pants down, freeing his now very hard cock. "But not now?" he asks, wrapping his hand around it.

Fucking hell. My nipples are hard, my pussy is pulsing, and my bottom lip is quivering.

"Still no?" His hands grab my legs and pull me towards him so my ass is just barely hanging off the edge of the table.

"No," I squeak out, sounding like a newborn bird in a nest looking for its meal.

He leans forward and his cock brushes along the inside of my knee and I moan out uncontrollably. His nose sweeps up my neck.

"My cock is weeping for your tight little pussy."

My body shudders as another whimper escapes.

His teeth latch onto my neck and he bites hard, but not hard enough to break the skin. My head falls to the side, giving him more access as my legs move to wrap around him and my heels dig into his back.

"We're doing this?" Knox asks, stepping forward. "We're going to fuck her in the kitchen with the windows that look into our other house where her parents, brother and Will are staying?"

"You're right," Jax says, standing up and pulling me with him. "To the Nest."

We're in our room a few minutes later. Jax carries me over to the bed and lays me gently on it. He would usually throw me, so I know he's still worried about hurting me.

"I'm not waiting," he says, ripping off his shirt and tossing it to the ground.

He climbs over the top of me and lines his cock up at my entrance. "We will fuck you, but you need to take it easy."

"Deal. Deal. Deal!" I glance at Emmett and hold my hand out. "Him too."

Jax's head falls to the side.

"What? I'm not pushing it. My vagina wasn't hurt during the accident, and having both of you inside of me means I don't have as much control and you both can't go as deep as you would alone. So really, I'm being cautious."

He laughs out and crashes his lips to mine as he shoves his cock inside of me. He lets out a deep, guttural groan and drags it out slowly before pressing it in again. A small whine escapes as pleasure and need flow across my body like hot embers. Something about the way he needs me right now causes a wave of pleasure to pass over my skin.

"Jax," Callum warns.

"I'm ok," I say, gripping onto Jax's back, holding him against me. I don't want him to stop. I need this. God, do I need this.

He presses in slowly, crawls over top of me and rolls us over. It's clumsy and uncoordinated, since he's guarded and trying not to hurt me. I want to yell at them to have their way, but I'm thankful they're looking out for me.

Emmett steps between Jax's legs and notches himself at my entrance, and we both freeze. Jax sucks his bottom lip into his mouth, wanting and waiting, as our eyes meet.

He wraps his hand around the back of my neck and pulls me down to him. "I love you, Ev."

Before I can say anything, his lips are on mine and his tongue is pressing into my mouth. The way this man, these men, kiss.

Jax bucks under me and lets out a groan just as I feel Emmett's hand at my entrance.

"Fuck, E," he groans out, digging his head back into the bed. When his eyes lock on mine, they are pure fire, as Jax adjusts, pulling his cock out a little. "E. You have... to stop."

I pull up and see Emmett rubbing his hand along Jax's cock while he's inside of me.

"Sorry." He runs his finger along Jax's cock and into me, stretching me wider. "Not sorry," he whispers.

His fingers work around Jax's cock and the idea of him getting us both off at the same time makes me so hot. Jax's eyes are dark and he's panting, obviously feeling the same as me. Needing to taste his kiss again, I lean forward and rock on Emmett's fingers and Jax's cock.

"She's going to come before you get your cock in," Callum says.

"Callum, I want to suck your cock."

"No, little love. I'm going to sink my cock in you tonight."

"I guess if I have to," Knox says, walking over.

I smile at him, licking my lips. Something about the fact that he'll be fucking my face right over Jax makes my stomach swirl in excitement. Knox must feel it too, but he doesn't say anything. He only glances at Jax and pumps his eyebrows.

"Don't come before her," Jax snaps.

"Well, you two do your job then."

"Are you ready for me?" Emmett asks, pressing his cock at my entrance.

"More than ready."

Jax pulls out his cock a little and they both press in slowly. Since it's been a couple of weeks, I can feel the tightness, but I try not to make a noise. I don't want them thinking it's anything other than being tight.

"Fuck, Trouble. We're snug as a bug in a rug in your pussy."

After a few thrusts, Emmett moves a little more freely. Jax stops rocking as much, so Emmett can fuck both of us, the ridges of his Jacob's ladder rippling over Jax's cock.

"Ok." I wave Knox to me.

"If pressing up on Jax is too much for your core, then let me know and we can stop."

"How about you not listen to Jax and come whenever you want to?" He smiles at me, then looks at Jax. "Don't look at him for approval. Listen to me."

His face snarls, then his resolve fades, and he agrees. Though I feel like Jax gave him a wink or a head nod or something.

With Emmett thrusting at a steady pace against Jax and me, I reach up and wrap my hands around Knox's base, and bring him to my lips. "Don't hold back." My eyes flick up to meet his as he studies me for a second. "I need this."

He nods. I'm not sure if it's in agreement or understanding, but it doesn't matter. I'll take it. His hands grip into my hair, gently at first, like he's just holding my head in place.

He presses his cock in slowly like he's unsure, but when he hits the back of my throat, a puff of air escapes between his lips, along with a moan. "I've missed your mouth." He drags it back out and lets me take over while he watches me. I run my tongue up the underside of his cock and swirl it around his head, before hollowing out my cheeks and sucking him back in again.

His head falls back like his neck is too weak to hold it up. His hands grip tighter and he pulses his cock in and holds it at the back of my throat for a second, making it hard for me to breathe, then pulls out. I suck in a breath and lick up his cock a few times.

"I just want to fuck your face."

With a small nod, I give him the ok.

"Babe, don't tempt me."

I hum around his shaft, then suck.

He whines out like he's fighting with himself. "Fuck it." His hands clamp to the sides of my head and I moan out as I push back onto Emmett and Jax's cock.

Callum lets out a chuckle as he watches us from the chair in the room. "I think she liked that, Knox."

Knox unleashes, pounding relentlessly into my mouth. My scalp is burning as he uses my hair as handles, pulling and pushing me onto his cock as he moves faster and faster. Emmett picks up speed, matching his pace, then slides his finger around and rubs on my clit.

My body is singing in pure joy right now. The only thing that would make it better is if Callum was with us, but I'll have him tonight, just the two of us.

Tingles shoot up and down my spine as my orgasm gets closer and closer. I grind down as best I can on Emmett's finger while his cock presses into me. When I start moaning, Knox loses it and thrusts faster. His cock presses at the back of my throat, cutting off my breath, and each time he does, I get this feeling that ripples through my body.

"Oh shit," he groans and his cock presses in deep and he holds it as he explodes. With my left hand, I reach up and wrap it as best I can around his ass, keeping him pressed in deep. My lungs begin to burn, crying out for oxygen, but I don't stop. He tries to pull back, but I dig my nails in to hold him there.

BAM!

My orgasm crashes into me, and I push him away, sucking in a deep breath. "Oh…" A mixture of moans and groans and other sounds come out of my mouth as I ride my high. Something between not being able to breathe and my orgasm just sent me… spiraling. My head is still swimming and my pussy pulses around their cocks. "My God," I pant out.

"Ev." Knox looks at me. "Did you just use my cock for breath play?"

My lips pull to the side, not exactly knowing the answer. I mean, I guess technically I did, but I didn't know it at the beginning.

My arms collapse and I fall onto Jax's chest.

"Jax?" Emmett asks.

"Yea. I'm ready."

Three more thrusts and Emmett goes first, followed quickly by Jax. They moan out as their come fills me, coating their cocks. Emmett pulls out, followed by Jax, and I roll over onto the bed, staring at the ceiling.

When I feel a body move between my legs, I jump and look down to see Emmett. He's staring at my pussy, then slowly presses his finger in as his teeth scrape over his bottom lip.

"Fuck, Everlee. I love seeing our come inside of you." He leans down and kisses the inside of my thigh as his finger continues to pulse in and out. "I fucking love it. I just want to sink my cock into you again. And," he growls. Before I know what's happening, he's pressing his tongue in, then sucks my clit into his mouth.

"Emmett," I say cautiously.

"I'm addicted to you. To your pussy."

He continues to suck on my clit while he presses two fingers in.

"More. I need more. Sit on my face."

"Emmett," I pant. His words and the way he's acting feral, makes me hot.

"I want our combined release to drip down my throat while you come again."

He slides his hands under my back, and lifts as I scramble up, helping him. As he lies on his back, I carefully position myself over his lips, feeling the warmth of his breath against my skin.

"I would destroy every chair in this world, so the only place you have left to sit is on my face. That is how much I love eating your pussy." He grabs my legs and pulls me down with a gentle force that tells me he's not playing around.

His tongue swirls as his moans grow louder. Our come feels slick on his lips as he swallows and something about that just makes my skin flush and feel like I'm sitting in a fire. His hands clamp onto my legs, and he pulls me closer to him as his tongue moves faster, like he can't get enough. Goosebumps erupt across my skin as my hands rove over my stomach and breast, needing to grab onto something.

The doorbell rings.

"Fuck!" I cry out.

"I'll go," Callum offers, walking over to give me a quick kiss on the forehead. "Hurry and don't be too loud."

"I'll come with," Jax and Knox both offer.

A low rumble rattles out of my chest as I continue to ride Emmett's face.

A few minutes later, my mom's voice filters from down-stairs, followed by my dad's.

"Emmett," I sigh again, as his finger presses on my clit and my orgasm rolls over me like a steamroller, slow and heavy. My teeth clamp onto my bottom lip as I slowly grind my hips onto Emmett's face, treasuring this release.

After another moment, he pushes me off his mouth so I'm sitting just over his neck area. "You taste so fucking good with our come inside of you." His eyes flash wildly. I wish I could slide down his body and sink onto his cock again.

A smirk curls my lips. "Fuck me again. I need you inside of me," I whisper.

He stares at me, knowing he should say no. Knowing he should say we need to go downstairs and be with my family, but he doesn't. Is it shitty of me to play on his breeding kink? Yes. But fuck it. I think I need it as much as him.

"Please." I slide down his body slowly, eyes locked onto his. "Put your cock in me and fuck me. Fill me with your come, Emmett."

His pupils explode, and his eyes darken.

I ease onto his hard cock and let the ripples of his rings shoot waves of pleasure across my body.

"Ev," he moans out slowly, while his hands clamp onto the side of my hips.

I continue to speak soft and slow. "Fill me, Emmett. I want your come leaking out of me." I rock my hips into him, his rings driving me wild. "Your come... so hot..." I slide my teeth over my bottom lip. "I love the way it feels inside of me."

"Goddamn, Trouble."

"The way it's slick." I sink back on his cock and lower my body so my nipples press against his chest and I suck on his neck.

"Fill me."

His hands clamp tight and he flips us over. "I fucking love you so goddamn much." He growls, thrusting his cock deep inside of me, causing my head to press into the bed. "You want me to explode inside of you?" He thrusts again and I nod. "You want to drip with my come?" He pounds into me with every question he asks.

"Yes Emmett. Fuck me, please," I whimper.

EMMETT - CHATTY CHARLES MCGURT

FIFTEEN MINUTES LATER, WE'RE all downstairs sitting at the bar. Those last several minutes with Everlee were some of the most intense I've ever had with her. I felt... uncontrollable. When I saw our come sitting on the edge of her pussy, I wanted to press it back inside of her. I wanted to rip her IUD out and fuck her until she's pregnant with my baby, Jax's baby. Fuck, I don't care whose baby. I just want her pregnant.

Never would I have ever thought I had a breeding kink, but her... she brought it out in me. I don't know how long they want to wait for the wedding, for kids, any of it. But I plan on making it known that I want it all immediately. Like I'm talking about marrying her this weekend, Monday at the doctor to remove the IUD and pregnant by next weekend. I know that's not how it works, but a guy can dream. I need to stop thinking about this before I pop a boner in front of her parents. It's bad enough I have to watch her walk around knowing she's full of my come and that it's leaking out of her.

Trying to distract myself, I look around the room. The table seems to be put back together and there is the fresh scent of the mint basil cleaner in the air.

"Nice to see you clothed this time, sister," Beckett says, holding his empty glass in the air.

"Looks like you have an empty glass," she retorts.

"Waiting for E to make me his special."

"Yes," Dave says. "I've heard so much about these drinks."

"They are divine, papa," Beckett says with an accent.

Knox leaps on Beckett's shoulders and puts him in a headlock, which then starts a wrestling match between them. It ends after Beckett has Knox pinned on the floor in the living room.

"I see you've been practicing," Knox cheers, grabbing Beckett's hand as he pulls him to standing.

"This is how they were most of the week at the beach," Donna coos.

"It's nice to see the closeness you all seem to have with Beckett and Will." Dave nods, no doubt a dig at Everlee's past boyfriends.

I glance at Callum, who picked up on it too. We had talked after we left Laurent that we were going to ask Dave for Everlee's hand in marriage while he was here. What we didn't discuss was when. When we were going to ask Dave and when we were going to ask Everlee. Part of me wants to do it while her family is here, but the other part of me wants it to just be us five.

"So mom, dad, Beckett, Will..." Everlee takes a seat at the end of the bar. "What happened? How did you get here? Last I spoke to mom... last night, mind you, you all weren't able to get flights."

"Your guys may have had something to do with it," Donna smiles at us. "They reached out to a friend and he let us borrow his plane. Such a fancy plane. Did you know the couch turns into a bed?" Donna asks, eyes wide with amazement.

"Really?" Everlee feigns.

She knows it does, because Jax and I had her bent over it, fucking her. That was a good flight.

The doorbell rings again, and I don't have to even answer it to know who it is.

"Did somebody say party?" Lizzy chimes, walking in without waiting for anyone to get the door.

"Yay. Lizzy's here," Jax says deadpan, and Everlee wraps her arms around his neck and gives him a quick peck on the cheek. He lets her get about an arm's length away, before he grabs her and pulls her back, causing her to yelp in surprise. "I love you," he whispers and kisses her on the forehead.

"Samesies," she says before walking over to Lizzy. "Did you know they were going to be here?"

"What? Me? No... Yes, yes, I did."

"You're telling me she didn't tell you?" Becks asks, walking up behind Lizzy to give her a hug.

"No," Everlee frowns, but her eyes still twinkle.

"Well, I'll be damned. I thought for sure, Chatty Cathy McGee here would spill the beans, although I guess thinking about it... I know for certain you didn't tell her."

"Why do you say it like that?" Lizzy asks.

"Nope. Beckett, not a freaking word."

Lizzy's hands clamp onto Beckett's arm. "All the words. Give me allll the words."

"Well, when we arrived–"

"Beckett," Dave cuts in. "If Everlee wants to share that with Lizzy, she will. You don't need to be a Chatty Charles McGurt or whatever you called it."

I hand him the Old Fashioned and pass the rest out to the guys and Everlee. When I was making drinks, I offered to make Donna one, but she passed, too enamored with Everlee, Lizzy, and Beckett.

Standing in the kitchen with a full house, watching Everlee glow makes my heart feel like it's going to explode out of my chest. She is so happy right now. She has us, her family, Lizzy. This is what the holidays are about. This right here.

When Jax catches me watching him watch Ev, he pumps his eyebrows. He feels it too. Sees it.

We've already bought the ring, and it's sitting somewhere in this house -likely the safe in the office, but if we hadn't bought it, we would after tonight. She completes us.

"Do you want to see the rest of the house?" Callum offers.

Obviously, I missed some of the conversation because I was envisioning Everlee waddling around the house in a robe and slippers, with a nice round belly.

"I'm going to start on dinner," I call after the rest of the group.

Beckett and Will stop on the stairs and walk back down.

"You aren't going up?" I ask, pulling some ingredients out of the fridge and preheating the oven.

"Please. We've already seen this place. How have you been?" Beckett's eyes narrow into thin slits as he studies me.

"Good, you? Why are you looking at me like that? I feel like you're fishing for something."

"No. No. No. Just wanted to talk to my favorite. Second favorite man," Beckett corrects when Will smacks his shoulder.

"What are you up to? You're acting sus, with a capital S."

"Sus? Look at you... all cool and stuff." Beckett walks around the island and stands behind the counter. "So..."

Hair tickles on the back of my neck. I pray he doesn't ask about proposing to Ev. There's no way he could know and I don't want to lie to him. And if he found out, there's no way he'd be able to keep his mouth shut.

No. No one can know until after we talk to Dave and then propose.

"How irritated are you that mommy dearest brought half her house with us?"

The muscles in my shoulders release as I blow out a cool breath. "That... yea. I mean, she can help if she wants. Or is she planning on doing the whole thing? Because honestly, I hadn't planned on her bringing stuff."

"Well, she will surprise you like that." Beckett laughs. "What did you think I was going to ask?"

"I don't know with you."

"How are things with you and Jax?"

My brow peaks.

"Ev said Jax's walls are coming down a bit. He's exploring."

"Good. I don't want you to think..." I pause, trying to figure out the words. "Just because Jax and my relationship has evolved... doesn't mean we don't love your sister. We both love her very much."

He chuckles. "I see the way you all look at her. The way you are around one another. You are a little polypod. You think she can love four guys, but the guys can't love one another? I get it." He looks at Will, "Well, not exactly the multiple lovers piece because there's only one for me." He grabs Will's hand and tugs him closer.

"How sweet," Will says.

"That's my middle name. Beckett Sweet McKinley."

"More like Beckett Pain in the Ass McKinley," Knox says, popping down the stairs.

"Yay, he's back," Beckett teases deadpan.

Knox rubs his knuckles along Beckett's head.

"You're like the brother I never wanted," Beckett says, pushing Knox away.

"Fine. I'll ignore you the rest of the time you're here."

"I doubt you can do that."

"Watch me." Knox crosses his arms indignantly.

"Not going to happen," I laugh.

"Whose side are you on, anyway?"

"Man, I'm just here for the family bonding and cooking," I say, throwing my hands up in the air. Hopefully, the latter. I don't want to tell Donna to stay out of my kitchen, but... I had a plan. That planned involved her oohing and aahing over Everlee and not wanting to cook. A dish here or there... sure... maybe. But with what she brought... wooo-sahhhh.

CALLUM - IMPRESSIONS

DINNER WAS A SUCCESS. Big group, but that's why we have such an enormous table in the dining room- to hold everyone. Not really. We never planned on having big family get-togethers during the holidays. It was us four and whatever girl we were seeing at the time and she most assuredly was not staying over for holiday dinners.

No. The table was big because the room was big and Emmett wanted to fill it and decorate it. Turns out, it was a good addition.

After dinner, I grab the guy's attention and point to the roof. They nod in understanding. It's really the best time to do this. To ask Dave for Everlee's hand in marriage. So antiquated, but I think Everlee and her family would appreciate it. Beckett had to run next door quickly, while Will, Everlee, Lizzy and her mom wash the dishes.

We offer Dave another Old Fashioned up on the roof and he takes us up on it.

As we ascend the stairs, the knot in my stomach grows larger and my throat grows tighter. I've been mulling over the list of things I want to say to Dave about his daughter, how wonderful she is, how she's the center of our universe.

Everything he wants to hear to say yes, because honestly, if he has reservations and says no... I don't know what we'll do. We're ready. If we don't have his blessing, then what does that mean? If we tell Everlee, then it creates a strain with her family and if we ignore it and still move forward, that would also create a strain.

No. All is going to be great.

Maybe we should have asked Donna instead... just throw the book out of the window.

"Dinner was great, Emmett," Dave says stepping on the deck.

"Yea? Thanks. Chicken Tetrazzini is my go-to for large groups." His voice is shaking. He walks around the bar and quickly makes us all a drink.

"Make one for me too," Knox calls.

We all look at Knox and his brows raise on his face. He's nervous too. It's one thing to think they like you, but to have definite proof... it's nerve-wrecking.

Emmett walks over to us with a tray of drinks, handing them to each of us. We sit around the small fire pit to the left of the hot tub. Knox flips the switch and we all stare at the flames for a while before Dave clears his throat.

"Seems like you boys are nervous."

Well, fuck. I see where Everlee gets her keen since of observation from.

I glance at the door, then to the guys, and lastly to Dave. "Yes. We... we wanted to ask you something."

Dave sits up in his chair, a small curl pulling on his lips.

Taking a deep breath and letting the cool air soothe my lungs, the guys nod at me. "Everlee... she is amazing. I don't know how much you know, but when we first met her, we didn't allow ourselves to have girlfriends." Shit. Shouldn't have said that. I basically just admitted we were only into casual fucks. "What I meant to say, is that..." Where the fuck are my words at? I had this all planned and recited.

Jax's hand clamps on my shoulder.

"Everlee has changed us. We thought we were headed down one path, and Everlee... she sort of blew it up and said no, *we're* going down this other path."

Everyone laughs, including Dave.

"We love her very much and can't see our lives without her in it. I know this-" I circle my hands around to the guys. "May not have been what you saw for Everlee's future... but... all I can say is that she will have more love and support and encouragement to explore her wildest fantasies."

"I'd say this one is pretty wild," Dave chuckles, taking a sip of his drink.

"Yes. Yes, this is. But with her, it feels so right. The guys and I sometimes joke that Everlee has molded herself into our family, filling cracks within each of us we didn't know existed." I pause, because the fear of rejection grips tight around my throat like a vice. Just a few simple words... stuck.

Knox steps forward. "What Callum is trying to say, what we're all trying to say, sir.... Is... We would love to marry Everlee and have your blessing."

I nod in appreciation at Knox, and his lips flatten as he nods, sitting back down.

It's so quiet outside as Dave looks at each of us. Even the wind has stopped blowing and the birds have stopped chirping.

"My Everlee has always been a big personality. A strong will. I always used to tease Donna and say when she grew up, she would change the world. We just had to survive her." He laughs. "That girl is more stubborn than her mama, and that's saying something. But you better not tell Donna I said that."

"Yes, sir, she is," Knox smiles, leaning forward in his chair.

"Now, truth be told, when Donna told me about the men in Everlee's life a few months ago," he pauses, tapping his empty glass on the handle of the chair. "I didn't know how to take it. I didn't like it. Everlee- my Everlee- with four men." He laughs, "Though Donna, of course, already had my mind made up for me, I just didn't know it yet." His hand waves in the air. "She was singing your praises about how wonderful you all were with Everlee. She was hemming and hawing about how attractive you all were and I just ignored that bit of course. But she also explained when Everlee was in trouble in the water, you all went in after her, with little to no regard for your safety. According to Donna, you put Everlee on a pedestal, and whenever she's around you, she radiates with joy." He laughs and points at Knox. "Then here you come to the airport dressed in a suit."

"I just wanted to make a good impression on you," he mumbles, as his cheeks tinge a light shade of pink.

"Son," he says simply and matter-of-factly. "My impression of you was made well before this trip. It was made in the way Donna talks about you, the way Everlee's eyes light up when she sees you. Hell, even in the way Beckett talks about you. My impression of you, of all of you, was made through their eyes, not mine." He takes in a deep breath. "My Everlee is not the kind of woman who needs a man, rather, she is the woman a man needs. Or in this case, the woman you men need."

"Yes, sir," Knox says and we all nod.

"I don't think I'd make it on the plane back home if I didn't give my blessing, but know that I give it without fear of my wife's wrath if I don't. You men have my Everlee's heart and I couldn't see her with anyone else but you four. I know it's not easy being in your kind of relationship, but I have full confidence that you five will get through it together."

"Everlee means the world to us. She is our northern star. Guiding us, leading us. We didn't know what it was to love someone before we loved her and we will never know what it's like to love anyone after her. She is it for us," I say.

"Yes. I believe that. I guess she won't be *my* Everlee much longer."

"Thank you, sir."

"Please stop calling me, sir. Call me Dave, or dad, but not sir. We're family."

"Yes, Dave."

We all hug Dave and shake his hand. Just as we pull away, Beckett, Lizzy, and Everlee burst through the door, eyes wide and anxious.

Had they been listening the entire time?

EVERLEE - BESTFRIENDS

AFTER DINNER, THE GUYS disappeared with my dad up on the roof. Mom voluntold Lizzy and me for dishes, and Beckett dipped out rather quickly. He gave me a quick hug and whispered for me to keep Will busy. My stomach tightened and my hands tingled.

This was it.

It took me a few days after I woke up from the accident to remember what Beckett and I had talked about. He's going to propose to Will and I couldn't be more excited. He didn't tell me when, at least, I don't think he did. It's been a bit of a whirlwind the last couple of days, or weeks, rather.

When we finish washing up the dishes, I grab a drink out of the fridge and sit at the bar. "So Will. How's the firehouse?" I ignore Lizzy's curious brow.

He sits beside me. "It's good. Bunch of good men and women. I know Becks was excited to show you all around."

"Yea. I was really bummed when we couldn't come down."

"It's understandable. You scared a lot of people."

"None of this hubbub. We are here to have fun and celebrate and spend time with family. Let's go upstairs to see the men," mom chimes in.

Lizzy jumps up. "Let's..." Her eyes flicker to me and I give my head the slightest little shake. "Stay here for another second. I wanted to hear about these men at the firehouse. Why has Beckett never offered to show me around?"

She glances back at me and shrugs her shoulders.

"Oh, Lizzy. We can talk about this later. Plus, you have a man. Speaking of... where is Tony?"

Well, there's another second of chatting. When I see the door closed behind me, my heart beats a little harder in my chest. Where is he?

"Tony," Lizzy speaks slower, like it's almost a question.

A puff of air blows from my nose as I laugh. I love her so much. She has no idea why we can't go upstairs, but she doesn't care. She's the kind of best friend that knows when they become your best friend, they automatically get pulled into all of your lies, cons, or whatever else without ever knowing why. Just a look or a head shake tells them the game is afoot and they pick up the baton and run, never knowing where they're running to. "Yes. Tony is finishing up a contract for the big job in California. Deadline is tonight, but he will be here tomorrow. He's excited to see all of you again. It's like a beach trip reunion. Did you have fun at the beach, Mama McKinley?"

I scoot to the side to look out of the window and see Beckett walking back and breathe a sigh of relief. A moment later, the door is opening, and he glances around at all of us.

"Oh. Were we waiting for Beckett? You should have said something," mom says.

"We weren't," I snap a little more quickly than seemed normal. "I was just trying to talk to Will a little."

"Guys upstairs?" Beckett asks, pointing.

"Yea."

"Cool, cool. Let's go upstairs," he says a little too quickly. Mom and Will both look at me and Lizzy's eyes get big. She knows. Fuck, how does she know? I swear she's like a witch or a sorceress or something.

I hurry after Beckett, with Lizzy right behind me. Mom is saying something to Will about the shenanigans we three used to get into and how we were probably up to something now. I was fairly certain she knew about Beckett proposing, so either she has no clue or is a master deception artist.

We burst through the door and see all the guys standing around the fire, with strange looks on their faces. I don't think it helped that Beckett burst through the door in a fit or worry or panic. Thank God it's cold outside, because he looks like he's sweating.

"Hey boys! What'cha up to?" I ask, trying to take pressure off Beckett.

"Nothing." All five of them say too quickly to be believable.

My gaze narrows on their faces, but no one speaks. After a moment, I break the silence. "Emmett, can you make us some drinks?"

"Me too," Dad calls, raising a glass. "I have a feeling it's going to be a long night."

"What does that mean?"

His neck jerks back and he's quiet for a moment. "Only that I've heard the stories about how you all like to play poker."

"Oh. Yea. I didn't think about that. I'm always down for a game of poker."

"So you can take their money," Beckett retorts.

"Our money is her money," Callum says.

My head sort of does this weird bobble head thing as I jerk it to look at him. Their money is not my money. I know we have the businesses, but...

He quickly adds, "Only meaning that whatever she wants, she can have."

"Spoiling her. Nice," Will chimes laughing.

"Do you want to be spoiled, my love?" Beckett asks Will, looping his arm around him.

"Being with you each day is enough." Will smiles.

"True story. That's a lot for one person to take," I tease.

We all grab our drinks from Emmett a few minutes later and are just standing in a circle while everyone looks at one another. It is awkward as fuck.

My eyes catch Becketts and I raise my brow at him. He shakes his head. Oh my God. This is horrible. Having to wait for him to propose. What is he waiting for?

Emmett walks over to me and loops his arm around my waist and buries his nose in my ear, causing goosebumps to erupt across my skin and my nipples to become hard. He plants a kiss softly on my neck, then looks back at everyone with his arm still wrapped around me. Wanting to be close to him, I lean my head against his chest.

"Well, aren't you two just the cutest?" Mom says, smiling. "Oh darn. I should get a picture of this. Dave. Dave, darling. Where's the camera?"

"Donna." He chuckles. "I didn't bring it. It's outdated compared to what's on your phone."

"Oh, right. These things. I don't understand how you kids keep up with all the changes. I feel like I'm always so far behind." She pats her pants. "Where's my phone?"

"I think you left it on the counter in the kitchen. I can go get it for you," Will offers.

"Would you? I'm not as young as I once was and those stairs make my ankles pop."

"Not a problem."

When Will closes the door, Lizzy and I both wait a second, then pounce on Beckett.

"Will you two stop?" he says, batting his hands in our face like he's batting away a mosquito.

"What's going on?" mom asks, as the boys draw nearer.

"Nothing," Beckett snaps, pushing us both away, giving us the look that says back the fuck off for real.

We both huff and back away just as the door is opening again.

"Did you superman down those stairs and back up?" Lizzy asks, astonished.

"I ran down them and back up. Trying to stay fit."

"You don't have a problem there," I say just before Callum wraps his arms around me.

"What does that mean?" he whispers in my ear.

I turn to look at him. "It means exactly how it sounds. He's fit."

"Should I be jealous?"

"If you want to be, but it's a waste. I only have eyes for four men. No more." I lean in closer to him so my lips are brushing against his ear. "I have no more holes to fill, anyway."

He bursts out in laughter, then quickly regains control.

"Should we all move by the fire? It's getting a little cold out here..."

"I will warm you, my love," Callum says, squeezing me tighter.

"Wait," Beckett says, then stops and turns to look at him. "Wilhelm."

He laughs awkwardly. "I didn't do it."

"Wilhelm Cavish. I just wanted to tell you that... you... you have been an unexpected light in my life. Quite literally the light in the dark. When I kissed you on black out night... my entire world changed. You changed me for the better."

Will looks around at all of us, fear behind his eyes. Not fear of what's happening, but fear that what he thinks is happening isn't.

Beckett grabs Will's hands and holds his gaze for a moment. "I... I love you so much... I had all these words planned. I've been rehearsing them for weeks now and had it all memorized... but looking at you... here. Tonight. Right now. Words escape me. I realize there aren't enough words in the dictionary that describe how you make me feel. So, all I can say is this... Wilhelm, will you make me the happiest man in the world and marry me?"

Beckett drops down on one knee and pulls out a ring to present up to him.

My gaze flickers around to all the guys who are watching Beckett, then they look at me and their expression is hard to read. It's a mixture of happiness, but something else. Something I can't put my finger on right now. Not wanting them to feel guilty, I pump my eyebrows and smile at them. Did they think I would be upset seeing this? Did they feel guilty?

I'd have to talk to them later, so they knew I was ok with all of this. I don't need a ring and a wedding to feel confident in our relationship. And that's not meaning that others do... I'm just saying I know what we have, and that's good enough for me.

"Yes. Yes, Beckett. I will marry you." He falls to his knees and presses his lips to Becketts, taking him in a passionate kiss.

Callum steps behind me and wraps his arms around my chest and gently squeezes, like a silent 'I love you'. Reaching up, I grab his forearms and squeeze back, then step out of his grip. "I think this calls for a celebration! I think we have some champagne in the cellar downstairs!"

"I'll help," Callum offers.

When we get to the cellar, I walk past the rows of wine bottles tipped in their slots on the shelf. I've not been down here a ton and I've never counted, but they have to have close to one hundred bottles of wine in their cellar. At the end of the row is a small glass door refrigerator with bottles of champagne chilled and ready to serve. Before I can get there, a hand grabs around my wrist and pulls me backward. Callum spins me around and presses me up against the wall of wine bottles.

"Callum, what are you doing?" I ask, my words slow, studying his face.

He brushes my hair behind my ear, taking a step forward and closing the gap between us, placing his thigh between my leg.

"Callum." His name comes out in a heady pant.

"I just wanted to make sure you're ok." He leans forward slowly and places his lips on my collarbone.

My head falls to the side, loving when he kisses me gently there. "Callum..." I puff out.

His hand slides up my shirt and under my bra, grabbing my breast.

A whimper of desire escapes my lips. "What are you doing?" I whisper.

"I'm glad your family is here with us, but I just want to sink my cock in you so bad it almost hurts."

My eyes pulse, and my pussy is getting wet. "Callum." I don't know what I was trying to say with his name. Callum stop, Callum keep going.

"I want to taste you." His lips travel up to just under my jaw, then to my ear as he sucks it in his mouth. My body is on fire right now, full of need.

His hand releases my breasts and slides down my stomach, past the hem of my pants.

"Callum, what if someone comes..." my words fade into a moan and my head presses back against the wine bottles as his finger slowly glides inside of me.

"I plan to make you come," he teases, knowing that's not what I was going to say.

My hands grab on his arms, his muscles rippling under my grip as his finger slides in and out of me.

"I love that you're always so wet for us. It makes me just want to live on my knees in front of your pussy."

My knees buckle at his words and incoming orgasm.

He adds another finger in, as his hand moves faster, rubbing over my clit. His warm breath blows quickly over my neck and down my chest.

"Callum." My fingers squeeze tight on his arms, my breaths shallow.

"Come for me, baby." His lips crash to mine just as my orgasm hits. My legs get weak, but Callum's free arm wraps around my body, holding me up and pressing our bodies together while I ride out my orgasm on his finger. His tongue pulses in and out as he swallows my moans.

After another minute, he drags his fingers out and sucks my arousal off them with a satisfied grin on his face. "Now we can get the champagne." He presses off me and gives his legs a little shake.

"But…" I look at his hard cock pressing against the seam of his pants.

"Later. After your parents leave, I plan to use it all night on you." He winks and grabs two bottles from the fridge. "We'll use the plastic flutes upstairs."

Grabbing his arm, I spin him around. "I love you."

"I love you." He leans forward and kisses my forehead before we walk upstairs.

When we get through the door, mother looks at me. "Everlee. You shouldn't have gone down there. You're looking flush in the cheeks. Here, sit down," she says, offering a chair at the bar.

Callum is on the other side of the bar, opening the champagne bottles when he tosses me a knowing glance, then winks. My stomach tightens as a hand clamps around my shoulder.

"So flush… you little horn toad," the voice whispers, their head right beside mine.

Lizzy.

"It's really amazing to me how many times one can orgasm in a day. I feel like studies should be done on you."

"Shut up," I whisper back, then kiss her on the cheek.

"I'm going to take off soon. It's getting late."

"You aren't staying for champagne?"

"Hell yea, I am. Moët and Chandon? Count me in. But after… I need to go get a few O's on the tally board." She nudges my arm with her elbow.

"You're too much."

"But am I?" She reaches across the bar and grabs a set of three glasses in each hand, and walks around the deck to deliver them. I grab three more, leaving one for Callum, and hand them out to Knox and Jax.

"We can help you get champagne next time," Knox says, winking.

Waiting for a snide comment from Jax, I look at him, but his brows just raise on his face. "Oh, stop."

We toast the happy couple and sit around the fire sharing funny stories. Again, mostly at my expense, since everyone loves to pick on me, but I don't care. I am happy. So happy. My family is here, Beckett is getting married, and everything is just great. Perfect.

EVERLEE - EYES ON ME

IT'S CLOSE TO MIDNIGHT when we decide to call it a night. Lizzy took off a couple of hours ago, and with her leaving, my parents also retired to the other house. Beckett and Will stayed on the roof with us, and we all ended up in the hot tub. Well, the guys did, while I sat on the edge with my legs hanging in. I don't think tonight could have been any more perfect.

For me, this is what the holidays are all about. Family getting together and just hanging out. When Lizzy tried to talk about wedding dates and other stuff, Will and Beckett both shut her down.

"Did you have a good night?" Callum asks after I spit my toothpaste out in his sink.

My eyes find his in the reflection in the mirror, watching me from the bathroom door. He's only wearing a pair of tight black boxers, and I try to stay focused. "Yes. It was great. I'm very excited about Will and Beckett. I never thought he was going to get married."

"Well, I guess things change and surprise you." He stalks towards me slowly, his eyes darkening and the air in the room shifts.

A mangled chuckle vibrates from my chest. Fuck being focused. "Callum, what are you doing?" Excitement is pulsing over my skin in waves.

"Nothing," he says in a low and sultry voice that causes the hair on my arms to stand and my stomach to tighten.

We haven't had sex in weeks, and I miss him and his cock. I miss looking at the tattoos trailing across his entire body, a map of who he is and what he's been through. A map that says the words that he doesn't speak. Protector, fighter, lover. He's the alpha of the house, and the guys look to him for direction, but that also means he's usually the last one to eat, always putting others above himself.

This man.

His arms wrap around me from behind as our eyes stay locked in the mirror.

"Let me help you get ready for bed," he says, sliding his hands under my shirt, not waiting for an answer. He rubs my stomach for a brief second before he runs them up my chest and over my bra, lifting the hem of my shirt with it.

My head falls against his shoulder and my eyes close, basking in the feel of his touch.

"No, baby girl. You're going to watch me."

Oh damn.

My stomach tightens like a vice at his words and my pussy... there's no saving these panties. The only reason I put them on was because I was loaded with Jax and Emmett's come and didn't want it dripping down my leg all evening.

He slips my shirt over my head and just stares at my body through the mirror, as his hands rove over my breast. "I know you like people watching you when you're being fucked, so you're going to watch yourself be fucked." My breasts bounce free of their constraints at his last word, causing me to suck in a breath.

"Callum," I whisper, body ready to explode.

"Shh," he hushes me, rubbing his hand up my back, then around my neck, whispering in my ear. "Do you want me to squeeze? I saw you earlier... with Knox. You were using his cock for breath play." His hand grips tighter, but I'm still able to breathe. "Eyes on me," his voice commands, pulling my eyes back to the mirror to watch us.

The sight of his hand wrapped around my throat sends a jolt of electricity through my body and causes my heart to thump wildly in my chest. His eyes, dark pools of Caribbean blue waters, stare at me.

"I'm going to fuck you while you watch and just before you come, I'm going to squeeze your throat hard enough so you can't breathe." His words are low and pulsate through me like a vibrator, pushing my body so close to the edge of an orgasm that I'm left speechless. Our eyes lock like he's waiting for me to say something, but... my tongue. It doesn't move.

As his hand slides from my throat to my breast, I can feel the pressure of his thumb and forefinger on my nipple. The mixture of pleasure and pain makes me moan and causes my back to arch, my head pressing into his arm.

"Use your words."

"Callum," I pant, so fucking needy that I'm nearly dripping down my leg.

"Your safe word..."

"Cupid."

"Now, what's your safe action? You won't be able to talk with my hand around your throat."

My mind is like a blank space. A large white board with nothing written on it.

"Tap my leg four times," he suggests.

I nod, too excited to speak. Jax has grabbed me around the throat before, but it's more for dominance or control, not to stop my breath.

Callum kisses my neck and continues to whisper, "I'll stop if I feel you're taking it too far. Your safety is my only concern. If you still like it, then we'll hire a breath play expert to do demonstrations at Allure."

"Yes, sir."

His eyes twinkle with satisfaction. "That's my good girl."

"Now watch me fuck you." He slides his hand down my body, too slow. I want to grab it and put it on my pussy, but I'm a good girl and wait. I know I'm not a great submissive, I've tried.

But damn.

"Look at your sexy body. I fucking love it so much." His left arm hooks around the top of my chest, pulling me to him while his right hand still inches further down. "I can't wait to press my cock inside of your pussy," he groans out. "Then fuck you and feel your orgasm pulse around it." He nibbles on my earlobe at the same time his finger brushes over my clit.

My head rolls back onto his shoulder until his left arm comes up and pinches my cheeks, and pulls my head back down. "Watch."

He presses his finger inside of me and my lips part and my body jerks. His eyes watch me with a smile pulled across his face. He curves his head and sucks on the side of my neck, while his right hand slides down and plays with my breast and his other hand inserts another finger inside of me. "You're so fucking wet. Do you enjoy watching yourself?"

My eyes are glued on us. On me. The way my bottom jaw juts out ever so slightly with each thrust of his finger. The way my chest pulses with each pinch of the nipple or suck on my throat. My body is so responsive to him- seeking his touch.

"Do you see how addicting you are to watch? This is why you drive us wild." His cock slides between my legs and my eyes pulse before they fall to his length jutting out between my legs. He rubs his fingers over the head and angles it towards my pussy. "This is my favorite right here. The first thrust." He pushes in and my head bobbles, but doesn't stop watching.

My mouth falls open and my eyelids flutter.

"You feel so fucking good." His head falls back for a moment as he savors the feeling of my pussy wrapped around him. He groans out and his cock pumps harder inside of me, angled in such a way that he hits my g spot and I'm crying out, moaning. My breasts bounce against his arm and his eyes watch us.

He says I like when people watch me being fucked, but he likes watching me be fucked just as much. His eyes are glued on us and haven't looked away once.

His hand releases from my breast and slides around my back and presses it down so I'm leading onto the counter. "Keep watching," he commands with a low and gravelly voice.

My nipples brush across the cool countertop and feel like ice against my flushed skin.

Callum stands up straighter and both of his hands grip around my hips and he punches into me, causing my mouth to part and a moan to escape. "That's my good girl. Take my cock."

My teeth clamp around my bottom lip as my orgasm builds. When we're like this, I swear he's somehow hitting my lungs. Emmett's been the only one to give me a cervical orgasm, but the way Callum is tonight, he may do just that. Fuck me, he's deep.

He chuckles, bringing me back to the present. "You're getting close. Do you still want me to wrap my hands around your neck?"

"Yes, sir."

"What's your safe action?"

"Four taps on the leg." As I say the words, I pray I don't have to use them. I'm too excited.

"Good girl." He removes his hands from my hips, slides them up my back and around my throat, and clamps just hard enough to slow my breathing.

He pumps into me faster and faster, using my neck to drive my body onto his cock. His teeth are biting on his bottom lip as he watches himself fuck me, pulling me off the counter just enough so my nipples are no longer on it.

He's mumbling a mixture of words and commands as his own orgasm builds. My breaths get shallower as my orgasm is cresting, then it stops. My lungs start to burn. Callum's eyes are watching me like a hawk.

FUCK ME!

My orgasm hits, my pussy clenches tight around his cock and he releases. The rush of everything hitting me all at once sends me on such a high I cry out the loudest moan I may have ever made... in my entire life. It's a guttural, deep moan that just pulses out of my mouth.

Two pumps and he's exploding inside of me with our eyes locked on one another through the mirror. These men have made me orgasm so many times and in a lot of different ways, but this... tonight... definitely makes the list of top five.

"Oh my God."

Callum leans over me, palms pressed to the counter, eyes on me. "I love you."

"I love you." My chest tightens, and his brow furrows. It's almost scary how easily he can read me. He's one step away from hearing my thoughts, which is...

"What's wrong?"

I guess no time like the present–post coitus with his cock still half hard inside of me. "Earlier tonight. The engagement."

His head tilts to the side.

"I don't need that. You know?"

"You don't?"

"No. I know your rules and I get we can't really get married since it's illegal. I just don't want you thinking that I need that. I don't. I need you all and I have you. A ring doesn't change that. You just... all of you... you looked at me and the expressions on your face. I just don't want you thinking that you're taking anything away from me. Really." I know I'm rambling, but I'm super emotional right now for some reason.

"Everlee. You have us- all of us–now and always. We want to give you everything. I once told you that if you said sir, I'd give you the whole goddamn world on a platter. I meant it then, and I mean it now. We love you and we will give you everything you want."

A tear trickles down my cheek, but I fight the urge to brush it away- to move.

"Do you hear me? *Anything.*" His gaze holds on mine like he's trying to send his thoughts into my head, so they wrap around me so tight that I never question what he's really saying.

Anything.

Kids??

Is that what I want? Really want?

I do.

I want a whole family. Little versions of the guys running around.

"I hear you."

He slides his cock out of me, turns me around. "Let's get you washed up and into bed. It's going to be a long day tomorrow. Emmett's going to be in a tizzy cooking dinner for everyone while trying to figure out how to work around your mom in the kitchen."

"It will be interesting, that's for sure." When he turns to walk away, I grab his arm and spin him around. "Thank you. For this. For my family."

"Anything, love."

"You are ours and we would move heaven and earth just to see a smile on your face."

Overcome with emotion, I nearly jump on him, wrapping my arms and legs tight. "I love you Callum McCall."

EMMETT - SHARING IS CARING... BUT NOT IN MY KITCHEN

FUCKING HELL.

We spoke to Everlee's dad last night and got his blessing to marry Everlee, but today... Shit biscuits!

I'm going to ruin it.

We're going to lose his blessing because of me. God love Donna, but she's in my fucking kitchen. Floating around, grabbing my dishes, and changing my plan.

In the days leading up to dinner today, I had planned everything out. A nice Thanksgiving gravy fountain with hors d'oeuvres, like skewered vegetables, stuffing bites, and some little mashed potato croquettes to start, followed by a nice pumpkin soup. For dinner, we'd have a cranberry and citrus chutney, an oyster casserole with cracker crumbs, smoked sweet potatoes with a chorizo butter, lobster mac and cheese, a spatchcocked smoked turkey with an apple flambé pie for dessert. Sounds great...

Nope.

She wants to do cranberry sauce... out of a can because the ridges from the can make it easy to cut, mac and cheese... with cheese that's not even a real cheese, and a green bean casserole.

Now don't get me wrong, I don't have a problem with want she wants to cook–well, maybe the cranberry sauce out of a can, but it's the fact that she wants to change my plan.

"I can't believe I'm cooking Thanksgiving with the great Emmett Monroe today."

Me either. "I'm so happy to have you here, Donna."

"Mom?" Everlee asks cautiously, walking down the stairs, followed by Callum.

"Good morning, darling. Sleep well?"

"Yes." Her words are slow, like she's still trying to figure out a puzzle. "What are you doing in Emmett's kitchen?"

I fucking love her. She gets me. She really gets me.

"Emmett's?"

"Yes. I mean, technically it's everyone's, but on special occasions, it's his."

"Emmett?" Donna looks at me, brows pinched into a v.

Shitsticks! Am I going to be the bad guy and tell her to get out... or let her stay, knowing how excited she is? I imagine for her it's the same problem I'd have. She's probably cooked Thanksgiving every year for who knows how many years and now she's being asked to just sit down? The internal groans echo around in my head before I speak.

"She's fine. Two cooks are better than one.

"Are you sure?" Her hand smacks her forehead. "And here I come, trying to change your plans. I never asked what you wanted to cook. I'm so sorry. I'm sure it's going to be fantastic. Here I am in the kitchen of one of the best chefs in the world talking about simple mac 'n cheese and cranberry sauce out of a can. You must think I'm a blistering idiot." Her cheeks flush a red as dark as the cranberry sauce.

Feeling guilty, I walk over to her and open my arms wide, and she walks in for a hug. "Mama McKinley, you don't need to feel bad at all. I love you are comfortable enough around me to speak your mind and tell me what you want. Many people in my kitchen at Bo's aren't like that. If I could replicate another twenty of you..."

"Oh, you're making me blush." She pushes away and looks up at me. "Your arms are like... well, I can't think of anything comparable. With all the talk of food, all I'm envisioning are like two long gigantic pieces of bread and, well, that just doesn't make sense." She blushes again and wipes her hands on her face. "I don't even know what I'm saying. I'm just a flustered mess, all out of sorts."

"Let's get to cooking. I'd love your help."

"That's bullsh-eisse," Knox says, coming around the corner, then correcting himself when he sees Donna. "Sorry. I thought you were talking to Everlee or someone else. Apologies, madame."

"Madame?" Everlee asks, taking a seat at the bar.

"I freaked." Knox shrugs, sitting beside her.

"What time are we wanting to eat?" I ask.

Everyone looks around without saying anything. Then I look at Donna, hoping she will have an opinion.

"We always eat around two, but we can do later."

"Two is perfect." Wanting to say my good mornings to Ev, I walk around, slinging my towel over my shoulder. "Good morning, love." I wrap my arms around her chest and plant a quick kiss on the crown of her head.

"Good morning."

"Don't mind me. I'm not jealous," Donna says, laughing.

Everlee's cheeks blush a light pink, so I give her should a light squeeze. "Lizzy, Tony, Betty and Gerald are coming over today."

"Betty, too? I imagined Lizzy would, but Betty?"

"Knox handled all the logistics around that."

"I will call them and tell them what time," she says, reaching for her phone.

"Already on it." Knox waves his phone in the air. "The three of us *gals* are on a group chat together."

"Oh Knox. You're such a hoot," Donna laughs, slapping at the air.

"What can I make you for breakfast? I was going to fix pancakes and such, but your mother scolded me. No big breakfasts on the morn of Thanksgiving."

Everlee shrugs. "I'll just take a hard-boiled egg with some butter." She looks at Donna, "like she fixes it." Her neck slowly retreats like she's in trouble, while her finger curls around her bottom lip.

My stomach tightens. I love when she plays innocent, because she's so far from it. I clear my throat, trying to play off the morning congestion, but Everlee's eyes snap to mine and she knows what it really means. It means move your fucking finger from your mouth before I take you away and have my way with you.

She drags it down and tosses me a little wink before I go back into the kitchen.

"Of course I will make you an egg, darling. I'll let chef Monroe do his thing."

The rest of the morning goes by in a flash. I've set the table with chargers, plates, bowls, glasses, a full setting of silverware, and decorations. Callum made some passing remark about it looking nice, but a little over the top, before he and Jax escorted the guys to the roof. They've lined up a day of playing corn hole, watching football, smoking cigars and drinking Old Fashioneds. Ev is playing go-between making sure everyone is happy and bringing me drinks.

She's really nailed the recipe, which makes my chest swell with pride. Knox started playing Christmas music through-out the house, making it more festive. It's irritating Jax, which seems to be Knox's motivation all along.

To be fair, Jax said Knox had to wait until Thanksgiving and even though we haven't had dinner yet... he waited. I give it to the weekend before he's pulling out all the decorations and planning a trip to a Christmas tree farm.

The door bell rings, and Donna answers it, while I continue to cook. She's stayed out of my way, lending a helping hand when I need it. To my surprise, it's been nice. She knows how to work and move around the kitchen and knows how to anticipate what's next. A shrill cackle echoes through the house and I know it's Lizzy. There is another female voice, which must be Betty. A few minutes later, they're all walking into the kitchen, with their men following just behind.

"Well, I'll be. You're busier than a cat on a hot tin roof! Look at all this, Gerald!" Betty smacks his arm. "Ooh, we're in for a treat today!" She rubs her hands together.

"Everyone is on the roof, if you want to join them?" Donna says, leading them up the stairs.

Sometime later, while I'm at the pot stirring the gravy, a pair of arms wraps around me.

"Donna, I don't think Everlee would approve of this."

A giggle is replaced by the sharp crack of the slap on my back. "Hilarious," Everlee says.

"Oh, it's you." Laying the whisk to the side, I turn around and wrap my arms around Ev, then give her a kiss on her forehead. I don't know how we got so lucky to find someone who fits so perfectly with us, but damn.

"I thought you could use this," she says, handing me another Old Fashioned.

Grabbing the glass from her, I hold it to my nose, inhaling the sweetness and the oak smell of bourbon, then hold it to my lips, barely taking a sip.

"Will you stop?" She laughs, swatting at my arm.

"Did you make this?"

"Who else would?"

"Well, Knox would try, but..."

"No. I wouldn't do that to you. Plus, he's too busy talking about Christmas with Lizzy and Betty."

"It's not even Thanksgiving yet. I mean technically yes, but we haven't had dinner yet."

"You know him. He's just trying to get under Jax's skin. Honestly, I'm a little scared about what he's planning for Christmas."

I throw my head back, laughing, then take a sip of my drink. An appreciative moan escapes from my lips.

"Are you ok?" Ev asks staring at me with her head tilted to the side.

"Yes."

"Emmett?"

I sigh. She won't let up until I just spit it out. "I'm just nervous."

"Nervous?"

"Everything needs to be perfect. This dinner, the food, the table. Everything."

"Why? I mean, it all looks great. You've decorated the table beautifully with all the pumpkins and gourds scattered throughout."

"Thank you. I just... I want to impress your parents- your dad."

"My dad loves you all."

"He's hardly spent any time with me. He loves the others, I'm sure. I mean, Callum is, well, Callum, so you sort of just love him and you don't know why. Knox is always so happy and irritatingly funny to a point where you just want to punch him in the face, but you can't because he's just so happy. And then Jax. He was a SEAL, so you sort of like him because you're scared of him. And then me. I'm just a cook and if I don't-"

"All of those things above may be true, but you aren't just a cook. You are motherfucking Emmett Monroe, chef extraordinaire. My mother is upstairs right now singing your praises."

I pick at the string on the corner of my apron.

"You are wonderful, and this is going to be wonderful." She grabs my chin and presses her lips to mine.

"Oh, look at you two lovebirds. I remember when your dad and I couldn't stand to be apart for even a second." She shrugs her shoulders... "And now..." She laughs awkwardly, "But anyway..."

"Everything ok?"

"Oh yes, sweetie. It's just so nice to see you and Beckett so in love and just at the beginning of your relationships. It just reminds me of those days." There's a long pause while her mind clearly drifts back to memories. A moment later, her eyes refocus on us. "I tell you... that Betty is a hoot. I've heard stories, but nothing prepares you for the real thing."

"No, I suppose not." Everlee smiles, rubbing my back.

The gravy on the stove starts to boil, so I turn back to it, giving it my full attention. After a few moments, I pull the whisk up to try a small taste, then call over my shoulder, "Hey babe, you want to get everyone down here? We'll be eating in about ten minutes."

"What can I do?" Donna asks, as Everlee walks upstairs.

I rattle through the list that has been running on repeat in my head. Today has to be perfect. *This dinner* has to be perfect. No, I don't think her dad will change his mind about us marrying her if he doesn't like the way I cooked something, but...

"Smells delicious," Knox says, bouncing downstairs a few minutes later. "What can I do to help?"

"Ideally, not touch anything. You have a knack for causing trouble when you don't mean to."

Knox bats his hand in the air, then takes a seat at the table.

"Find your place tag."

"You gave us assigned seating?" Jax questions as he walks into the dining room.

"Well, yes. I wanted Ev's parents in the middle so they could talk to everyone. I would hate if they got stuck at one of the ends."

"Where am I boo thang?" Lizzy sings, latching onto Jax's arm. He looks down at her with a quizzical brow, but doesn't say anything.

"At the end."

Lizzy clutches her chest. "I thought I meant more to you than that," she delivers in an overdramatic fashion.

"I'm just kidding. You're near the middle to Donna's left."

"Please don't tell me I'm near her." Jax's eyes lock on mine.

"Would I do that to you?" I smirk back at him.

His gaze narrows when I don't answer the question. I can't help but laugh, because I know he really does like Lizzy. She may get on his nerves, but like Knox, Lizzy and Jax, have a complicated relationship- a bond that is beneath the surface. I saw it at the hospital.

"You're down there on the other end. Callum is at the head and you are to his right, across from me." I toss him a casual wink before I pour the gravy into the dish.

"Wow, Emmett. This looks great," Dave says, walking downstairs and Everlee casts a side eye at me that screams 'I told you so'.

"Thank you."

Everyone takes their seats at the table. Dave and Donna are in the middle, with our group to their right, Beckett and Will to the right of Dave, with Betty and Gerald sitting across from one another at the ends.

"Has anyone cleaned this table?" Beckett chimes.

"Beckett!" Donna scolds.

"Just asking." He shrugs nonchalantly, swiping his finger across the edge of the table like he's inspecting for dust, or smut.

Lizzy casts me a knowing glance and all I can do is roll my eyes.

I take a seat at the table and just stare at all the food and all the people before landing on Everlee. She's so happy, she's glowing. This is what she was terrified of missing out on, and I can see why. But she was willing to give it all up for us. My heart feels like it's going to burst in my chest with my love for her.

Her gaze falls on mine, and she smiles.

Can she hear my thoughts? Does she know what I'm thinking?

Wouldn't that be some shit?

She winks at me, then reaches for my hand. "This all looks wonderful, Emmett."

EVERLEE – WHEN THE TURKEY IS MOIST, IT MUST BE SHOUTED

THIS IS IT.

My perfect day.

My hand is still holding Emmett's when Callum clears his throat and pushes away from the table. "Friends, family. I just wanted to say how thankful I am for each and every one of you. This year has been a year of change for us. A year where rules were broken and truths were told. If you would have told me on January first that this is where we would be eleven months later, I would have laughed at you. Words can't even begin to express how happy I am that Everlee walked into our club at Valentine's. I know some people want to call it an instalove, but that came later- once we would allow ourselves to admit what we were feeling all along." He laughs. "While it may not have been instalove, it was definitely an instaconnection. There was something about her from the moment she walked in that called to me." When he looks at me, he casts the warmest smile. "Because of her, we all know what it feels like to love a little more and allow ourselves to be loved. We know that it's ok to take risks and to try something outside of our comfort zone." He holds his glass in the air. "Thank you all for sharing this amazing woman with us." He takes a seat after everyone cheers.

Beckett stands up, holding his glass in the air. "I want to just say that I, too, am thankful for my sister. She has a weirder relationship than me and made gay look like a cakewalk." Mom swats at the air in front of him and mumbles something under her breath, scolding him. He shrugs then continues, "In seriousness though, I am thankful for her, because we are here with all of these men." He pauses, "I'm trying to be serious and not make a joke, at least right now." He sighs, "With these men. They are all pretty cool, and I'm thankful for my boo." Lizzy ruffles her shoulders. "Will," Beckett clarifies, and Lizzy's mouth drops open. "I'm also thankful for Lizzy, but mostly for Will. He's accepted me for who I am, faults and all, though there aren't many, but like the one he's found, he's accepted it." Will mumbles something and my dad chuckles. "Thank you Everlee's harem, for hosting. Thank you Everlee, for not dying in that car crash. Thank you Lizzy, for... just being you. And thank you Will, for agreeing to marry me."

Everyone takes a sip, and just before I stand, Betty stands.

"Well, hi all." She waves at the group. "I's just wanted to say something too. You all got me over here boo hooin' harder than a snail on ice cream day." Her analogy is lost on the table and Gerald simply pats her leg. "I just want to say I'm thankful for all yuns. Now I know I haven't known Dave and Donna very long, but man. You both raised some good 'uns. Beckett and Everlee, and of course I can't forget to mention Lizzy Lou, are just absolute salt of the earth. A little coo coo cachoo, and Everlee if I didn't say it before, I'm sorry I thought you's a hooker."

Lizzy snort chuckles and I'm stunned as both of my parents look at me, faces blank.

Betty blushes and tries to clarify. "Well, I guess I could have provided better context. She wasn't really dressed like a hooker, I just..." She blushes. "I's just nervous speakin' up here in front of all you beautiful people. I just wanted to say thank you for inviting me into your home and lettin' me partake in all this wonderful food with you all." She hurriedly sits down and catches my attention, pulling her bottom lip in apology.

Just before I stand up, my dad stands. Fuckin' aye. I just want to speak!

"I won't take very long because I don't want the food to get cold, but I just wanted to say I'm thankful for you all. Men," he looks at my men. "Thank you," he nods and pauses like he's referring to an unspoken conversation, then continues, "Thank you for loving my daughter so fiercely and for accepting her wild parents into your lives. Will. Thank you for loving Beckett and making him the happiest man last night. This time last year... let's just say we were all in a much different spot in our lives, but this year has brought love, learning, and family. Tony. While Lizzy may not have been born to us, we still consider her very much a part of this family, so thank you for loving her. She can be a lot for anyone, but my goodness, she is loyal and she will love with everything she has. So, thank you. We love you Lizzy, and are so thankful you're in our lives."

Lizzy doesn't even wait for dad to sit down before she stands. Fuckballs!

"I'm going to keep this short and sweet, like me." She bobbles side to side with her hand in the air and lips quirked in sass. "I just want to say thank you to Everlee's harem. You love my girl and you take care of her. She deserves so much and you all give it to her. Beckett, I love you like the brother I never had, Betty. Girl, next to Ev, you are my ride or die. You're wild and I love it! And Tony. My lovebug. You saw me, the real me, behind all the sarcasm and jokes. You love me for me and I love you for you. I can't wait to do life with you."

"Fuck!" I yell, standing and the table looks at me, shocked. I freeze for a moment, realizing that was an inside thought that slipped out. Go with it? "Sorry. I'm just... so excited to be here today with my loves and my family. Thank you, guys, not Everlee's harem, for loving me so unconditionally. Thank you for everything you have shown me, taught me, and instilling self-confidence in me. Thank you, Lizzy and Betty, for always being there. Lizzy, you are the butter to my bread, the jelly to my peanut butter. You are my forever sister from another mister. Beckett. I love you. You are my brofriend. You are my brother, but also my best friend. I'm so happy you found Will and can't wait to plan your wedding! And mom and dad. Thank you. When I first met the guys, I didn't want to let myself love them. Fear had a grip on my heart because I was terrified I would eventually have to choose between them and you. But your openness and acceptance," I take a deep breath. "It has truly meant so much. I love these men with everything, and I can't wait to see what our future holds."

"Hopefully lots of babies," Mom chimes and the table laughs.

"Who knows where we'll be this time next year. So much changed this year, so..." I laugh. "Thank you all for being here and thank you, Emmett and mom, for this amazing meal. It looks and smells absolutely divine."

"It was all Emmett. He's a wonderful cook."

With drinks raised high, we finish our final toast. The clinking of glasses sounds the bell for a frenzy of arms as we pass food around and fill plates. I glance at Emmett as I pass him the turkey. "You've really outdone yourself. This all looks absolutely amazing."

He gives me a subtle wink, pulling a slice of turkey off the plate, and passes it to Callum.

After everyone has their food, the air fills with a mixture of silence and moans of appreciation at Emmett's cooking.

Mom speaks up, "Well, this just settles it. We're coming here every year. This is delightful. Absolutely the best thanksgiving food I've ever put in my mouth."

Dad chimes in, "Yours is pretty amazing, too."

"Honey. Not this good. I appreciate you trying to have my back, but hot damn!" She laughs at her slip of a cussword.

"Mama McKinley's cussing. It must be good!" Lizzy cheers and the table erupts in laughter.

Mom thrusts her fist into the air. "Well, it is!" Her eyes roll into the back of her head as she slouches in her chair. "The flavors, the turkey... it's so moist."

Beckett chimes, "I don't know if moist is the right word to use..."

Lizzy and I chuckle, but mom just huffs. "Well Beckett, what would you call it? It is very moist. So moist." She moans out.

"Oh God," Beckett cries out. "Everlee," he pleads.

"Oh, for heaven's sake, Beckett, are you being a perv?"

"Not a perv... just..."

"Moist!" Mom shouts, then holds her hands up in the air. "There, I'm done saying that word even though I don't know why I can't say it. Seems like the silliest thing I've ever heard."

"Thank you, Mama McKinley. You are a wonderful chef yourself, so your praise means the world to me," Emmett says, clutching his chest.

KNOX – COCKWARMING

- -

AFTER DINNER AND DESSERT, we all come to the roof to sit around the fire pit, watch some football, and relax in the hot tub. Everlee insisted Emmett hang up his chef's apron for the rest of the night so she's looped me in to helping her make and disperse drinks for the group. We're behind the bar while everyone else is spread across the deck. Looking around one more time to make sure no one has snuck up on us, I nudge her arm and wait for her to look at me.

"What's up, Knoxxy baby?"

"So, I have that thing you ordered. It was sitting at the office since before Halloween. I thought you may want it."

"Oh," her cheeks blush. "Do you think it's stupid?"

"I think Emmett will love it."

"You do? You aren't just saying that?"

"I'm not. When have you known me to say something I don't believe?"

"True." She pauses for a moment, then looks at me. "Where is it?"

"It's in your room, in your closet, under that stack of shirts you refuse to hang up or put in a drawer."

"I don't know if I want to get rid of them."

"Do you wear them?"

"No."

"So then get rid of them."

"But what if I want to wear them one day?"

"Then buy one when you need it."

"That's wasting money."

"I can't with you." I spin her, then grab both of her shoulders and lightly shake until she's laughing.

"What's going on over here?" Emmett asks, walking up.

"Nothing," Everlee fires back, a little too quick to be casual.

"Yea, so that's a lie."

"Stop," she pleads. "It's a surprise for you. And maybe Jax."

"Go on."

"I'm not right now."

"Is this that thing that was on the tray at Halloween?"

"Yes."

"What is it?"

"I'm not telling you."

"That's bullshit. I thought you loved me."

"Emmett. That is so not fair. You know I love you. Which is why I'm not going to tell you."

His eyes narrow at hers, but she doesn't back down.

"This weekend. We'll find some time this weekend."

Jax walks up a moment later and rubs his hand across Emmett's shoulders. "What's going on over here?"

"Nothing," Everlee and I both shout at the same time.

"Nothing," Emmett says.

"Well, I know that's horse malarky. Oh God. What the fuck was that? I think between your parents and Betty. Fuck me. Don't let me say that ever again." Jax wipes his tongue like that can wipe the words away.

How can I incorporate horse malarky into a Christmas gift for Jax? I already have a couple of ideas that I think are going to be outstanding.

Most everyone heads out around nine. Beckett and Will stay until almost ten, but then they leave too. It's been a long day and everyone is tired. Just as Everlee is about to go to her room, I grab her hand and drag her with me. "Bath time. You and me."

"Knox," she yawns.

"No funny business. Promise. I'm exhausted too."

She stares at me, trying to figure out if I'm lying or not.

"I promise." I cross my hand over my heart.

"I can't take a long bath. My incision is mostly healed, but..."

"Say less."

She takes a deep breath and follows me. While I run the bath water and put some lavender in, she undresses. Goddamn. She's a fucking vision. She looks at my hardening cock and her brows raise on her face.

"What! You can't blame me. Fuck. You look at yourself in the mirror and tell me you don't turn yourself on."

Her eyes pulse for a second, then she smiles.

"I'm not going to use it, but it has a mind of its own."

A few minutes later, we step into the hot water. For good measure, I threw a few purple flowers on top of the creamy colored water so it looked nice for her. It was from the dozens of actual flowers she got from the hospital, not vibrators.

She leans against me, smooshing my cock against my stomach. I promised her this was a no sexy time bath, and I meant it. I should have made the promise after I saw her naked. Before was stupid on my part. Missed opportunity.

"Did you have a good thanksgiving?" I ask her, running the sponge up her arms and over her shoulder.

"I did. It was really great. I'm so happy my dad likes you all and is ok with this. He didn't say anything to you, did he?"

"Your dad? About us?"

She nods, not looking at me. Was she worried?

"No, he didn't. Well."

Her body tenses.

"He said I was his favorite one."

"No, he didn't."

"Is it so hard to believe?"

"No, but I know my dad and he wouldn't say that."

Pushing her forward, I rub the sponge over her back.

"I love you," she says.

"I love you, too. What's wrong?"

"Nothing... I'm just happy. That's all."

If she's happy now, just wait until we propose to her. I thought we were going to do it today. Hell, I thought Callum was going to do it at dinner, but he didn't. He mentioned this morning he wanted to wait until it was just us because he didn't want to take away from Beckett and Will's proposal, which I understand, but fuck. It's killing me.

When we get out of the bath, a few minutes later, she's staring at me.

"What?"

"You didn't try anything."

"I told you I wouldn't and I am a man of my honor."

"You are."

She starts to grab her clothes, but I race across the room and bat them out of her hand. "What do you think you're doing?"

"Knox."

"I'm not going to fuck you, but I want to sink my cock inside of you and go to sleep."

"What?"

"Cockwarming. After we did it last time, I looked it up because I really liked it and figured there had to be a name for it." I pull her to my bedroom. "I'll give you one of my shirts, but that's all you're wearing tonight."

She smiles and my stomach tightens with excitement. I toss her a shirt and after she slips it on, we hop into bed.

"How does this work?" she asks with intrigue furrowing her brow.

"It's like spooning... only more intimate." I hop in bed behind her and wrap her in my arms. "Are you ready?"

"Yes," she mumbles. "But just so you know... this is going to suck for me."

Without speaking, I grab my cock and slide it between her legs. Oh, fuck me, this was not a good idea. She's so wet. You can do this, Knox. You are a fucking SEAL.

With a renewed confidence, I glide my cock into her pussy and we both let out a moan.

"Knox," she seethes.

I scoot my legs up, folding them into hers, pressing as far in as I can go. "You feel so fantastic," I mumble against her back.

"So do you. Why in the hell did you say no sex?"

"We're tired."

"Well, I'm pretty fucking awake right now."

A chuckle slips out, causing her to gasp as my cock shifts inside of her.

"Damn you Knox."

"How about this?" I ask, sliding my hand around her hip and down between her legs. She lets out a gasp of appreciation as I press gently on her clit.

"Knox?"

"We still aren't having sex, but I will get you off with my cock inside of you so I can feel your pussy squeeze around it, then we will go to sleep."

"How is that fair to you?"

"Fair? Love, I want to fall asleep with my cock inside of you and you are giving that to me. Don't worry. I said I wouldn't fuck you tonight, but tomorrow morning is another story." I kiss the back of her head and start to work my finger around her clit, swirling.

"Try not to move. Too much rocking may constitute a fucking."

She laughs, causing her pussy to tighten around me.

Why did I have to come up with this silly idea? Because I loved the way it felt last time and I wanted to recreate it. But I also know if she doesn't pee after sex, that could cause problems with her lady bits, and she's already gone through enough over the last few weeks.

My other hand moves the hair off her neck, so I can kiss and suck on it while I bring her to orgasm. I wish I could also play with her breasts, but the position we're in is making me choose- breast or clit. Me or her.

Always her.

My lips and tongue play with the back of her neck, and she moves her hips as her orgasm gets closer. "Everlee."

"Sorry," she pants out. "Your cock... it just feels so good inside of me and your lips and your finger."

My finger never stops, only slows. This will not be a fast orgasm, but one I plan to draw out as long as possible, so when she comes, she will come so fucking hard.

"Knox." The tone of her voice is threatening and I love it.

"Yes, love?"

"If you don't give me release, I'm going to take my own," her words filter out through gritted teeth.

"You won't. And if you try, I will handcuff your wrists to the bar at the top of my bed and then take even longer. I don't want to do that, so please don't make me."

She gasps. "Knox!"

"Just because I'm always bubbly doesn't mean I don't have a dark side that wants to play every once in a while. It's not the role I take in group play because we have Jax and Callum. I don't always enjoy it either, but tonight... tonight I may enjoy it a little too much because I know how much you like it. So don't make me let him out."

Her moans come closer together and I can feel the slight quiver of her pussy. I don't really have a dark side, but I know she enjoys hearing those words. Hell, I'd probably love to handcuff and torture her. I say torture loosely, because she'd love every fucking second of it, but that's not for tonight. When, and if, I do that, I plan on fucking her.

"Knox," she pants, so I move my finger a little faster and latch onto the back of her neck. "Oh Knox, oh Knox," she puffs outs.

Her pussy is pulsing around my cock as her orgasm washes over her and it takes all the self-control I have not to fuck her right now until I explode inside of her. I remove my hand from her clit and slide it up her body, nestling the side of my hand between her breasts, and cup the one on top.

"Good night, my love."

She hesitates, no doubt trying to figure out if I'm serious about not fucking her tonight. After a moment, she answers, "Good night."

The wet warmth of her pussy around my cock feels amazing and within minutes, the darkness is creeping in.

EVERLEE - LET'S PLAY A GAME

THIS WEEKEND HAS BEEN absolutely amazing- better than I could have ever dreamed of or imagined. Everyone I love and care about was at our house for Thanksgiving, which went off without a hitch. After Beckett and Will left early Friday morning, Knox was a little bummed. He seems to really like Beckett and Will, or at least making jabs at Beckett. Though, Beckett gives as good as he gets.

Saturday was a lot of family time, almost too much. Mom somehow got Emmett to agree to let her cook dinner for everyone as a thank you. This only made Knox jealous, which then started an entire story about how he almost burned the entire house down trying to boil a pot of water. While she was cooking, dad was talking with guys about a variety of things–businesses, sports, embarrassing stories about me and Lizzy. Overall, it was just a great time until we got into the great Christmas debate of when you put up decorations- the day after Thanksgiving or December first, or in Knox's opinion after the fourth of July.

For breakfast this morning, we all walked down to the corner café Knox frequents when he wants to fix breakfast but isn't allowed to cook. We took over all the seating along the back wall. It's a small little café with a few tables inside and out, but with the weather getting cooler, there aren't really outside tables anymore. After breakfast, we walked around for a bit and made it all the way to Bo's. Emmett unlocked the doors and showed my dad around, who was super impressed. He, of course, had to get a picture of mom in a Bo La Vie apron with her standing at the oven with a pot in hand. They said it was definitely going on the Christmas card this year.

Brady pulls up to a stop at the airport, so we all climb out. The guys were really nervous with me driving, but they were going to let me. But I couldn't start the car. Flashbacks of the accident paralyzed me with fear and I started shaking, so Brady was standing by the back door ready to jump in. They both give me a hug and tell me their goodbyes, thanking me profusely for the wonderful time they had. They kept oohing and aahing over the guys, talking about how wonderful they are and how much they love me. My parents said several times they are so happy I found men that love and cherish me like they do, and hearing those words really made my heart soar. Their love and acceptance for the guys has been equal part shocking and overwhelming.

Just before they turned to go inside, mom started talking about the future and babies. Dad laughed at her and guided her away, winking at me. When I climbed back in the car, I sat there for a moment, just breathing in the silence. Brady is good about that- never feeling like he needs to fill silence with words.

Just as he pulls away from the curb, his phone dings with an incoming text and then another.

"Do you need to get that?"

"No, it's ok. I'll look at it when we stop," he says matter-of-factly, hands at three and nine on the wheel. Never phased. He definitely didn't have FOMO, more like WRMO (would rather miss out).

Even after all this time, he remains elusive and hard to figure out. He was gone all week, getting back late last night, and I have no idea where he was. He could have been visiting family or he could have been in another country on some sort of contracted military op. If I'd seen him come home last night, then I would've had a better idea. At least I think I would have. Last time he was on an op, he came home with a full beard and he was a lot darker. Though I guess every op, he's on doesn't have to be outside. I made up some pretty interesting stories after his last trip, since I was curious and he wouldn't talk about it. Somehow, I don't believe my made-up story was any crazier than reality, but I guess we'll never know.

"So, did you have a good Thanksgiving?" I ask, trying to be more social and less nosy.

"Yea. How was yours? Your parents seemed to like the guys."

Divert back to me. Well done, Brady.

"They do, which is such a relief. That was one thing I was most scared of when we first started this relationship. I love my family and especially love the get-togethers during the holidays. I didn't know how I would manage that and still keep our relationship a secret."

"Well, now you don't have to."

"No. Thanks to Beckett in some ways."

"Your brother?"

His question is more confusion about how my brother was involved and less about the status of Beckett being my brother. I get the feeling Brady probably has dossiers on my family and me and knows more about us than we know about each other.

"He accidentally invited my mom down to the beach for the fourth."

"Oh, right," he chuckles, and his skin creases behind his black beard.

He pulls over to the side of the road and turns the car off.

"What are we doing?" I ask, looking around.

"We are doing nothing. *You* are staying in the car while I run inside really quick." The car door closes with a thud and I turn to watch him walk behind the car and down the sidewalk.

"Well, this sucks," I mumble to myself. He didn't say where he was going or how long he'd be gone. Grabbing my phone out of my pocket, I text the guy's group chat and wait, but nothing. I send a funny meme about Christmas just to rile up Jax and Knox, but nothing.

When I text Lizzy, she doesn't pick up either.

What in the hell is going on? I flip back and forth between my text messages, looking for those irritating bubbles that pop up and tell you someone's typing. Irritating because you can't see through them and are even more irritated when they start, stop, start, stop.

To pass the time, I pull up a game on my phone and start playing. It's like a fast-paced version of solitaire and I love it. I found it when I was in the hospital with nothing to do and I'm now on level 523. The thunk of the trunk closing brings me back, just as Brady is opening the driver's side door.

"Did you get what you needed?"

"I did."

"A man of few words."

"Why say more than you need to?"

"True. What did you have to stop for?"

His eyes cut at me and a smile curls his lips. A smile that says he's not answering that question because it's none of my business. The smile that is going to drive me crazy now, because it only makes me want to know what's in the trunk by tenfold. Before it was just a question for conversation, but now... now I need to know. I must know.

My stomach grumbles and I check my watch. "Hey."

He eyes me cautiously before he answers, "Yes?"

"Would you mind if we stopped by Flint's? I can run in and pick up some dinner and surprise the guys."

"I don't think so."

My brow pinches together in a hard v. "No?" Did he just tell me no? He's not one for ever joking, so I don't think he's being coy. He legit told me no.

He continues, clearly picking up on the shock and confusion that is skittering across my face, "I believe the guys have dinner plans for you tonight."

I glance at my watch again. "It's four o'clock. We never eat dinner this early."

"I didn't say you were eating dinner now. Only that they have plans."

"You said you believed they had plans and now you're saying they do have plans. Which is it, Brady?"

He sighs and stares at me without speaking.

"I see. Clamming up. A little clam action. A little snappy snappy mouth shutty." I have no idea what I'm saying or why I keep talking.

Brady nods slowly.

"Yea. I'm sorry about that. I'm just a little off... and tired. Probably tired. You know... mentally exhausted."

"No need to apologize, Ms. Everlee."

"Why do you do that? Call me Ms. Everlee? Why not just Everlee?"

"I don't know. It feels weird to call you Everlee."

"Can you make it unweird? I get you may not want to be my friend, because of some bro code or something, but we can pretend. I call you Brady. You call me Everlee. Miss just seems so formal."

"I'll try."

"Please."

The rest of the car ride to the house is silent. My head keeps looping through ideas about what's in the trunk, what the guys have planned for dinner, and why they haven't responded to any texts. There are four of them! How is it that not even one of them has responded? What's the point of dating four guys if they act like one?

When we pull up to the house a few minutes later, he pulls the car to a stop, then waits a minute before he gets out.

"Do you want me to help you get the thing out of the trunk?" I ask as he closes my door.

"No, Everlee. I can handle it." He stands beside the back passenger door and doesn't move.

"Ok..." What's going on? The hairs on the back of my neck stand on end. "Brady? Is there something you need to tell me?"

"No."

I should have rephrased the question. Amateur hour Everlee.

When I walk up the stairs, I peek through the small window beside the door and notice the lights are mostly out. Only a few are on in the kitchen, casting a soft glow to the surrounding rooms.

My heart hammers in my chest, and as I push the door open, I look over my shoulder at Brady. He's standing by the car, hands clasped in front of him like he's a member of the secret service or something.

"Hello?" I call out, and my voice echoes through the empty silence. The door shuts behind me with a soft thud, and I quickly remove my shoes, placing them neatly in the cubby by the back door. "I swear, if one of you jumps out and scares me, I'm going to punch you in the balls. Halloween is over and I don't like being scared. It's Christmas time... mostly."

A flickering candle on the island captures my attention, so I walk over to it and see a piece of paper folded up.

Hello our love,
We are going to play a game and at the end, there will be a surprise for you.

Clue 1: We love how wet we make you. It drives us wild. Where was the first place you were wet, that drove us wild?

Love, us

"The surprise better be you four men naked with a bow wrapped around your dicks," I mumble to myself, then reread the clue. "The first place that I was wet? Like are we talking moist wet, or wet wet?" I ask the air.

Silence.

"What even is moist wet? Now I'm making up things. The first place? Callum's shower? I was wet there, literally and then physically, after Callum barged in... because you all heard me. Did that drive you wild?"

With apprehension, I walk upstairs and go to Callum's bedroom. It's dark with a single light on in the center of his shower, shining down... on a paper! Another piece of paper! I nearly break my neck running across the room to the shower.

Good job, babe,
You found the first clue! When we heard you in the shower
that first time you
came to our house, we nearly lost our minds. Here you were
masturbating in
one of our showers with the speaker on. That's when we
realized you were going
to be trouble.

Clue 2: This one may be a little harder. We thought we had
lost you, but
it only made us realize how much we needed you in our lives.
Where did we reconnect?
Love, us

"Where did we reconnect? We reconnected at the church at my parent's house and I'm fairly certain you don't want me to jump on a plane and head there." I wait for an answer, knowing I won't get it. "It would be a lot easier if you all would talk to me, because I'm fairly certain you can hear me and are probably watching me." A wicked idea passes through my mind and a sinister smile creeps onto my face. "If you're watching me, then enjoy this." I take off my shirt, bra, and pants. I don't wear panties, so I'm standing completely naked in Callum's shower. "Should we recreate the first time I was wet?"

A voice comes over the intercom, making me jump. "Everlee," Callum warns. "Behave or you will lose your surprise."

"No fun."

"Trust me. There will be plenty of fun to be had tonight."

"What kind?"

Silence.

My heart is racing now with excitement, so I go back to the clue. "Where did we reconnect? It was definitely the Easter event... Oh!" There's a picture on the Living room sofa table of us at the egg toss. Will had apparently been taking pictures of Beckett and captured all of us in it. Beckett sent it to me and I had it printed and framed.

With my heart pounding in my chest, I dash down the stairs and into the living room. Hidden under the frame is another white piece of paper.

"Yes!" I scream, hurriedly unfolding it and praying Brady doesn't come in.

Good job, babe,
You did it! We had no idea that you were going to be at that event, and
when we saw you with that guy... Let's just say we all felt the fangs
of jealousy bite us hard. You were ours, you just didn't know it yet.
We all swore from that day forward, we would do what was needed, to give
you the confidence to stay.

Clue 3: You have grown so much since you have come into our lives, and
to watch your transformation becoming the woman you are today has been
so amazing. This is the place where we squashed any reasons of doubt you may
have had and made you part of us. Part of our family.
Love, us

"Squashed doubts?" For some reason kumquats comes to mind. I think because of squash, squash Thanksgiving, Thanksgiving table, table sex, sex kumquats. But I don't think that's it. As I walk into the dining room, I don't see a note on the table. "Part of us? Part of our family?" I repeat the words over and over again. "The contract? Sammie and Allure?"

With cautious steps, I enter the office and my eyes immediately land on a note resting on the desk. "Yes!"

Racing over to it, I grab it and flip it open.

You're doing great, babe!
When Sammie came to us and gave us first right of refusal for Allure, we
knew we wanted to go on this new "again" venture with you. The growth we've seen
in you, is the exact reason we started Allure to begin with. It seemed only fitting
that you help others find what makes them happy too.

Clue 4: I know one of your biggest concerns with dating us was your family. You were
scared they wouldn't accept you- us. These last few days showed us what you were
willing to give up when you made the decision to stay. Your family is great.
Your mom coming to the beach ended up being a happy surprise.
Because of that trip, we were able to introduce ourselves and she got a chance

to know us for us and nothing more. Last clue. We may not be near a beach or
a pool, but we still have water none-the-less. This is where you will find your surprise.

Love, us

My feet are planted to the ground as their words play on repeat, trying to figure out what the surprise is going to be. I can already tell that whatever it is, I'm going to cry, because they've put so much thought into this game. Replaying pieces of our history together, but in a fun way, knowing my affinity for games.

Taking a few deep and shaky breaths, I make my way up the sets of stairs to the door that leads to the roof. Gripping the handle, my body freezes as nerves surge through me, weighing down my limbs like cement. It feels like there's an electrical current coursing through my body, creating a buzzing sensation. My stomach is twisting and turning, tying itself into knots before unraveling again. My palms are moist with sweat... I don't understand what's going on.

When I finally get the courage to push the door open, I'm greeted by all my men, standing in a semi-circle wearing full on tuxedos. Black pants and jacket, with matching bowties over a crisp white button up. My breath gets caught in my throat and I can't breathe. Lit candles behind the men create a soft glow that spreads across the decking, while the bistro lights above add to the ambiance. Rose petals blow in the cool breeze, which reminds me I'm not wearing anything.

The men are staring at me and I'm staring at them, neither of us speaking. Unable to stand the silence anymore, I offer, "I feel like I'm underdressed."

"You're naked," Callum whispers, walking over to me and shrugging out of his jacket to lie around my shoulders.

"Well, had I known I was going to end up on the deck with you four dressed like sexy super spies, then maybe I wouldn't have undressed."

Callum grabs my hand, leading me closer to the fire pit, then turns me around. All four guys are there, expressions unreadable.

"What's going on?" I meekly whisper out.

Callum starts, "Everlee," he sighs, shaking head. "You... you came into this house with a force that none of us were prepared for. You broke all the rules and made me break a few, too." He scowls at me and I smile. "You have been mine... ours... from the moment you walked into Vixen with your red wings on."

Emmett steps forward. "Trouble... that's what you were and what you are. From the moment your eyes sparkled at me at the bar, you had me entranced. The way you moaned over my food the first time you came to Bo's. You have been so supportive of every part of my life and have showed me it's ok to let love in."

Jax steps forward. "Everlee. You are... the part of me I didn't know was missing. I never let myself truly want something or love something. I pushed everyone away for fear of getting hurt, but you didn't care. You saw *me* and you loved *me*. Your presence by my side has been a constant source of love and support. You've helped unlock a piece of me I buried forever ago and probably would still have buried if it wasn't for you. You accept me for all my faults and for all the things I want to give you, but can't yet. You only take what I can give and never ask for anything more. You know me better than I know myself at times and..." he sighs. "We were a family that was from broken homes and we pieced ourselves together. We thought we were whole until we met you and you fit in those cracks and showed us we weren't. You melded to each of us so perfectly..."

My chest tightens listening to their words.

Knox steps forward, nervously running his hand through his hair. "Ali. I'm not one for words and I have thought about these words a lot. About what I wanted to say to you. When you left, it felt like a piece of me was ripped out. I was in a bad spot and making poor decisions. Alcohol has been a weakness for me, something I've turned to in times of heartache or pain, but you... you are my addiction now. Everything about you- your hair, your smell, the way your body moves, the taste of you... I could drink you up all day. An ocean full of Emmett's Old Fashioneds couldn't intoxicate me as much as a single drop of you. I love you so completely that it sometimes hurts. I get the privilege of running Allure with you and being with you nearly every hour of every day, and I couldn't be more thankful for that."

Tears are streaming down my cheeks. Not just because of Knox's words, but all of their words. All of their truths laid out so bare.

"I feel like I should say something." I rub the back of my hand across my cheek and stare at them. "They say... they say things happen for a reason. And that's what I told myself after every breakup, every heartache. I told myself that it was happening for a reason- it was teaching me some lesson, or setting me on a better path. Through all of my ups and down, through all the tears, every decision that I made led me on a path to you all. If I had done one thing differently, who knows where I would have ended up? And I don't want to think about that because I'm here with you. You all are my home and I love you so incredibly much that it takes my breath away."

"We feel the same. Which is why we want to ask you something," Callum says, and they all step forward in unison.

Before I can say or do anything, they all take a knee in front of me. I clutch my chest, willing my lungs to breathe air.

They all speak in perfect unison, "Everlee McKinley. Will you do us the honor of marrying us?"

Tears are gushing out of my eyes. This is definitely not a picture that will go on the Christmas card. Me standing buck ass naked in front of a fire with tears streaming down my face looking like I've just had an exorcism, with four deliciously hot men in tuxedos on their knees in front of me.

Fuck! They are waiting for an answer.

"Yes. Yes, of course I will marry you!"

I want to ask if this has anything to do with Beckett's proposal, but before I can get the words out of my mouth, Callum is pulling out a ring box with a ring perched inside.

"Holy forking shirtballs. Wow. Shit. Wow." I grumble out a series of incoherent moans. "Wow. That is beautiful. And big. Holy shitballs. Sorry I keep cussing. Not the ladylike thing to do while you're proposing, even though I'm fully naked. But wow."

Callum reaches for my shaky hand, pulls the ring out of the box, and slips it on my finger. "We picked this ring out especially for you- for us. It's a five-diamond layout with the center being an Asscher cut- unique like you, and on each side are two emerald cut diamonds, symbolizing the four of us."

"It's absolutely beautiful. Stunning. I have no words." I stare at the ring on my finger and a heat flushes through my body. "Are you sure? Marriage?"

"One thousand times, yes, without question. It would be more of a commitment ceremony, since polyamorous weddings aren't legal. But it doesn't matter. We already knew before the holidays we wanted to marry you, but seeing you with your family..." Callum shakes his head in disbelief. "You were willing to give up everything for us, and we don't want you to give up a single thing. We want to give you everything you have ever wanted and dreamed about and more. You have made our life whole, but I feel like this is all just the beginning. We can't wait to do life with you and see where we are. Because babe. You are it for us. The end all, be all."

I fall forward, latching my arms around all of them as they hug me back.

After a few minutes, Knox pulls away and asks, "So, who's ready to go celebrate?"

"Shut the fuck up," Jax mumbles.

"What? Our girl is wearing nothing but our ring. If that doesn't make you hot for her pussy, then you're broken," Knox retorts, taking off his jacket and tossing it on the back of the closest chair.

"We'll be in the Nest, waiting or not waiting for you all!" He says, grabbing my wrist and leading me away.

My heart melts all over again when I look at my ring.

I'm getting married.

EVERLEE - FOREVER

THREE HOURS LATER, WE'RE all walking downstairs happily fucked and satiated with grumbling bellies. The guys are only wearing their joggers, and I'm wearing one of Jax's shirts. Knox and Emmett dig through the refrigerator, pulling out leftovers while Callum and Jax pull out plates and silverware, setting the bar top. A large pink box sits in the middle of the island and I realize this must have been what Brady had retrieved. Catching Callum's gaze, I playfully tiptoe over to the box and wait for him to tell me I can peek. Once he nods, I lift the lid and inside are five cupcakes lined up in the front with congratulations written in chocolate along the back.

"Awfully presumptuous of you to buy the cupcakes before I said yes," I tease, pumping my eyebrows.

"Well, a man can dream, can't he?"

Feeling overwhelmed with emotion, I loop my arm around him and hug, pressing my face against his bare chest. "I love you," I mumble out, holding my hand up again to look at my ring.

I can't believe it.

"I imagine your mom is probably anxiously waiting by the phone for your call," Jax says, grabbing me around the waist and pulling me off of Callum. He kisses my cheek from behind, then releases me.

"They know?"

"We asked your dad several nights ago. Our plan was to propose that night, but your brother unexpectedly popped the question to Will. We didn't want to steal their spotlight, so we waited until it was just us. Poor Knoxxy was climbing out of his skin."

When I look at him, he shrugs.

"You asked my parents?"

"Your dad, only because we thought your mom would be too excited and blow the lid off the can. Same reason your dad didn't tell her until they were at the airport."

Tears form on the rim of my eyes. "Guys..."

Jax brings me back in for a hug and kisses my forehead. I grab my phone off the counter and face time my mom. She picks up on the second ring, but I keep my cool. "Hey mom.

"Everlee!" Her smile is spread wide across her face.

"Is everything ok?" I ask with mock concern.

Her face falls with confusion and she tries to reel it back in. "Yes. You?"

"Yea. All good here. I was just calling to see if y'all got home?"

"You were? That's why you called?"

"Yea. Why else would I call?" I chuckle.

She frowns and looks behind the phone like she's staring at dad. "Oh. I thought... nevermind what I thought. Yes. We got home about fifteen minutes ago. Thank your guys again for such a wonderful trip."

"I will. Ok. Well, I will let you get to unpacking. Tell dad I love him."

Looking like a dejected kid on a playground, she nods.

"Oh, I love you too."

She sighs, "I love you too, baby."

"Oh, one more thing... I got engaged." I flip my hand on the screen.

She takes a minute for the words to sink in and she looks at my ring, then me and screams. "Oh Everlee! Why did you do that? You're playing with my heart! Dave! They did it! They proposed! Oh my goodness, look at that ring." She pulls the phone closer to her face. "Wow. It's beautiful. Do they need one more in the harem? Just kidding. I love your father, but wow. That ring."

"It's stunning," I say, lowering it back down to look at it one more time.

Dad pops on the phone. "Congrats, honey. I'm thrilled for you. You got some good men there."

"Thank you." My face falls as more tears form. "Seriously, thank you. Thank you for being so open and accepting. I know this is not what you expected for me, but you didn't let your love for me waver. So really. Thank you."

"Oh baby. You're our baby girl. You're more important to us than anything else in the world."

"Even Beckett?" I tease.

"You stop that!" Mom scolds. "You know what we mean. Trying to start trouble," she puffs.

"But in all seriousness. Thank you. Your love and acceptance has allowed me to have everything I've ever dreamed of and wanted."

"Oh stop. You're going to make me cry," Mom says, batting her hand.

"We don't want to do that again," Dad chimes in. "I made the mistake of telling her at the airport and let's just say she made quite the scene, screaming and crying. People thought I was hurting her, so we had to awkwardly tell people that she just found out her daughter was getting engaged."

"Oh, it wasn't that bad." She shoves my dad on the shoulder.

"Donna. We had three security agents walk over and they were questioning you on if you felt safe around me."

"Mom." I laugh.

"I can't help I was just so excited. Once I explained to them what was going on, they were fine and left us alone."

"Yes, but they still gave me weird looks, and I swear one was following us around."

"Ok. Well, I just wanted to call and tell you all the news. We're going to grab a bite of food, then I'm going to call Beckett and Lizzy."

"Ooh," Mom mumbles.

"Ooh what? What ooh?"

"Who are you going to tell first?" her mouth pulls.

"Ohh."

"Yea."

Thinking about it for a moment, weighing out the pros and cons of each, I decide to video chat them both at the same time.

"Good luck," Mom says. "And I love you. Now go get a wedding date planned so I can get me some babies."

"Mom."

"Love you, ta ta." She disconnects the call before I can say anything else.

I still haven't told her that babies may not be in the cards, but something tells me maybe they changed their minds on that too? I don't want to bring anything up about it yet. If they haven't changed their mind, I would be ok with it because I have them, but...

"Trouble," Emmett calls, breaking my reverie. "We still have a few minutes before dinner is ready if you want to call Liz and Becks."

I nod, trying to build up the courage. I know Lizzy can't physically come through the phone, but if she could... she would be the one to find a way. Pressing the nerves down, I dial both of them. Lizzy picks up first.

"Good evening," she answers, wearing a top hat and a black vest. I'm fairly certain that may be all she's wearing.

"Seems like you are."

"Just bit of role play. I'm a ringmaster."

"And what's Tony?"

Lizzy doesn't answer, but just pumps her eyebrows.

"I see." I really don't, well, not exactly. I imagine he's some animal, but really it could be any of them. If I had to guess a lion, but still not sure.

Beckett answers. "Well, what do I owe this honor? Do you already miss me?"

"We did. When are you and Will going to move here? Now that you're getting married, you'll have to move out of mom and dad's house."

"Har har. We still haven't set a date, so I have time. Did you two call me to harass me?"

"I didn't call you," Lizzy scoffs.

"What are you wearing?" Beckett asks, finally noticing her outfit.

"TLDR," Lizzy claps back.

"I don't think that's how that works..."

"I called you both because..." Suddenly, I didn't know how I wanted to tell them. The words sort of slipped out of my mind. So I just hold up my hand and flinch, waiting for Lizzy to lose her shit.

"Shut the back door! Ev! You're getting married? They proposed?" She's looking around the phone like she can see them behind me. "I don't see them, but I know they're there. Well done, boys. Way to make an honest woman out of her! She was a little hoe bag before!"

"Lizzy!" I yell.

"Ok. Just kidding, she wasn't. But still! Wow, that ring!"

"Yea, they've had it for a while." I add, so Beckett doesn't think it was because of him.

"Sis. Congrats. I'm so happy for you. The ring is beautiful."

"Thanks."

"It makes sense why Knox was acting so cagey. I ruined the proposal, didn't I? When I proposed?"

"No, not at all. They had a scavenger hunt planned out tonight, which led me through all our times together."

"Of course they would do something super romantic," he teases. "Babe, come here." He waves Will over. "The guys proposed to Ev."

Will's head pokes into the frame, so I show him my ring.

"Congrats Ev! Wow, that ring is gorgeous... way better than what Beckett picked out." He laughs when Beckett slaps his arm. "Only teasing, of course."

"If you want a gazillion diamonds too, I will buy it for you, babe!"

"No, what you got me is perfect." He kisses Beckett on the cheek.

"How did the firehouse take it when you told them?" I ask, happy to move the conversation off me. I may like all eyes on me when I'm fucking, but attention outside of that... no thanks.

"Beckett, being Beckett, called a group meeting at a local bar after work on Friday with both of our firehouses and announced it."

"They were all very excited for us," Beckett coos, looping his arm inside of Will's.

"Do you have a date yet?" Lizzy asks.

"No, we just got engaged," Beckett laughs.

"Well, it has to be after mine... rules and what not... first to be engaged, so first to be married."

"Seriously?" Beckett scoffs playfully.

"What? I'm teasing... kind of." She pouts and stomps her feet. "I don't want your wedding before mine to be all gay and great, making me change everything at the last minute."

"I can't with you." Beckett laughs and Will walks off camera.

"I don't have a date either, but it will be after both of yours, I'm sure." I smile.

The guys make choking sounds in the kitchen, pulling my attention. When I look at them, they are looking around at the ceiling or staring at some non-existent thing on the floor.

"Apparently, the guys have an opinion, so I'll have to get back to you on that."

Emmett clears his throat and holds up my plate.

"Dinner time. Thank you both for coming over for Thanksgiving. It was great seeing you and spending time with all of my loved ones. Love you, both."

They each return the sentiment before we hang up.

"Baby... we aren't waiting until the end of next year to marry you... so we need to get Lizzy on board with that."

"We could do a double wedding... 6-9 is really the best date..."

"Fuck no!" Jax declares. "I'm not... no... nope... hell no. I'm not going to have a dual wedding with Lizzy." He shivers his shoulders.

"It was just a joke... but now that I know how you really feel... we may need to make it happen."

Jax nearly throws down his plate and swoops across the room and lifts me in his arms. "You will not. Or you will be so punished," he growls.

"You know that doesn't scare me and only turns me on."

He chases me around the kitchen until Callum grabs me. I think he's going to protect me, but he turns on me.

"It's time to eat, boys."

When I catch his darkened eyes, I realize he's not talking about dinner.

These are going to be my men for forever.

What's Coming Next?

Next will be a Christmas/New Year's book that will continue the story. After that, there will be at least one more in the main story line (no holiday attached to it yet). I am also hoping to release a 2nd edition of Cupid's Contract (it will likely have a new name) that will include chapters from the guy's POV so it falls more in line with the other books in the series. There will also be at least 1 story published next year in Beckett's POV, probably 2. And then Lizzy... I am hoping to get one for her as well next year.

About the Author

HI FRIENDS! FOLLOW ME below for all the updates, behind the scenes and bonus content!

You can always email me at authorsnmoor [at] gmail.com or message me below. I do rely more on facebook, Insta and TT for most of my communication.

Website
Etsy Shop AuthorSNMoor
Tiktok@authorsnmoor
Instagramsn_moor
FacebookSN Moor Author — Author SN Moor Fan Group
GoodreadsS.N. Moor
Amazon